"*Popular Music from Vittula* is a tale of boyhood friendship elastic enough to include numerous digressions, some fantastical, some so precise in their sociological observation . . . that an anthropologist could make good use of them. . . . In British translator Laurie Thompson's hands, Niemi's language is a constant, fresh poetic surprise. . . . Even the alphabet—'a scary army of sticks and half-moons'—comes strangely alive in this marvelous book."
—Michael Upchurch, *The Seattle Times*

"Mikael Niemi comes from Pajala, Sweden, the scene—perhaps even the main character—of his remarkable book. . . . The book is filled with eccentric, grotesque, even unsavory characters, but Niemi shows large tolerance, kindly spirit and even clear pleasure in these odd neighbors. They are human, too."
—Bill Holm, *Star Tribune*

"A beautiful, poignant, often very funny novel about growing up in a remote area. Niemi writes with real poetry as he strings together the culturally rich vignettes of Matti's experiences, snapshots of childhood that are at the same time intensely personal and universal . . . all rendered pure and convincingly as a young boy's perceptions. Niemi also seasons the book well with the mysticism of childhood that suffuses the usually hidden psychological space where the transformation from child to youth occurs. An exquisitely beautiful novel, artfully translated."
—Paula Luedkte, *Booklist*

Popular Music *from* Vittula

a novel

MIKAEL NIEMI

TRANSLATED FROM THE SWEDISH BY
LAURIE THOMPSON

SEVEN STORIES PRESS
NEW YORK

Seven Stories Press
140 Watts Street
New York, NY 10013
http://www.sevenstories.com

In Canada:
Publishers Group Canada
50A Carlton Street
Toronto, ON M5A 2LI

Library of Congress Cataloging-in-Publication Data

Niemi, Mikael, 1959-
[Populärmusik från Vittula. English]
Popular music from Vittula / Mikael Niemi ; translated from the Swedish by Laurie Thompson.
p. cm.
ISBN 1-58322-523-4 hc / 1-58322-659-1 pbk
I. Title.
PT9876.24.I29P6713 2003
839.73'8—dc21

2003002496

9 8 7 6 5 4 3 2 1

College professors may order examination copies of Seven Stories Press titles for a free six-month trial period. To order, visit www.sevenstories.com/textbook, or fax on school letterhead to (212) 226-1411.

Book design by Jess Morphew

Printed in Canada.

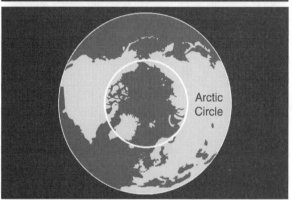

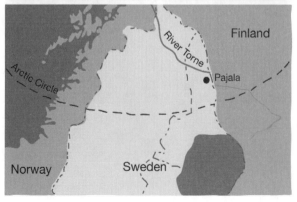

PROLOGUE

The narrator wakes up, starts his climb and finds himself in a fix in the Thorong La Pass, whereupon the story can commence

It was a freezing cold night in the cramped wooden hut. When my travel alarm started peeping I sat up with a start, unlaced the top of my sleeping bag and reached out into the pitch-black cold. My fingers groped around on the rough wooden floor, through all the splinters and grains of sand and the naked draft from the gaps in the floorboards until they found the cold plastic of the clock and the off-button.

I lay there motionless for a while, semi-conscious, clinging on to a log with one arm trailing in the sea. Silence. Cold. Short panting breaths in the thin air. Still lingering in my body was an ache, as if I'd spent the whole night with muscles tensed.

It was then, at that very moment, that I realized I was dead.

The experience was difficult to describe. It was as if my body had been emptied. I had been turned into stone, an incredibly big, bleak meteorite. Embedded deep down in a cavity was something strange, something long, thin and soft, organic. A corpse. It wasn't mine. I was stone, I was merely embracing the body as it grew ever colder, encompassing it like a colossal, tightly closed granite sarcophagus.

This feeling lasted two seconds, three at most.

Then I switched on my flashlight. The alarm clock display showed zero and zero. For one awful moment I had the feeling that time had ceased to exist, that it could no longer be measured. Then it dawned on me that I must have set the clock to zero when I was fumbling for the off-button. My wristwatch said twenty past four in the morning. All around the breathing hole of my sleeping bag was a thin layer of frost. The temperature was below freezing, even though I was indoors. I braced myself against the cold, wriggled out of my sleeping bag, fully clothed, and forced my feet into my icy walking boots. Somewhat uneasily I packed my empty notebook into my rucksack. Nothing today either. No draft, not even a single note.

Up with the metal catch on the door and out into the night. The starry sky stretched away into infinity. A crescent moon was bobbing on the horizon like a rowing boat, and the jagged outlines of the Himalayan giants loomed dimly on all sides like spiky shadows. The starlight was so strong that it drenched the ground—sharp, white spray from a colossal shower head. I maneuvered into my rucksack, and even that little effort left me panting for breath. The lack of oxygen sent tiny spots dancing before my eyes. A rasping cough scraped through my throat, grating bellows, 14,450 feet above sea level. I could just make out the path running steeply up the stony mountainside before disappearing into the darkness. Slowly, ever so slowly, I started climbing.

* * *

The Thorong La Pass, Mount Annapurna in Nepal. Seventeen thousand seven hundred sixty-five feet above sea level. I've conquered it. Up there at last! My relief is so great, I flop down on my back and lie gasping for breath. Lactic acid is making my leg muscles ache, my head is throbbing, I'm in the early stages of altitude sickness. Daylight is worryingly blotchy. A sudden gust of wind is a warning that nastier weather is on the way. The cold bites into my cheeks, and I can see a handful of hikers quickly shouldering their backpacks and starting their descent to Muktinath.

I'm left all alone. Can't bring myself to leave, not yet. I sit up, still gasping for breath. Lean back against the cairn with its fluttering

Tibetan prayer flags. The pass is made up of stones, a sterile expanse of gravel with no vegetation. Mountain peaks loom up on all sides, rough black façades dotted with heavenly white glaciers. Gusts of wind fling the first snowflakes into my anorak. Not good. If the path gets buried in snow, it can be dangerous. I look back over my shoulder: no sign of any other hikers. I'd better get back down quickly. But not just yet. I'm standing at the highest point I've ever been in my life. Must bid it farewell first. Must thank somebody. A sudden urge takes possession of me, and I kneel down beside the cairn. Feel a bit silly, but another look around confirms that I'm on my own. I bend quickly forward, like a Muslim with my bottom in the air, lower my head, and mumble a prayer of gratitude. I notice an iron plate engraved with Tibetan writing, a text I am unable to understand but one that exudes solemnity, spirituality, and I bend further down to kiss the text.

At that very moment a memory comes back to me. A vertiginous pit down into my childhood. A tube through time down which someone is shouting out a warning, but it's too late.

I'm stuck fast.

My damp lips are frozen onto a Tibetan prayer plaque. And when I try to loosen my lips by wetting them with my tongue, that sticks fast as well.

Every single child from the far north of Sweden has no doubt been in the same plight. A freezing cold winter's day, a railing, a lamp post, a piece of iron coated in hoar frost. My own memory is suddenly crystal clear. I'm five years old, and my lips are frozen onto the keyhole of our front door in Pajala. My first reaction one of vast astonishment. A keyhole that can be touched without more ado by a mitten or even a bare finger. But now it's a devilish trap. I try to yell, but that's not easy when your tongue is stuck fast to the metal. I struggle with my arms, trying to tear myself loose by force, but the pain compels me to give up. The cold makes my tongue numb, my mouth is filled with the taste of blood. I kick against the door in desperation, and emit an agonized:

"Aaahhh, aaahhh..."

Then Mum appears. She's carrying a bowl of warm water, she pours it over the keyhole, and my lips thaw out and I'm freed. Bits of skin are still sticking to the metal, and I resolve never to do that again. "Aaahhh, aaahhh," I groan as the snow starts lashing into me. Nobody can hear me. If there are any hikers on their way up, they'll no doubt turn back now. My bottom is sticking into the air, the wind is whipping up and making it colder by the minute. My mouth is starting to go numb. I pull off my gloves and try to warm myself loose with my hands, panting away with my hot breath. But it's all in vain. The metal absorbs the heat but remains icy cold. I try to lift up the iron plaque, to wrench it loose, but it's firmly anchored and doesn't shift an inch. My back is covered in cold sweat. The wind worms its way inside my anorak collar and I start shivering. Low clouds are gathering and enveloping the pass in mist. Dangerous. Bloody dangerous. I'm getting more and more scared. I'm going to die here. I'll never last the night frozen onto a Tibetan prayer plaque.

There's only one possibility left: I must wrench myself free.

The very thought makes me feel sick, but I have no choice. Just a little tug first, as a test. I can feel the pain right back to the root of my tongue. One... two... *now...*

Red. Blood. And pain so extreme I have to beat my head against the iron. It's impossible. My mouth is stuck just as firmly as before. My whole face would fall apart if I tugged any harder.

A knife. If only I had a knife. I feel for my backpack with my foot, but it's several feet away. Fear is churning my stomach, my bladder feels about to burst. I unzip my fly and get ready to pee on all fours, like a cow.

Then I pause. Feel for the mug that's hanging from my belt. Fill it full of pee, then pour the contents over my mouth. The urine trickles over my lips, starts the thawing process, and a few seconds later I'm free.

I've pissed myself free.

I stand up. My prayers are over. My tongue and lips are stiff and tender, but I can move them again. At last I can start my story.

CHAPTER 1

In which Pajala enters the modern age, music comes into being,
and two little boys set out, traveling light

It was the beginning of the sixties when paved roads came to our part
of Pajala. I was five at the time and could hear the noise as they
approached. A column of what looked like tanks came crawling past
our house, digging and scratching at the pot-holed dirt road. It was
early summer. Men in overalls marched around bow-legged, spitting
out wads of snuff, wielding crowbars, and muttering away in Finnish
while housewives peered out from behind the curtains. It was incredibly exciting for a little kid. I clung to the fence, peeping out between
the rails, and breathed in the diesel fumes oozing out of those
armored monsters. They prodded and poked into the winding village
road as if it were an old carcass. A mud road with lots and lots of
holes that used to fill with rain, a pock-marked surface that turned
butter-soft every spring when the thaw came, and in summer was
salted like a minced meat loaf to prevent dust flying around. The dirt
road was old-fashioned. It belonged to a bygone age, the one our parents had been born into but were now determined to put behind
them, once and for all.

Our district was known locally in Finnish as *Vittulajänkkä*, which means something like Cuntsmire. It's not clear how the name originated, but it probably has to do with the great number of babies being born here. There were five children in some of the houses, sometimes even more, and the name became a sort of crude tribute to female fertility. Vittulajänkkä—or Vittula, as it's sometimes shortened—was populated by villagers who grew up during the hardship years of the thirties. Thanks to hard work and a booming economy, they worked their way up the ladder and managed to borrow money to buy a house of their own. Sweden was flourishing, the economy was expanding, and even Tornedalen in the far north was being swept along with the tide. Progress had been so astonishingly fast that people still felt poverty-stricken even though they were now rich. They occasionally worried that it might all be taken away from them again. Housewives trembled behind their home-made curtains whenever they thought about how well-off they were. A whole house for themselves and their offspring! They'd been able to afford new clothes, and the children didn't need to wear hand-me-downs and patches. They'd even acquired a car. And now the dirt road was about to disappear under a layer of oily-black asphalt. Poverty would be clothed in a black leather jacket. What was being laid was the future, as smooth as a shaven cheek. Children would ride along it on their new bikes, heading for welfare and a degree in engineering.

The bulldozers bellowed and roared. Gravel poured out of the heavy trucks. Enormous steamrollers compressed the hard core with such incomprehensible force that I wanted to stick my five-year-old foot underneath to test them. I threw big stones in front of a steamroller, then ran out to look for them when it had rumbled past, but there was no sign of the stones. They'd disappeared, pure magic. It was uncanny and fascinating. I lay my hand on the flattened-out surface. It felt strangely cold. How could coarse gravel become as smooth as a newly pressed sheet? I threw out a fork taken from the kitchen drawer, and then my plastic spade, and both of them disappeared without a trace. Even today I'm not sure whether they are still concealed there in the hard core, or if they did in fact dissolve in some magical way.

* * *

It was around this time that my elder sister bought her first record player. I sneaked into her room when she was away at school. It was on her desk, a piece of technical wizardry made of black plastic, a shiny little box with a transparent lid concealing remarkable knobs and buttons. Scattered all around it were curlers, tubes of lipstick, and aerosol cans. Everything was modern, unnecessary luxuries, a sign of our new riches heralding a future of waste and welfare. A lacquered box contained photographs of film stars and cinema tickets. Sis collected them, and had fat bundles from Wilhelmsson's cinema, each one with the name of the film, a list of its leading actors, and grades out of ten written on the back.

She'd placed the only single she owned on a plastic contraption that looked like a plate rack. I'd been made to cross my heart and promise never even to breathe on it. Now, my fingers tingling, I picked it up and stroked the shiny cover depicting a handsome young man playing a guitar. He had a dark lock of hair dangling down over his forehead, and was smiling straight at me. Ever so painstakingly I slid out the black vinyl. I carefully lifted the lid of the record player. Tried to remember how Sis had done it, and lowered the record onto the turntable. Fitted the hole of the EP over the central pin. And, so full of expectation that I'd broken into a sweat, I switched it on.

The turntable gave a little jerk, then started spinning. The tension was unbearable. I repressed the urge to run away. With my awkward, stumpy, boy's fingers I took hold of the snake, the rigid black pick-up arm with its poisonous fang, as big as a toothpick. Then I lowered it onto the spinning plastic.

There was a crackling, like pork frying. I just knew something had broken. I'd ruined the record, it would be impossible to play it ever again.

BAM-BAM... BAM-BAM...

No, here it came! Brash chords! And then Elvis's frantic voice.

I was petrified. Forgot to swallow, didn't notice I was slavering. I felt dizzy, my head was spinning, I forgot to breathe.

This was the future. This was what it sounded like. Music like the bellowing of the road-building machines, a neverending clatter, a commotion that roared away toward the crimson sunrise on the far horizon.

I leaned forward and looked out the window. Smoke was rising from a tipper truck, they were starting the final surfacing. But what the truck was spewing forth was not black, shiny-leather asphalt. It was oil-bound gravel. Grey, lumpy, ugly, bloody oil-bound gravel.

That was the surface on which we inhabitants of Pajala would be bicycling into the future.

* * *

When all the machines had finally gone away I started going for cautious little walks around the neighborhood. The world grew with every step I took. The newly surfaced road led to other newly surfaced roads, the gardens stretched away like leafy parks with giant dogs standing guard, barking at me and rattling their running chains. The further I walked, the more there was to see. The world never seemed to end, it just went on and on, and I felt so dizzy I was almost sick when it dawned on me that you could go on walking for ever. In the end I picked up courage and went over to Dad, who was busy washing our new Volvo:

"How big is the world?"

"It's enormous," he said.

"But it must stop somewhere, surely?"

"In China."

That was a straightforward answer that made me feel a bit better. If you walked far enough, you'd eventually come to an end. And that end was in the realm of the slitty-eyed ching-chong people on the other side of the globe.

It was summer and roasting hot. The front of my shirt was stained by drops from the ice-pop I was licking. I left our garden, left my safe little world. I occasionally looked back over my shoulder, worried about getting lost.

I walked as far as the playground, which was really an old hayfield that had survived in the middle of the village. The local authority had installed some swings, and I sat down on the narrow seat. Started heaving enthusiastically on the chains to build up speed.

The next moment I realized I was being watched. There was a boy sitting on the slide. Right at the top, as if he were about to come down. But he was waiting, as motionless as a hawk, watching me with wide-open eyes.

I was on my guard. There was something worrying about the boy. He can't have been sitting up there when I arrived, it was as if he'd materialized out of thin air. I tried to ignore him, and forced the swing up so dizzyingly high that the chains started to feel slack in my hands. I made no sound and closed my eyes, and could feel my stomach churning as I hurtled down in a curve faster and faster toward the ground, then up toward the sky on the other side.

When I opened my eyes again he was sitting in the sandbox. As if he'd flown there on outstretched wings: I hadn't heard a thing. He was still watching me intently, although he was half-turned away from me.

I allowed the swing to come slowly to a stop, then I jumped down onto the grass, did a forward roll, and lay on my back on the ground. Stared up at the sky. Clouds were rolling over the river in patches of white. They were like big, woolly sheep lying asleep in the wind. When I closed my eyes I could see little creatures scuttling about on the insides of my eyelids. Small black dots creeping over a red membrane. When I shut my eyes tighter I could see little violet-colored fellows in my stomach, clambering over one another and tracing patterns. So there were animals inside me as well, a whole new world to explore in there. I felt giddy as it dawned on me that the world was made up of masses of pockets, each of them enclosing the previous one. No matter how many layers you penetrated, there were more and more still to come.

I opened my eyes and gave a start. I was astonished to see the boy lying beside me. He was stretched out on his back right next to me, so close that I could feel the warmth of his body. His face was strangely small. His head was a normal size, but his features had been crammed into far too small a space. Like a doll's face glued onto a large, brown, leather football. His hair had been snipped unevenly at home, and a scab was working its way loose on his forehead. His face was turned toward me. He was screwing up one eye, the upper one that was catching the sun. The other was lying in the grass and wide open, with an enormous pupil in which I could see my own reflection.

"What's your name?" I wondered aloud.

He didn't answer. Didn't move.

"*Mikäs sinun nimi on?*" I repeated the question in Finnish.

Now he opened his mouth. It wasn't a smile, but you could see his teeth. They were yellow, coated with bits of old food. He stuck his little finger into his nostril—the others were too big to fit in. I did the same. We each dug out a booger. He stuck his into his mouth and swallowed. I hesitated. Quick as a flash he scraped mine off my finger and swallowed that as well.

I realized he wanted to be my friend.

We sat up in the grass, and I had an urge to impress the boy in return.

"You can go wherever you like, you know!"

He was listening attentively, but I wasn't sure if he'd understood.

"Even as far as China," I added.

To show that I was serious I started walking toward the road. Confidently, with an affected, pompous air of self-assurance that concealed my nervousness. He followed me. We walked as far as the yellow-painted vicarage. There was a bus parked on the road outside, no doubt it had brought some tourists to see the Laestadius House. We bowed our heads in acknowledgment of the Bible-thumping evangelist who once lived there. The bus doors had been left open because of the heat, but there was no sign of the driver. I grabbed the boy and pulled him over to the steps, and we climbed aboard. There were suitcases and jackets lying on the seats, which smelled a bit damp. We sat right at the back and crouched down behind the seats. Before long some old ladies got in and sat down, panting and sweating. They were speaking a language with a lot of waterfall sounds, and gulping down big swigs of lemonade straight from the bottle. Several more retirees eventually came to join them, and then the driver turned up, pausing outside to insert a wad of snuff into his mouth. Then we set off.

Wide-eyed and silent, we watched the countryside flash past. We soon left Pajala behind and breezed off into the wilds. Nothing but trees, trees without end. Old-fashioned telephone poles with porcelain insulators and wires sagging in the heat.

We'd gone several miles before anybody noticed us. I happened to bump against the seat in front, and a lady with pincushion cheeks turned around. I smiled expectantly. She smiled back, rummaged around in her handbag, and then offered us a sweet from an unusual cloth-like bag. She said something I didn't understand. Then she pointed at the driver and asked:

"*Papa?*"

I nodded, my smile frozen.

"*Habt ihr Hunger?*" she asked.

Before we knew where we were she'd thrust a cheese roll into each of our hands.

After a long and shaky bus ride we pulled up in a large parking lot. Everybody got off, including me and my friend. In front of us was a big concrete building with a flat roof and high, spiky, metal aerials. Beyond it, behind a wire fence, were some propeller-driven airplanes. The bus driver opened a hatch and started pulling out bags and suitcases. The nice lady had far too much luggage and seemed to be under a lot of strain. Beads of sweat were forming under the brim of her hat, and she started making nasty smacking noises, sucking at her teeth. My friend and I gave her a hand as a way of saying thank-you for the sandwiches, and we lugged her heavy cases into the building. The flock of retirees crowded round a desk, jabbering away loudly, and started to produce no end of papers and documents. A woman in uniform tried patiently to keep them in order. Then we passed through the gate as a group and made our way toward the aircraft.

It was going to be my first ever flight. We both felt a bit like fish out of water, but a nice brown-eyed lady with gold heart-shaped earrings helped us fasten our seat-belts. My friend landed a window seat, and we grew increasingly excited as we watched the shiny propellers start spinning, faster and faster, until they disappeared altogether in a round, invisible whirl.

Then we started moving. I was forced back into my seat, could feel the wheels bumping, and then the slight jerk as we left the ground. My friend was pointing out of the window, fascinated. We were flying! There was the world down below us. People, buildings, and cars shrunk to the size of toys, so small we could have popped them into our pockets. And then we were swallowed up by clouds, white on the outside but grey inside, like porridge. We emerged from the clouds and kept on climbing until the aircraft reached the sky's roof and started soaring forward so slowly we hardly knew we were moving.

The nice stewardess brought us some juice, which was just as well, as we were very thirsty. And when we needed a pee she ushered us into a tiny little room and we took turns to get our willies out. We peed into a hole, and I imagined it falling down to the ground in a yellow drizzle.

Then we each got a book and some crayons. I drew two airplanes crashing into each other. My friend leaned his jaggedly cropped head further and further back and soon dozed off with his mouth wide open. The plane window misted over as he breathed.

We eventually landed. All the passengers pushed and shoved their way out, and in the mêlée we lost the old lady. I asked a man in a peaked cap if this was China. He shook his head and pointed us in the direction of an endless corridor, where people were hurrying to and fro with their bags. We walked down it, and I had to ask politely several times before we came across some people with slitty eyes. I reckoned they must be going to China, and so we sat next to them and waited patiently.

After a while a man in a dark blue uniform came over to us and started asking questions. We were going to be in trouble, you could see it in his eyes. So I smiled shyly and pretended not to understand what he was saying.

"Dad," I mumbled, pointing vaguely into the distance.

"Wait here," he said, and strode off purposefully.

The moment he'd gone we moved to another bench. We soon discovered a black-haired Chinese girl in knee-length socks who was playing with a sort of plastic puzzle. It seemed to be fun. She laid the pieces out on the floor and showed us how you could make a tree, or a helicopter, or whatever you liked. She talked a lot and waved her thin arms around, and I think she said her name was Li. She sometimes pointed to a bench where an elderly fellow with stern eyes was reading a newspaper, next to an older girl with raven hair. I gathered she was the girl's sister. She was eating a messy red fruit, and kept wiping her mouth with a lace-edged napkin. When I went over to her she gave me a guarded look, then offered me some pieces that had been neatly cut with a fruit knife. It tasted so sweet that I started to get butterflies in my stomach: I'd never tasted anything so good in my life, and I prodded my friend into trying some as well. He was ecstatic, his eyes half-closed. As a sort of thank-you, he suddenly produced a matchbox, opened it, and let the Chinese girl have a look.

Inside was a large, shimmering green beetle. Big sister tried to feed it a little piece of fruit, but then it flew off. Buzzing softly, it flew over all the slitty-eyed people in their seats, circled two ladies with long pins in their hair who gazed up in astonishment, swerved around a mountain of suitcases with some carelessly wrapped reindeer antlers on top, and headed down the corridor just under the florescent lights, the same way we had come in. My friend looked sad, but I tried to console him with the thought that it was no doubt going back home to Pajala.

At that very moment there was an announcement over the loudspeakers, and everybody started moving. We packed the puzzle into the girl's bag of toys and passed through the gates in the midst of the jostling crowd. This aircraft was much bigger than the previous one. Instead of propellers this one had big drums on the wings that made a whistling sound when they started up. The noise grew and grew until it was a deafening roar, and after we'd taken off it reduced to a booming rumble.

We got to Frankfurt. And if my silent traveling companion hadn't all of a sudden needed to relieve himself and started doing his number twos under a table, we would certainly, we would quite definitely, without a shadow of a doubt, we would have gotten to China.

CHAPTER 2

About living and dead faith, how nuts and bolts give rise to violence, and a remarkable incident in Pajala church

I started seeing quite a lot of my taciturn friend, and before long I went home with him for the first time. His parents turned out to be Laestadians, members of the revivalist movement started by Lars Levi Laestadius a long time ago in Karesuando. He was only a little man, but his sermons were red-hot and peppered, when he attacked strong drink and debauchery, with almost as many curses as the sinners used. He spoke with such force that the reverberations are still rumbling on even today.

Faith is not enough for a Laestadian. It's not just a question of being baptized or confessing your sins or putting money in the collection plate. Your faith has to be a living faith. An old Laestadian preacher was once asked how he would describe this living faith. He considered for quite a while, then answered thoughtfully that it was like spending the whole of your life walking uphill.

The whole of your life walking uphill. It's not easy to imagine that. You're ambling casually along a narrow, winding country road in Tornedalen, like the one from Pajala to Muodoslompolo. It's early

summer and everything is fresh and green. The road passes through a
forest of weather-beaten pines, and there's a smell of mud and sun from
the bog pools. Capercaillies are eating gravel in the ditches, then take
off with wings flapping loudly and disappear into the undergrowth.
Soon you come to the first hill. You notice that you're starting to
climb and you can feel your calf muscles getting tense. But you don't
give it a second thought, it's only a gentle slope after all. When you
reach the top, quite soon, the road will level out again and the forest
will be flat and dry on each side, with fluffy white reindeer moss in
among the soaring tree trunks.

But you keep on climbing. The hill goes on longer than you thought it
would. Your legs grow tired, you slow down and you look more and more
impatiently for the crest, which has to come at any moment now, surely.

But it never does come. The road just keeps on going up and up. The
forest is the same as before, with stretches of bog and brushwood and
here and there an ugly clear-felled patch. But it's still uphill. It's as if
somebody has broken off the whole landscape and propped it up on
one edge. Lifted up the far end and stuck something underneath it, just
to annoy you. And you start to suspect that it will keep on going uphill
for the rest of the day. And the next day as well.

You keep on climbing stubbornly. The days gradually turn into
weeks. Your legs start to feel like lead, and you keep wondering who it
was who thought he'd be smart and prop up the landscape on one end.
It's been pretty skillfully done, you have to admit that, grudgingly. But
surely it will level out once you get past Parkajoki, there are limits after
all. And you come to Parkajoki, but the road is still going uphill and so
you think it will be Kitkiöjoki.

And the weeks turn into months. You work your way through them
one stride at a time. And the snow starts falling. And it melts, and falls
again. And between Kitkiöjoki and Kitkiöjärvi you're pretty close to
giving up. Your legs are like jelly, your hip joints ache, and your last
reserves of energy are practically used up.

But you stop for a while to get your breath back, then keep battling on. Muodoslompolo can't be far away now. Occasionally you come across somebody going in the other direction, that's inevitable. Somebody skipping along merrily on the way to Pajala. Some of them even have bikes. Sitting on their seats without needing to pedal, freewheeling all the way down. That does raise your doubts, you have to admit that. You have to fight a few inner battles.

Your strides get shorter and shorter. And the years pass. And now you must be nearly there, very nearly there. And it snows again, that's how it should be. You peer through the snow flurries, and you think you might be able to see something. You think it might be getting a bit lighter just over there. The forest thins out, opens up. You can make out houses among the trees. It's the village! It's Muodoslompolo! And in mid-stride, one last short and shaky stride…

At the funeral the preacher bellows on about how you died in the living faith. No doubt about it. You died in the living faith, *sie kuolit elävässä uskossa*. You got to Muodoslompolo, we all witnessed it, and now at long last you are sitting on God the Father's golden luggage carrier, freewheeling down the eternal slope accompanied by fanfares of angels.

* * *

The kid turned out to have a name: his mother called him Niila. Both his parents were strict Christians. Although their house was teeming with kids, there was a dreary, church-like silence wherever you went. Niila had two elder brothers and two younger sisters, and there was another child kicking away in his mother's stomach. And as every child was a gift from God, there would be even more as time went by.

It was unreal for so many young children to be so quiet. They didn't have many toys—most of what they did have were made of rough wood by their elder brothers, and unpainted. The kids just sat there playing with them, as silent as fish. It wasn't only because they had been brought up in a religious way. It was something you found in other

Tornedalen families: they'd simply stopped talking. Possibly because they were shy, possibly because they were angry. Possibly because they found talking unnecessary. The parents only opened their mouths when they were eating; at other times they would nod or point when they wanted something, and the children took after them.

I also kept quiet whenever I went to visit Niila. Children have an instinctive feel for that sort of thing. I took my shoes off and left them on the mat in the hall and tip-toed into the kitchen with head bowed and shoulders slightly hunched. I was greeted by a mass of silent eyes, from the rocking chair, from under the table, from by the pot cupboard. Looks that stared, then turned away, sneaked off around the kitchen walls and over the wooden floor but kept coming back to me. I stared back as hard as I could. The face of the youngest girl puckered up with fear, you could see her milk teeth gleaming in her gaping mouth, and tears started to flow. She was sobbing, but even her sobs were silent. Her cheek muscles trembled and she clung to her mother's beskirted leg with her chubby little hands. Mum was wearing a headscarf even though she was indoors, and had her arms plunged up to the elbows in a mixing bowl. She was kneading vigorously, flour swirled up and was turned into gold dust by a sunbeam. She pretended not to notice that I was there, and Niila took that as a sign of approval. He led me over to a settee where his two elder brothers were exchanging nuts and bolts. Or perhaps it was some sort of game, involving a complicated pattern of shifting nuts and bolts around various compartments in a box. The brothers were growing increasingly annoyed with each other, and without speaking tried to wrench bolts from the other's hands. A nut fell onto the floor and Niila snapped it up. Quick as a flash the eldest brother grabbed him by the hand and squeezed until Niila was in so much pain he could hardly breathe, and was forced to drop the nut into the transparent plastic box. Whereupon the other brother turned it upside down. A clatter of steel as the contents rolled all over the wooden floor.

For one brief moment everything stood still. Every eye in the kitchen homed in on the brothers like rays of the sun through a magnifying glass. It was like when a film gets stuck in a projector, blackens over, goes crinkly, and then turns white. I could feel the hatred even though I couldn't understand it. The brothers lashed out and grabbed each other's shirt front. Biceps bulging, they exerted the force of industrial magnets and the gap between them closed inexorably. All the time they stared at each other, coal-black pupils, two mirrors face to face with the distance between them expanding to infinity.

Then their mum threw the dishtowel. It flew across the kitchen trailing a thin wisp of flour behind it, a comet with a tail that squelched into the elder son's forehead and stuck there. She eyed them threateningly, slowly wiping the dough from her hands. She had no desire to spend the whole evening sewing on shirt buttons. Reluctantly, the brothers let go. Then they stood up and left through the kitchen door.

Mum retrieved the dishtowel that had fallen to the floor, rinsed her hands, and went back to her kneading. Niila picked up all the nuts and bolts, put them in the plastic box, and stuck the box in his pocket with a self-satisfied expression on his face. Then he glanced furtively out of the kitchen window.

The two brothers were standing in the middle of the path. Trading punches in rapid succession. Heavy punches jerking their crew-cut skulls around like turnips in a hopper. But no shouting, no taunts. Biff after biff on those low foreheads, on those potato noses, bash after bash on those red cabbage ears. The elder brother had a longer reach, the younger one had to slot in his blows. Blood poured from both their noses. It dripped down, splashed about, their knuckles were red. But still they kept going. Biff. Bash. Biff. Bash.

We were given juice and cinnamon buns straight out of the oven, so hot that we had to keep what we bit off between our teeth for a while before we could chew it. Then Niila started playing with the nuts and bolts. He emptied them out onto the sofa, his fingers were trembling, and

I realized he'd been longing to do this for ages. He sorted them out into the various compartments in the plastic box, then tipped them out, mixed them up and started all over again. I tried to help him but I could see he was annoyed, so after a while I left to go home. He didn't even look up.

The brothers were still at it outside. The gravel had been kicked around by their feet to form a circular rampart. Still the same frenzied punches, the same silent hatred, but their movements were slower now, weariness was creeping in. Their shirts were soaked in sweat. Their faces were grey behind all the blood, powdered lightly with dust.

Then I noticed they had changed. They weren't really boys any more. Their jaws had swollen up, their canines were sticking out from between their swollen lips. Their legs were shorter and more massive, like the thighs of a bear, and so big their trousers were splitting at the seams. Their fingernails had turned black and grown into claws. And then I realized it wasn't dust on their faces, it was hair. They were growing a pelt, dark hair spreading over their fresh, boyish faces, down over their necks and inside their shirts.

I wanted to shout a warning. Rashly took a step toward them.

They stopped immediately. Turned to face me. Crouched slightly, sniffed my scent. And then I saw their hunger. They were starving. They were desperate to eat, craved meat.

I stepped back. An icy chill ran down my spine. They growled. Started advancing shoulder to shoulder, two vigilant beasts of prey. They sped up. Stepped outside their gravel circle. Dug in their claws then pounced.

A dark cloud loomed over me.

My scream was stifled. Terror, whimpering, the squeaking of a stuck piglet.

Ding. Ding dong.

Church bells.

The holy church bells. *Ding dong. Ding dong.* A white-clad being cycled into the courtyard, a shimmering figure ringing his bell in a cloud of floury light. He braked without a word. Grasped the beasts with his enormous fists, lifted them by the scruff of their necks, and banged their turnip-heads together so hard that sparks flew.

"Dad," they gasped, "Dad, Dad…"

The bright light faded, the father flung his sons to the ground, grabbed them by their ankles, one son in each hand, and dragged them backward and forward over the gravel, smoothing out the surface with their front teeth until everything was nice and tidy again. And by the time he had finished, both brothers were crying their eyes out, sobbing, and they'd turned back into boys again. I raced home, galloping as fast as I could. In my pocket I had a bolt.

* * *

Niila's dad was called Isak and came from a big Laestadian family. Even as a little boy he'd been dragged along to prayer meetings in the smoke-filled hut where dark-suited smallholders and their wives in knotted headscarves sat bottom to bottom on the wooden benches. It was so cramped that their foreheads hit against the backs of those in front whenever they were possessed by the Holy Spirit and started rocking back and forth as they intoned prayers. Isak had sat there, hemmed in on every side, a delicate little boy among all those men and women being transformed before his very eyes. They started breathing more deeply, the air grew damp and fetid, their faces turned crimson, their glasses misted over, their noses started dripping as the two preachers sang louder and louder. Their words, those living words weaving the Truth thread by thread, images of evil, of perfidy, of sins that attempted to hide underground but were torn up by their hideous roots and shaken like worm-eaten turnips before the congregation. In the row in front was a little girl with braids, fair golden hair gleaming in the darkness, squashed in by grown-up bodies riddled with dread. She was motionless, pressing a doll to her heart as the storm raged over her head. It was horrific to see her mother and father weeping. Watching her grown-up relatives being transformed, crushed. Sitting there hunched up, feeling the fall-out dripping all over her and thinking: it's all my fault. It's my fault. If only I'd been a bit better behaved. Isak had clenched his boyish hands tightly together, and inside them it felt as if a swarm of insects were creeping around. And he thought: if I open my hands we'll all die. If I let them escape we're all finished.

And then one day, one Sunday after a few years had passed, he crawled out onto the thin nocturnal ice. Everything crumbled away, his defenses collapsed. He was thirteen and could feel Satan beginning to grow deep inside him. Filled with a fear that was greater than the fear of being beaten, greater than the urge for self-preservation, he'd stood up in the middle of the prayer meeting and, holding onto people's backs, he'd swayed back and forth before collapsing nose-first into the lap of Christ. Callused hands had been placed on his brow and his chest, it was a second baptism, that's the way it was done. He had unbuttoned his heart and been drenched by the flood of his sins.

There was not a single dry eye in the congregation. They had witnessed a great event. The Almighty had issued a summons. The Lord had taken the boy with His very own hand, and then given him back.

Afterward, when he learned to walk for the second time, as he stood there on trembling legs, they had propped him up. His corpulent mother had hugged him in the name and blood of Jesus, and her tears flowed down over his own face.

Obviously, he was destined to become a preacher.

* * *

Like most Laestadians Isak became a diligent worker. Felled trees and piled the trunks up on the frozen river during the winter, accompanied the logs down to the sawmills in the estuary when the ice melted in the spring, clearing jams on the way, and looked after the cows and potato fields on his parents' smallholding during the summer. Worked hard and made few demands, steered well clear of strong drink, gambling and Communism. That sometimes caused him a few problems with his lumberjack colleagues, but he took their mockery as a challenge to be overcome, and didn't say a word during the working week, merely read books of sermons.

But on Sundays he would cleanse himself with saunas and prayers, and put on his white shirt and dark suit. During the prayer meetings he could cut loose at last, sail forth to attack filth and the Devil, brandish the Good Lord's two-edged sword, aim His law and gospel truth at all the world's sinners, the liars, lechers, hypocrites, the foulmouthed, boozers, wife-beaters, and Communists who flourished in the accursed valley of the River Torne like lice in a blanket.

His face was young, energetic, and smooth-shaven. Eyes deep-set. With consummate skill he grabbed the attention of his congregation, and was soon engaged to a fellow believer, a shy and well-polished Finnish girl from the Pello district, smelling of soap.

But when the children started to come, he was forsaken by God. One day there was nothing but silence. Nobody answered his pleas.

He was left with nothing but confusion, tottering on the edge of the abyss. Filled with sorrow. And festering malice. He started to sin, just to discover what it felt like. Minor little wicked acts, aimed at his nearest and dearest. When it dawned on him that he quite enjoyed it, he kept going. Worried members of his church tried to engage him in serious conversations, but he put the Devil's curse on them. They turned their backs on him, and did not return.

But despite being abandoned, despite feeling hollow, he still regarded himself as a believer. He maintained the rituals, and brought up his children in accordance with the Scriptures. But he replaced the Good Lord with himself. And that was the worst form of Laestadianism, the nastiest, the most ruthless. Laestadianism without God.

* * *

This was the frosty landscape in which Niila grew up. Like many children in a hostile environment, he learned how to survive by not being noticed. That was one of the things I observed the very first time we met in the playground: his ability to move without making a sound. The chameleon-like way in which he seemed to take on the background color, making him practically invisible. He was typical of the self-effacing inhabitants of Tornedalen. You hunch yourself up in order to keep warm. Your flesh hardens, you get stiff shoulder muscles that start to ache when you reach middle age. You take shorter steps when you walk, you breathe less deeply and your skin turns slightly gray through lack of oxygen. The meek of Tornedalen never run away when attacked, because there's no point. They just huddle up and hope it will pass. In public assemblies they always sit at the back, something you can often observe at cultural events in Tornedalen: between the spotlights on stage and the audience in the stalls are ten or more rows of empty seats, while the back rows are crammed full.

Niila had lots of little wounds on his forearms that never healed. I eventually realized that he used to scratch himself. It was unconscious, his filthy fingernails just made their own way there and dug themselves in. As soon as a scab formed, he would pick at it, prize it up, and break it loose, then flick it away with a snapping noise. Sometimes they would land on me, sometimes he just ate them with a faraway look on his face. I'm not sure which I found more disgusting. When we were at my place I tried to tell him off about it, but he just gaped at me with a look of uncomprehending surprise. And before long he was at it again.

Nevertheless, the oddest thing of all about Niila was that he never spoke. He was five years old after all. Sometimes he opened his mouth and seemed to be about to come out with something, you could hear the lump of phlegm inside his throat starting to move. There would be a sort of throat-clearing, a gob that seemed to be breaking loose. But then he would change his mind and look scared. He could understand what I said, that was obvious: there was nothing wrong with his head. But something had got stuck.

No doubt it was significant that his mother was from Finland. She had never been a talkative woman and came from a country that had been torn to shreds by civil war, the Winter War, and the Continuation War, while her well-fed neighbor to the west had been busy selling iron ore to the Germans and growing rich. She felt inferior. She wanted to give her children what she had never had. They would be real Swedes, and hence she wanted to teach them Swedish rather than her native Finnish. But as she knew practically no Swedish, she kept quiet.

When Niila came around to our place we often sat in the kitchen because he liked the radio. My mum used to have the radio mumbling away in the background all day, something unknown in his house. It didn't much matter what was on, so we had a potpourri of pop music, *Woman's Hour*, *Down Your Way*, bell-ringing from Stockholm, language courses, and church services. I never used to listen, it all went in one ear and out the other. But Niila seemed to be thrilled to bits just by the sound, the fact that it was never really quiet.

One afternoon I made a decision. I would teach Niila to talk. I caught his eye, pointed to myself and said:

"Matti."

Then I pointed at him and waited. He also waited. I reached out and stuck my finger between his lips. He opened his mouth, but still didn't say anything. I started stroking his throat. It tickled, and he pushed my hand away.

"Niila!" I said, and tried to make him say it after me. "Niila, say Niila!"

He stared at me as if I were an idiot. I pointed at my crotch and said: "Willy!"

He grinned, thought I was being rude. I pointed at my backside. "Bum! Willy and bum!"

He nodded, then turned his attention back to the radio again. I pointed at his own backside and made a gesture to show something coming out of it. Then I looked at him questioningly. He cleared his throat. I went tense, waiting impatiently. But nothing happened. I was annoyed and wrestled him down to the floor.

"It's called poop! Say poop!"

He slowly extricated himself from my grip. Coughed and sort of bent his tongue around inside his mouth to loosen it up.

Then he said: "*Soifa.*"

I held my breath. That was the first time I'd ever heard his voice. It was deep for a boy, hoarse. Not very attractive.

"What did you say?"

"*Donu al mi akvon.*"

There it was again. I was flabbergasted. Niila spoke! He'd started talking, but I couldn't understand what he said.

He rose to his feet with great dignity, walked over to the sink and drank a glass of water. Then he went home.

Something very remarkable had taken place. In his state of dumbness, in his isolated fear, Niila had created a language of his own. Without conversing, he had invented words, begun to string them together and form sentences. Or wasn't it just him alone, perhaps? Could there be something deeper to it, embedded in the deepest peat layer at the back of his mind? An ancient language? An ancient memory, deep frozen but slowly starting to melt?

And before I knew where I was, our roles had been reversed. Instead of me teaching him how to talk, it was him teaching me. We would sit in the kitchen, Mum pottering around in the garden, the radio buzzing in the background.

"*Ĉi tio estas seĝo,*" he said, pointing at a chair.

"*Ĉi tio estas seĝo,*" I repeated after him.

"*Vi nomiĝas Matti,*" he said, pointing at me.

"*Vi nomiĝas Matti,*" I repeated, good as gold.

He shook his head.

"*Mi nomiĝas!*"

I corrected myself.

"*Mi nomiĝas Matti. Vi nomiĝas Niila.*"

He clicked his tongue enthusiastically. There were rules in this language of his, it was ordered. You couldn't just babble on in any way you liked.

We began using it as our secret language, it grew into a space of our own where we could be all to ourselves. The kids from round about grew jealous and suspicious, but that only increased our pleasure. Mum and Dad got a bit worried and thought I was losing my powers of speech, but when they phoned the doctor he said that children often invented fantasy languages, and it would soon pass.

But as far as Niila was concerned, the blockage in his throat had been cleared once and for all. Our make-believe language overcame his fear of talking, and it wasn't long before he started speaking Swedish and Finnish as well. He understood quite a lot already, of course, and had a big passive vocabulary. It just needed translating into sounds, and his mouth movements had to be practiced. But it proved to be more difficult than one might have thought. He sounded odd for ages, his palate had trouble with all the Swedish vowels and the Finnish diphthongs, and he was constantly dribbling. Eventually it became possible to understand more or less what he was saying, although he still preferred to stick to our secret language. That was where he felt most at home. When we spoke it he would relax, and his body movements were less awkward, more natural.

* * *

One Sunday something unusual happened in Pajala. The church was full. It was a routine service, the clergyman taking it was Wilhelm Tawe as usual, and in normal circumstances there would have been plenty of room. But on this particular day it was full to overflowing.

The reason was that the inhabitants of Pajala were going to see their first real, live African.

There was so much interest that even Mum and Dad were induced to turn up, despite the fact that they very rarely went to church at all apart from on Christmas Eve. In the pew in front of us were Niila and his parents and all his brothers and sisters. Just once he turned around and peered at me over the back of the pew, but was immediately prodded quite hard by Isak. The congregation included office workers and lumberjacks, and even a few Communists, all whispering among themselves. It was obvious what they were talking about. They were wondering if he'd turn out to be really black, pitch black, like the jazz musicians on record sleeves. Or would he just be a sort of coffee-brown?

There was a ringing of bells and the vestry door opened. Wilhelm Tawe emerged, looking a little bit on edge behind his black-framed spectacles. And there behind him. Also in vestments. A glittering African mantel, oh, yes…

Pitch black! Whispers spread swiftly among the Sunday School mistresses. No trace of brown, more a sort of bluish black. Trotting alongside the African was an old deaconess who had been a missionary for many years, thin as a rake and with skin like tanned leather. The men bowed in the direction of the altar and the woman curtsied. Then Tawe got the service under way by bidding all present welcome, especially the guest who had traveled all the way from the war-stricken Congo. Christian parishes there were in crying need of material assistance, and today's entire collection would be sent straight to the aid of our brothers and sisters in Africa.

Then the rituals commenced. But everybody just stared. They couldn't take their eyes off him. When the hymn-singing started they heard the black man's voice for the first time. He knew all the tunes, they seemed to have the same hymns in Africa. He sung in some native language or other, with a deep and somehow passionate voice, and the congregation sang softer and softer in order to listen to him. And when it was eventually time for the sermon, Tawe gave a sign. The unheard-of happened. The African and the deaconess both climbed the stairs into the pulpit.

There was widespread alarm—we were still in the sixties, and women were supposed to take a back seat and keep silent in the churches. Tawe explained that the lady's role was to translate what our guest said. It was a little on the cramped side in the pulpit as she tried to establish herself next to the imposing form of the newcomer. She was sweating profusely under her deaconess's hat, took hold of the microphone, and looked nervously around the congregation. The African was calm and collected as he contemplated the worshipers before him, and he seemed even taller than he was, thanks to his high pointed hat, in blue and yellow. His face was so dark that all anybody could see was the glint in his eyes.

Then he started preaching. In Bantu. He ignored the microphone. He sort of shouted, loud and alluring, as if he were trying to contact somebody in the jungle.

"I give thanks to the Lord, I thank the Lord my God," according to the deaconess's translation.

Then she dropped the microphone, slumped forward moaning loudly, and would have hurtled over the pulpit rail had it not been for the African, who grabbed hold of her and hung on.

The sacristan was the quickest of all to react. He raced forward, skipped up the stairs, folded the deaconess's bony arm round his bull-like neck, and levered her down into the aisle.

"Malaria," she gasped. Her skin had turned deep yellow, and she was on the point of collapse. Several members of the church council hastened forward and helped to carry her out of church and into a car that sped off in the direction of the cottage hospital.

The rest of the congregation and the African were still there. They were all somewhat confused. Tawe stepped forward to assert his authority, but the black man was still dominant in the pulpit. He'd travelled halfway across the globe, and he ought to be able to cope with this. In the name of God.

He thought for a moment, then switched from Bantu to Swahili. Many millions speak Swahili, including many Africans up and down their continent. Unfortunately, not many people in Pajala are acquainted with it. He was confronted by a mass of blank faces. He changed language once again, and tried Creole. His dialect was so specialized that not even the local French teacher could work out what he was saying. He was getting a little heated and tried a few sentences in Arabic. Then, in desperation, a couple of phrases in Flemish that he'd picked up while in Belgium on ecumenical business. But contact was zero. Nobody could understand a word he said. In remote areas like this, you had to speak Swedish or Finnish.

He was desperate by now. Tried one final language. Bellowed it out so that it rebounded from the organ loft, roused an old lady from her slumbers, scared stiff a small child, who burst out crying, and set the pages of the lectern Bible a-flutter.

Then Niila stood up in the row in front of me and answered him back.

A deathly silence descended on the whole church. Every single member of the congregation turned around and glared at this impertinent little brat. The African focused on the little boy in the midst of the congregation before him, just as Niila was being given a good thump by Isak. The African gentleman raised his hand to indicate a halt to any such action. The palm of his hand was remarkably white. Isak felt the eyes boring into him, and let go of his son.

"*Ĉu vi komprenas kion mi diras?*" bellowed the African.

"*Mi komprenas ĉion,*" replied Niila.

"*Venu ĉi tien, mia knabo. Venu ĉi tien al mi.*"

Niila edged his way hesitantly along the pew and into the aisle. For a moment it looked as if he might run away. The African beckoned to him with the pale palm of his hand. All eyes were on Niila as he took a few trembling steps. Shoulders hunched, he tip-toed toward the pulpit, a bashful little boy with an awful haircut. The black man helped the slip of a lad up the stairs. Niila could barely manage to peer over the edge of the pulpit, but the African lifted him up in his strong arms. Held him like he would a little lamb. In a quaking voice, the black clergyman resumed his sermon:

"*Dio nia, kiu aŭskultas niajn preĝojn...*"

"O Lord our God, who hears our prayers," said Niila without the slightest hesitation. "Today Thou hast sent unto us a boy. We thank Thee, O Lord, we give unto Thee our thanks."

Niila understood every word the African said. The citizens of Pajala were thunderstruck, the boy translated the whole of the sermon as the African delivered it. The faces of Niila's parents and those of his brothers and sisters were etched with dismay, they sat in their pew like statues of stone. They were in shock, they realized they were witnessing a wondrous act of God. Many of the congregation burst into tears from sheer rapture, everyone was deeply moved. Whispers of jubilation spread throughout the chapel until the whole place was buzzing. The hand of God! A miracle!

As for me, I couldn't understand what was happening. How had the African learned our secret language? For that was what they were speaking, him and Niila.

News of the incident spread rapidly, and not just in ecclesiastical circles. For a long time afterward there were calls from newspapers and the television people, wanting to interview the boy, but Isak forbade it.

I didn't see Niila again until several days later. He sneaked into our kitchen one afternoon, still looking staggered. Mum gave us each a sandwich and we sat there chewing. Niila occasionally pricked up his ears in that awkward way he had.

The radio was mumbling away in the background, as usual. I suddenly had a strange suspicion, and turned up the volume.

"*Ĝis reaŭdo!*"

I gave a start. Our secret language! A brief snatch of a signature tune, and then an announcer said:

"You have been listening to today's installment of our course in Esperanto."

A course in Esperanto. He'd picked it up from our radio.

I turned slowly to look at Niila. He was miles away, staring out of the window.

CHAPTER 3

*On dramatic occurences in the Purly-Girly School shed
and an unexpected meeting that takes us way ahead of events*

Next to the children's playground was a big wooden building, almost a mansion, with lots of windows all over its façade. It used to be the hostel that housed pupils at Pajala School who lived too far away to travel to and fro every day. Then it became a college where teenage girls were trained in such things as cookery and knitting. Instead of being unemployed, the girls were able to become well-qualified housewives. We boys imagined the girls being taught how to "knit one, purl one," and called it the Purly-Girly School. Next to it was an old, red-painted shed, full of scrap metal and discarded school stuff that we youngsters found exciting to rummage through. There were some loose boards at one of the gable ends that could be prized open far enough for us to crawl inside.

It was a scorching hot day in high summer. A canopy of heat weighed down on the village, and the smell of hay from the grassy parts of the playground was as strong as tea. All alone, I sneaked up to the wall of the shed, keeping my eyes peeled for the school caretaker. We children were scared stiff of him. An athletic type in paint-stained overalls, he hated kids nosing around. He would materialize out of thin air with his radar eyes on alert. He used to wear wooden clogs that he kicked off before pouncing on his prey like a tiger. No kid ever managed to get away. He would clamp his hand around their necks like a pair of pliers round a nail, then wrench them up into the air and very nearly sever their heads from their bodies. I had seen with my own eyes one of the lads down our street, a teenage tough guy as hard as steel, cry like a baby after daring to ride his moped where he shouldn't.

I took the risk even so. I'd never been in the shed before, but I'd heard about others who'd been bold enough to sneak in. With nerves at breaking point, I peered cautiously around. It seemed all clear. I dropped down on all fours, prized open the wooden boards, stuck my head through the dark opening and edged my way inside.

After the sunshine, everything was pitch black. The darkness and blindness made my eyes swell up. I stood there motionless for an age. Then, gradually, I was able to start making out shapes. Old bookcases, broken desks. A pile of wood, a stack of bricks. A cracked lavatory bowl with no lid. Boxes of old electrical odds and ends. I started wandering about, being careful not to bump into anything. There was a smell of dried-out rubbish, sawdust, and mortar, and warm asphalt from the sun-drenched roofing felt above. I glided around, almost swimming through the dense darkness. It was olive-green, like the heart of a spruce forest. I was moving as if through a dormitory in the dead of night. Breathing silently through my nose, feeling the dust tickle my nostrils. My canvas shoes made no noise on the concrete floor, the soft paws of a cat.

Stop! A giant loomed up before me. I shrank back, a shadowy shape in the darkness. My body stiffened.

But it wasn't the caretaker. It was an old boiler. Tall and heavy, covered in metal plating. As fat as a housewife, with big, cast-iron doors. I opened the biggest of them. Peered into a cold, pitch-black opening.

Called softly. My voice reverberated inside. She was empty. An iron maiden, left with no more than the memory of an all-consuming inner fire.

I carefully stuck my head in the opening. Groped around with my hand and felt lumps of rust coming loose from the walls, or maybe it was soot. There was a smell of metal in there, oxide and old fires. I hesitated for a moment, plucking up courage. Then I wormed my way in through the narrow fire doors.

Now I was inside her. Crouching down in her rounded belly, curled up like a fetus. I tried to stand up but hit my head against the top. I closed the door quietly behind me, pulled it until the last faint strip of light was extinguished.

I was shut in. She was pregnant with me, protecting me with the bullet-proof iron walls of her womb. I was inside her, I was her child. It felt stimulating but unnerving. A feeling of security mixed with a strange sensation of shame. I was doing something forbidden. I was betraying somebody, my mother perhaps. Eyes closed, I curled myself up more tightly, resting my chin on my knees. She was so cold, but I was warm and young, a small, glowing ember. And when I pricked up my ears I could hear her whispering. A faint sighing through a damper or the remains of a cut-off pipe—tender, comforting words of love.

Then there was a clattering noise. The caretaker stormed into the shed. He was furious, threatening to beat the living daylights out of any bloody brats he found in here. I held my breath and listened to him charging around, searching, heaving aside furniture, shoving and kicking at piles of rubbish, as if hunting down rats. He charged round and round the shed, growling out threats: no doubt somebody in the Purly-Girly School had seen me and blabbed to the caretaker. And now it was all buggers and bastards and death threats, in both Swedish and Finnish.

He stopped right next to the boiler, and seemed to be sniffing the air. As if he were onto a scent. I could hear a scraping noise against the metal plating, and realized he was leaning against her. The only thing separating us was an inch and a half of iron skin.

The seconds ebbed away. Then another scrape, and the sound of footsteps fading into the distance. The shed door slammed shut with a bang. I stayed where I was. Didn't move a muscle as the minutes ticked by. Suddenly there was the clomping of the wooden clogs again. With the cunning of a grown man, he'd only pretended to go away in order to flush out his young prey. But now he gave up. This time he left for real: I could hear his footsteps fading away on the gravel outside.

At last I was able to move. My joints were aching, and I pushed at the door. It was stuck. I pushed harder. It wouldn't budge. I broke out in a cold sweat. Fear grew into panic. The caretaker must have accidentally brushed against the handle. I was locked in.

Once the immediate paralysis began to wear off, I started screaming. The echo magnified my voice. I stuck my fingers in my ears and yelled out over and over again.

But nobody came.

Hoarse and exhausted, I collapsed in a heap. Was I doomed to die? Die of thirst, shrivel up in my iron sarcophagus?

The first day was awful. My muscles ached, I had cramps in my legs. I had no option but to sit curled up, and my back grew stiff. Thirst was driving me mad. The heat given off by my body condensed on the sooty walls, I could feel it dripping and tried to lick it. It tasted metallic, and only made me feel even more thirsty.

The second day I was completely overcome by exhaustion. I dozed for hour after hour. The emptiness felt liberating. I lost all trace of time. I slid in and out of contented oblivion and realized I was dying.

The next time I came to my senses it was obvious that a considerable length of time had passed. The greenish light of day that seeped in through the ventilator was fainter now. Days were growing shorter. It was getting much colder at night, and soon there was frost as well. I kept warm by jerking my muscles one after another.

I don't remember much of winter. I curled up in a ball and slept most of the time. I was in a trance as weeks passed by. When the spring warmth finally returned, I discovered I had grown. My clothes felt tight and uncomfortable. I wriggled and squiggled and managed to take them off, and resumed my waiting, naked.

Gradually my body filled more and more of the cramped space. Several years must have passed. The damp given off by my body had started the iron rusting, and I had flakes of rust in my tousled hair. I could no longer move up and down, only sway from side to side like a duck. If the doors were to open now, the hole would be too small for me to climb out anyway.

Eventually it became almost unbearable. I couldn't even move from side to side any more. My head was jammed in between my knees. There was no room for my shoulders to grow any broader.

For several weeks I was convinced it was all over.

In the end everything came to a full stop. I occupied the whole of the space. There was no room to breathe properly any more, all I could manage was a series of short gasps. But I kept growing even so.

Then it happened one night. A faint cracking noise. Like when a pocket mirror breaks. A brief pause, then a slow crunching noise from behind me. When I tensed my muscles and pressed backward, the wall gave way. Bulged out, then burst open in a cloud of splinters, and I shot out into the world.

Naked, newly born, I crawled around through the rubbish. Stood up on very shaky legs and supported myself against a bookcase. To my surprise, I noticed that the whole world had shrunk. No, it was me who'd doubled in size. I'd sprouted pubic hair. I'd grown up.

It was a bitterly cold winter night outside. Not a soul in sight. I plowed my way through the snow and scampered barefoot through the village, still stark naked. At the crossroads between the chemist's and the newsstand, four youths were lying in the middle of the road. They seemed to be asleep. I stopped and stared down at them in surprise. Bent down to examine them more closely in the light from the street lamp.

One of the youths was me.

Feeling very odd, I lay down next to myself on the icy road. It was cold against my skin, melted and turned damp.

I started to wait. They'd wake up soon enough.

CHAPTER 4

*In which the village children start at the Old School and learn about
southern Sweden, and a homework session ends in a hell of a row*

One overcast morning in August the bell rang, and I started school.
Class one. Mum and I marched solemnly into the tall, yellow-painted
wooden building that housed the infants' section—an old school imag-
inatively named the Old School. We were piloted up a creaky staircase
and into a classroom on the first floor, strode over broad, yellowed
floorboards with a thick, shiny coat of varnish, and were each shep-
herded behind an antique school desk with a wooden lid, a pen box,
and a hole for an inkwell. The lid was covered in carvings made by the
knives of generations of pupils. The mums all trooped out, and we
were left behind. Twenty kids with loose milk teeth and knuckles covered in warts. Some had speech defects, others wore glasses, many
spoke Finnish at home, several were used to receiving a good beating if
they stepped out of line, nearly everybody was shy and came from
working-class homes, and knew from the start they didn't belong here.

Our teacher was a matron in her sixties with round, steel-framed
glasses, her hair in a bun contained by a net and pierced with pins, and
she had a long, hooked nose that made her look like an owl. She always

wore a woolen skirt and a blouse, often a cardigan buttoned halfway up, and soft, black shoes like slippers. She approached her duties gently but firmly, intent on carving out of the roughly sawed planks confronting her something neat and presentable, and capable of coping with Swedish society.

To begin with, we all had to go to the blackboard and write our names. Some could, others couldn't. On the basis of that scientific test, our teacher divided the class into two groups, called Group One and Group Two. Group One comprised all those who had passed the test—most of the girls and a few sons of civil service clerks. The rest were in Group Two, including Niila and me. We were only seven, but correctly classified right from the start.

Hanging from the wall in front of the class were the Letters of the Alphabet. A scary army of sticks and half-moons stretching all the way across. Those were the things we were required to wrestle with, one after another: force them down on their backs in our notebooks and make them do as they were told. We were given pencils as well, and chalks in a cardboard box, a reading book about Li and Lo, and a stiff sheet of cardboard with blocks of water-color paints that looked like brightly colored sweets. Then we had to get down to work. The inside of the desk had to be lined with paper, and the books as well: there was a deafening crackling and rustling from the rolls of wax paper we'd brought from home, and some eager snipping with blunt school scissors. Finally we stuck a timetable onto the inside of our desk lids with tape. Nobody had the slightest inkling what all those mysterious squares actually meant, but the timetable was an essential part of things, part of being Neat and Orderly, and it meant our childhood was over. Now we were faced with a six-day week with school from Monday to Saturday, and on the seventh day there was Sunday School for those who hadn't had enough of it.

Neat and Orderly. Stand in a line outside the hall when the bell rang for lessons. Walk in a line to the canteen, with the teacher at the front.

Raise your hand whenever you wanted to speak. Raise your hand whenever you wanted to leave the room for a pee. Turn the punched holes in your paper toward the windows on your left. Go out into the playground the moment the bell rang for break. Go back in the moment the bell rang for lessons. Everything done in that typically calm, Swedish manner, and only rarely was it necessary for some cheeky oaf in Group Two to have his hair tweaked by pincer-like magisterial talons. We liked our teacher. She really knew how to turn you into an adult.

Right at the front, next to teacher's desk, was the harmonium. It was used every morning when she took attendance and we sang hymns. She'd sit down on the stool and start pedalling away. Her fat calves bulged inside her beige knee-length stockings, her glasses misted over, she spread her gnarled fingers over the keyboard, and gave us a chord. Then a quivering dowager-soprano, with stern glances to left and right, making sure we were all joining in. Sunlight seeping in through the window panes, yellow and warm over the nearest desks. The smell of chalk. The map of Sweden. Mikael, who suffered from nosebleeds and sat with his head leaned back, clutching a roll of paper towels. Kennet, who could never sit still. Annika, who always spoke in a whisper, and with whom all the boys were in love. Stefan, who was brilliant at football but would ski into a tree on the Yllästunturi slalom slope three years later and kill himself. And Tore and Anders and Eva and Åsa and Anna-Karin and Bengt, and all the rest of us.

As a citizen of Pajala, you were inferior—that was clear from the very beginning. Skåne, in the far south, came first in the atlas, printed on an extra-large scale, completely covered in red lines denoting main roads and black dots representing towns and villages. Then came the other provinces on a normal scale, moving farther north page by page. Last of all was Northern Norrland, on an extra-small scale in order to fit onto the page, but even so there were hardly any dots at all. Almost at the very top of the map was Pajala, surrounded by brown-colored tundra, and that was where we lived. If you turned back to the front you could see that Skåne was in fact the same size as Northern Norrland, but colored green by all that confoundedly fertile farming land. It was many years before the penny dropped and I realized that Skåne, the whole of our most southerly province, would fit comfortably between Haparanda and Boden.

We had to learn that Kinnekulle was 1,004 feet above sea level. But not a word about Käymävaara, 1,145 feet high. We had to be able to ramble on about the Viska, the Ätra, the Vomit, and the Bile (or whatever they were called), four colossal rivers that flowed from the southern Swedish highlands. Many years later I saw them with my own eyes. I felt obliged to stop the car, get out, and give my eyes a good rub. Ditches. Tiny little brooks barely deep enough to paddle in. No bigger than Kaunisjoki or Liviöjoki.

I felt similarly alienated when it came to culture.

"Have you seen Mr. Chantarelle?" our reader asked us.

I could answer that question with an outright "no." Nor Mrs. Chantarelle, nor any other members of the family, come to that. Chantarelles didn't grow in our part of the world.

We sometimes used to receive *Treasure Trove*, the savings bank magazine, with a picture of the bank's oak tree logo. If we saved our money, it would grow and grow until it was as big as that majestic old oak, we were told. But there were no oak trees around Pajala, and so we realized there was something fishy about the ad. The same sort of things applied to the *Treasure Trove* crossword, where one of the clues that kept cropping up was a tall tree similar to a cypress, seven letters. Answer: juniper. But where we lived the juniper was a straggly little bush about knee-high.

Music lessons were a fascinating ritual. Our teacher would produce a big, clumsy tape recorder and put it on her desk—a gigantic chest dotted with spikes and knobs. She would slowly thread in and set up a tape, then hand out song books. Peer at the class with her owlish eyes, and switch the recorder on. The reels would start turning, then a bright and breezy signature tune would blare out from the loudspeakers. A brisk female voice spouting something or other in a Stockholm accent. The voice would go on to give us a perfect music lesson, peppered with sighs and squeals of enthusiasm. The pupils on the tape were from the Nacka School of Music in Stockholm, and to this very day I wonder why we were forced to listen to these southerners with angelic voices singing about bluebells and cowslips and other tropical vegetation. Sometimes one of the Nacka pupils would sing a solo, and the worst thing was that one of the boys had the same name as me.

"Now, repeat that tune for me, Matthias," the lady would chirrup, and a girlish boy soprano would ring out as clear as a bell. At which point the whole of our class would turn around to stare at me, grinning and giggling. I wished I could have gone up in smoke.

After several pedagogical repetitions, we were expected to sing along with the tape—the Kermit the Frog Ensemble joins the Vienna Boys' Choir. Our teacher's eyes took on a glint of steel, and the girls started to sing softly like the soughing of zephyrs through tufts of grass. But we boys stayed as silent as fish, moving our lips when our teacher glared at us, but that was all. Singing was unmanly. *Knapsu.* And so we kept quiet.

We gradually caught on to the fact that where we lived wasn't really a part of Sweden. We'd just been sort of tagged on by accident. A northern appendage, a few barren bogs where a few people happened to live, but could only partly be Swedes. We were different, a bit inferior, a bit uneducated, a bit simple-minded. We didn't have any deer or hedgehogs or nightingales. We didn't have any celebrities. We didn't have any theme parks. No traffic lights, no mansions, no country squires. All we had was masses and masses of mosquitoes, Tornedalen-Finnish swearwords, and Communists.

Ours was a childhood of deprivation. Not material deprivation—we had enough to get by on—but a lack of identity. We were nobody. Our parents were nobody. Our forefathers had made no mark whatsoever on Swedish history. Our last names were unspellable, not to mention being unpronounceable for the few substitute teachers who found their way up north from the real Sweden. None of us dared write in to *Children's Family Favorites* because Swedish Radio would think we were Finns. Our home villages were too small to appear on maps. We could barely support ourselves, but had to depend on state handouts. We watched family farms die, and fields give way to undergrowth. We watched the last logs floating down the River Torne when the ice melted, before it was banned; we saw forty muscular lumberjacks replaced by one diesel-oozing snowmobile; we watched our fathers hang up their heavy-duty gloves and go off to spend their working week in the far-distant Kiruna mines. Our school exam results were the worst in the whole country. We had no table manners. We wore woolly hats indoors. We never picked mushrooms, avoided vegetables, never held crayfish parties. We were useless at conversation, reciting poems, wrapping presents, and giving speeches. We walked with our toes turned out. We spoke with a Finnish accent without being Finnish, and we spoke with a Swedish accent without being Swedish.

We were nothing.

There was only one way out. Only one possibility if you wanted to be something, no matter how insignificant. You had to live somewhere else. We learned to look forward to moving, convinced it was our only chance in life, and so we moved. In Västerås you could be a person at last. In Lund. In Södertälje. In Arvika. In Borås. There was an enormous evacuation. A flood of refugees that emptied our village, but strangely enough it felt voluntary. A phoney war.

The only ones who ever returned from the south were those who died. Car crash victims. Suicides. And eventually also those killed off by AIDS. Heavy coffins dug down into the frozen earth among the birch trees in Pajala cemetery. Home at last. *Kotimaassa*.

* * *

Niila's house had a view over the river and was in one of the oldest parts of Pajala. It was a spacious, well-built house from the end of the previous century, with large, small-paned windows along the long walls. If you examined the façade closely, you could see traces of where it had been extended. There were still two chimneys from two separate hearths: the house had been too big to be heated by just one fire. When Laestadianism was at its peak, the house had been a natural grey color; but at some point in the 1940s it had been painted the traditional Swedish red, with white window trim. The rough corners had been sawed and planed in accordance with the new fashion, to make sure the house couldn't be mistaken for an overgrown barn—much to the distress of national archivists and other persons of good taste. On the river side were grassy meadows that had been fertilized for thousands of years with river silt every time the thaw came, and they produced abundant and rich hay, perfect for boosting milk production. At this very spot several hundred years ago, one of the earliest settlers had taken off his birch-bark backpack and created a smallholding for himself. But the grass in the meadows had not been harvested for years. Creeping bushes and undergrowth had thrust up their sauna twigs here, there, and everywhere. The place stank of gloom and decline. Visitors did not feel welcome there. There was a chill about the spot, like that of someone browbeaten so relentlessly as a child that all the bitterness had been directed inward.

The cowshed was still standing, and over the years it had been turned into a shed and a garage. School was out, and I'd gone home with Niila. We'd exchanged bikes for the day. He'd borrowed mine, which was rather flashy with a racing saddle and drop handlebars. I was riding his Hercules—"just the thing for knobbly knees," as the nastier element in class three used to shout at him when he rode past. As soon as we got to his house, Niila dragged me with him to the cowshed.

We sneaked up into the loft, up the steep, axe-hewn stairs that had been polished by a century's feet. It was semi-dark up there, with only one small, glazed window to admit the afternoon sun. There were piles of junk everywhere—damaged furniture, a rusty scythe, enamel buckets, rolled-up carpets smelling of mold. We paused by one of the walls. It was dominated by a huge bookcase full of volumes with worn, brown leather spines. Religious tracts, collections of sermons, books on ecclesiastical history in both Swedish and Finnish, row after row of them. I'd never before seen so many books at the same time, apart from in the library on the top floor of the Old School. There was something unnatural about it, something decidedly unpleasant. Far too many books. Who could possibly ever manage to read them all? And why were they there, hidden away in a cowshed, as if there were something shameful about them?

Niila opened his satchel and took out his reader starring Li and Lo. We'd been given an extract to prepare for homework, and he found his way to the place, turning the pages over with his clumsy, boyish fingers. Concentrating hard, he started mouthing the letters one after another, spending an enormous effort connecting them up to form words. Then he grew tired of it and slammed the book shut with a bang. Before I'd caught on to what was happening, he hurled it down the stairs with tremendous force. It landed awkwardly and the spine broke against the rough floorboards.

I looked doubtfully at Niila. He was smiling, with red patches on each cheek, reminiscent of a fox with long canines. Then he plucked a tract from the enormous bookcase, quite a small volume with soft covers. Defiantly, he flung that downstairs as well. The thin, silky pages rustled like leaves before it crashed to the ground. Then followed in quick succession a few volumes of collected works, heavy brown tomes that disintegrated with a crack as they landed.

Niila looked encouragingly in my direction. I could feel my heart starting to pound with excitement as I reached for a book. Flung it down the stairs and watched several pages flutter out before it thumped down into a rusty wheelbarrow. It looked outrageously funny. Growing more and more ecstatic, we hurled down more and more books, egging each other on, spinning them up in the air, kicking them like footballs, laughing until we choked as the shelves were emptied one after another.

All of a sudden Isak was standing there. Broad-shouldered like a wrestler, black and silent. Not a single word, just big, fleshy fingers trembling as he unfastened the buckle of his belt. He ordered me away with one brief gesture. I crept down the stairs like a rat then bolted for the door. But Niila stayed behind. As the cowshed door closed behind me, I could hear Isak starting to beat him.

* * *

Just for a moment I look up from the notepad I started filling in Nepal. The commuter train is approaching Sundbyberg. The morning rush hour, the smell of damp clothing. In my briefcase is a file with twenty-five corrected school essays. February slush, and over four months to go before the Pajala Fair. I sneak a look out of the train window. High over Huvudsta is a flock of jackdaws, circling excitedly round and round.

I switch my attention back to Tornedalen. Chapter five.

CHAPTER 5

About two hesitant winter warriors, chain thrashings,
and the art of stomping out a ski slope

Every day when lessons were over at the Purly-Girly School, hordes of sixteen- and seventeen-year-old girls would come swarming past our house. Pretty young things. This was the sixties after all, with lots of mascara, false eyelashes, miniskirts, and tight plastic boots. Me and Niila used to perch on the snowdrift outside our house and check them out. They would saunter past in bunches, chatting away, bare-headed no matter how cold it was, so as not to disturb their hairdos. They smoked like chimneys, and left behind a sickly-sweet smell of ashtrays and perfume that I associate to this day with desire. Occasionally they might say hello to us. We'd be incredibly embarrassed, and pretend we were building a snow fortress. Even though we were only seven, we were certainly interested in them, in a way. You couldn't really say we were horny, it was more of a vague longing. I'd have loved to have kissed them, to get close to them. Snuggle up to them like a little kitten.

Anyway, we started throwing snowballs at them. Mainly so they'd regard us as manly, I think. And believe it or not, it worked. These lanky sixteen-year-old Valkyries would scamper off like reindeer, screaming and shrieking, holding up their makeup bags as shields. They really made a meal of it. We were only throwing loosely packed little bundles of snow that rarely hit them, after all—fluffy lumps of snow that came floating down like woolly Lapp mittens. But it was enough to impress them. We were a force to be reckoned with.

It went on like this for a few days. We made a store of snowballs as soon as we got home from school. By now we felt like soldiers from Vittulajänkkä fighting in the Winter War, two battle-scarred veterans in action on a foreign continent. We bristled in expectation. Fighting brought us closer and closer to pleasures we could only dream of. Our cockscombs grew with every battle fought.

There came the flock of girls. Several bunches with irregular intervals between them. As they approached, we crouched down behind the ramparts of snow piled up at the side of the road by the snow plow. The plan was worked out in great detail. We used to let the first group pass by unscathed, then throw the snowballs at their backs while the other groups came to a halt in front of us. Create disarray and panic. And admiration, of course, of our manly deeds.

We crouched down in wait. Heard the girls' voices approaching, the smokers' coughs, the giggles. We stood up at exactly the right moment. Each of us with a snowball in our right hand. Like two fearsome Vikings we watched the girls scamper away, screaming. We were just about to heave our missiles into their midst when we realized that one of the girls was standing her ground. Only a couple of yards in front of us. Long, blond hair, neatly made-up eyes. She was staring straight at us.

"Just you dare throw one more snowball, and I'll kill you," she snarled. "I'll hit you so hard, you'll never walk again. I'll make such a mess of your faces that your mothers will burst into tears the moment they clap eyes on you…"

Niila and I slowly lowered our snowballs. The girl gave us one last, terrifying look, then turned on her heel and strolled after her friends.

Niila and I didn't move. We didn't even look at each other. We just felt we'd been terribly misunderstood, in spades.

* * *

As a boy in Pajala, one's life was dominated by chain thrashings. They were a means of adjusting the balance of power between the male citizens of the village. You were drawn into them as a young lad of five or six, and didn't escape until you were fourteen or fifteen.

Chain thrashings took something like the following form: a few little lads would start arguing. Anders punched Nisse, who started crying. I won't go into the cause of the argument, whether there was a history of animosity or some kind of family feud hovering in the background. A young lad simply hit another one, and then they went home.

That's when the chain reaction starts.

The one on the receiving end, Nisse, immediately tells his two-years-older brother about it. Big brother goes out into the village and keeps his eyes peeled: the next time he comes across Anders he gives him a good hiding and extracts revenge. Anders goes home crying his eyes out and tells his own four-years-older brother, who goes out into the village and keeps his eyes peeled. The next time he comes across Nisse or Nisse's elder brother, he gives them a good hiding and issues a series of threats into the bargain. (Are you still with me?) Nisse's five-years-older, burly first cousin hears an abridged version of what has happened and beats up Anders's brother, Anders himself, and a few friends who tagged along as bodyguards. Both Anders's two friends' six-years-older brothers go out into the village and keep their eyes peeled. The rest of Nisse's brothers, cousins, and other relatives hear an abridged version of what has happened, who has beaten up whom, and in what order; the same thing happens on Anders's side. Exaggerations in the interests of propaganda are common. Eighteen-year-old second cousins twice removed and even fathers receive urgent requests for assistance, but claim they couldn't care less about the petty squabbles of little kids.

That gives some idea of how things developed. The most elaborate of chain thrashings would involve classmates, neighbors, and an entire range of friends, especially if the two original combatants came from different parts of the village. In that case it was Vittulajänkkä versus Paskajänkkä, or Strandvägen versus Texas, and war was declared.

The duration of a chain thrashing could be anything from a few days to several months. The norm was a few weeks, following the pattern described above. The first stage was scuffling and an exchange of blows with little kids crying. Then came the threat stage, with the strongest ones involved roaming the village with their eyes peeled while the little kids stayed in hiding at home. If any of the little brats got caught, it was no laughing matter, believe you me. I used to think that was the worst stage, that non-stop terror between school and the relative safety of home. Last of all came the disarmament stage, when nobody could remember or be bothered to remember all those complicated patterns of punishment with all the subtle variations, and the whole thing ran out of steam.

But before that happened, life was dominated by the balance of terror. It's winter and you're on your own on your kick-sled, gliding over the tightly packed snow to the corner shop where you're going to buy a bag of mixed candy. It's mid-afternoon, but it's already quite dark, and scattered snowflakes are drifting down from the endless lead-grey sky, sparkling under the street lamps like stars. You're standing with one foot on the runner of your sled, clinging on to the handlebar and kicking with your other foot, skimming your way between the mountains of snow piled up on each side of the road by the plows. Your runners are being held back a bit by the newly fallen snow, and from the nearby main road to Kiruna you can hear the booming of a snow plow bludgeoning its way through the winter. And then, just ahead at the crossroads, one of the big boys materializes. The black silhouette of a pupil from the senior school. He comes toward you, you slow down and try to make out who it is. You consider turning back, but you see there's another big lad closing in from behind. Hard to make out who it is in the gloom, but he's certainly big. You're surrounded, a little boy on a kick-sled. All you can do is hope. Square your shoulders and advance toward the first of the big boys, who eyes you up and down. The street lamps are snowing, his face is in the shadows, and now he steps forward and your heart stands still. You try to prepare yourself for what's coming, snow down the back of your neck and all down your back and into your trousers, your ears boxed so hard you can feel your skull coming loose, your woolly hat thrown up into a birch tree, sobs and snot and humiliation. You stiffen up like a calf as the slaughterer approaches. And now he's right in front of you and you have to stop. He's as big as an adult, but you don't recognize him. He asks you whose boy you are, and you recall that there are at least three chain thrashings going on at the moment, your mind is working overtime, then you tell him who you claim to be, and hope you've hit upon the right answer. And the bloke puckers up his eyebrows and knocks your hat off into the snow. Then he says:

"Lucky for you!"

And you brush the snow off your hat, set off again, and wish to God you were a grown-up.

* * *

The end of winter was in sight, the worst of the cold was over. The days were still short, but in the lunch break you could occasionally catch a glimpse of the sun over the frosty rooftops, looking like a blood orange. We drank in the light in greedy gulps, and the fiery deep orange juice filled us with renewed lust for life. It was like crawling out of a burrow, waking up from hibernation.

One day Niila and I made up our minds to test Laestadius Hill. Straight after school we strapped on our wooden skis with cable bindings and took a short cut through the children's playground. It was getting dark. The skis sunk about a foot into the loose, deep top covering

of snow. Niila led the way, and I followed in his tracks, two blurred figures in the murky gloom. Over by the Laestadius House loomed two
rows of sky-high giant spruce firs like church steeples. Silent, ancient,
holy trees, preoccupied with greater thoughts than ours.

We crossed over the ice-covered Laestadiusvägen, our skis clattering
on the road surface; the street lamps were on already. We clambered
over the piled-up snow by the side of the road and slunk into the darkness that sloped steeper and steeper down toward the river. We skied in
silence past the statue of Lars Levi: he was staring out into the birch
trees, his head covered by a cap of snow. Soon the streetlights had faded
away behind us, but it wasn't completely dark even so. Light was
reflected by millions of ice crystals, and grew until it seemed to be hovering over the ground. Our eyes slowly became used to it. The slope
stretched out in front of us, swishing away down to the river. But it was
impossible to ski on as yet, covered knee-deep in soft snow. We turned
our skis at right angles to the slope, and started stomping. Ski-width by
ski-width we worked our way down the hill. Compressing the snow,
pounding it down with all the weight our young bodies could bring to
bear, making a furrow between the masses of snow on either side, all
the way down the long slope to the ice-covered river. We worked side
by side, sweat pouring off us under our clothes. And when we finally
got to the river, we turned back again. Stomped our way back over our
own tracks, with bull-like obstinacy. Compressed the snow still more,
made it as hard and smooth as we possibly could.

And finally we're standing there. Back where we started, after all that
strenuous effort. Our legs are shaking, our lungs heaving; but stretching
out below us is the tightly packed slope. A broad, smooth path, the
result of thousand upon thousand stomps with our skis. We stand side
by side, Niila and me. Gaze down into the darkness. The slope points
us down into a blurred, murky dream world, disappears like a fishing
line dropped through a hole in the ice. Vague shadows, silent movements down in the depths. A thin thread plunging down into our

dreams. We glance at each other. Then we crouch forward, dig in our bamboo poles. At exactly the same moment we thrust ourselves forward.

We're off. Glide away. Surge faster and faster through the night. Swishing. The cold burning our cheeks. Two steaming young boys, two newly cooked black puddings thrown into the freezer. Faster and faster, wilder and wilder. Side by side, mouths open wide, warm holes sucking in the winter. Perfectly stomped, couldn't be better! Knees flexible, feet firm in tightly laced boots. A roar penetrates our flesh, our speed approaches the impossible, snow flashing, wind howling, everything swirling.

And then it happens. A thunderous explosion rolls over the ice down Tornedalen as far as Peräjävaara and the air is smashed like a mirror. We break through the sound barrier. The sky is as hard and sharp as gravel as we hurtle down through it, side by side, each in our twirling cloud of snow, whirling round and round in powdery bounces, arms outstretched, our ski poles pointing to the sky, at outer space, at our shining stars.

CHAPTER 6

How an old biddy takes her place at the right hand of God,
and on the hazards involved in distributing worldly goods

One bleak day in spring Niila's grandma took her leave of this earthly
life. Still mentally alert, she had lain on her deathbed and confessed her
sins in a barely audible whisper before licking the bread with the tip of
her liver-brown tongue and having her shriveled lips sprinkled with
wine. Then she said she could see a bright light, and angels drinking
curdled milk from ladles, and when she drew her last breath her body
became half an ounce lighter, that being the weight of her eternal soul.

Close relatives were summoned to the *ulosveisu* the same day as she
died. Her sons carried her coffin around all the rooms in the house,
with the foot end first and the lid open so that she could take farewell
of her home; hymns were sung, coffee was drunk, and the corpse was
eventually driven off to the freezer at the mortuary.

Then the funeral arrangements were made. The Pajala telephone
exchange glowed red hot, and the post office started distributing invi-
tations all over Norrbotten, Finland, south Sweden, Europe, and the
rest of the world. After all, Grandma had filled as much of the world as
she could manage and had had time for. She had borne twelve children,

the same number as the apostles, and like the apostles the children had
gone off in all possible directions. Some lived in Kiruna and Luleå, others in the suburbs of Stockholm, and others yet in Växjö and Kristianstad
and Frankfurt and Missouri and New Zealand. Only one still lived in
Pajala, and that was Niila's father. All of them came to the funeral,
including the two deceased sons—the ladies of the parish in touch with
the other side had seen them. They had wondered who the two boys
were, standing with heads bowed by the coffin during the introductory
hymn, but then had realized that they were rather bright around the
edges and that their feet were hovering a finger's breadth over the ground.

Also present were grandchildren and great-grandchildren from all over
the globe, strange, elegantly dressed creatures speaking every Swedish
dialect you could think of. The grandchildren from Frankfurt had
German accents, while the Americans and New Zealanders chattered
away in Swenglish. The only ones from the younger generation who
could still speak Tornedalen Finnish were Niila and his brothers and sisters, but they didn't say very much anyway. There was a whole host of
languages and cultures assembled in the Pajala church, a very tangible
tribute to what a single fertile Tornedalen womb could give rise to.

Valedictory homilies delivered by the side of the coffin were numerous and lengthy. Tribute was paid to the deceased's life of honest toil,
in a spirit of devoted prayer and self-denial. She had lugged and heaved,
heaved and lugged, fed cattle and children, raked more hay than three
horse-drawn harvesters, woven five hundred yards of rag carpet, picked
three thousand buckets of berries, drawn forty thousand buckets of
water from the well in the yard, chopped firewood equivalent to a major
clear-felling in the Käymäjärvi forests, washed a mountain of dirty
linen as high as Mount Jupukka, and shoveled acres of shit from the
outhouse without so much as a word of complaint, and when she lifted
potatoes the clatter of them dropping into the tin bucket had frequently been mistaken for a salvo from a Finnish machine gun. To
mention but a few of her achievements.

In her last years, when she had been bed-ridden, she had read the Bible from cover to cover eighteen times—the old Finnish version, of course, uncontaminated by the modernizers and atheists who work for the Bible Commissions. Naturally, the written Word was nothing compared to the Living one, the two-edged sword wielded with such fervor at prayer meetings; but it might as well be read as she had nothing else to do.

As usual at Tornedalen heroic burials, the preachers spoke mostly about Hell. They described in minute detail the endlessly burning charcoal stack where sinners and heretics were fried like pork in tar in the Devil's red-hot skillet, while he prodded them with his trident to bring out the juices. The congregation cowered in their pews, and the old lady's daughters, especially, shed many a crocodile tear into their permanent waves and fashionable dresses, while the men who had married into the family shuffled uneasily with hardened hearts. But here was an opportunity to sow the seeds of penitence and mercy over almost all the globe, and it would have been unpardonable not to try. Besides, Grandmother had filled a whole notebook with instructions on how the funeral was to be conducted, and there was to be much Holy Writ and a modicum of the Gospel in the service. None of your forgiveness scattered glibly hither and thither on an occasion like this.

But when the heavenly gates finally opened at the end of the ceremony, when the angels breathed sweet-smelling Grace into the Pajala church and the earth trembled and Grandma was delivered unto the Heavenly Father, the women sniffled into their handkerchiefs and wept and quivered and hugged one another in the name and blood of Jesus Christ amen, the pews and aisles were filled with the scent of freshly mown hay, and the whole church rose half an inch from its foundations before crashing back in place with a resounding, deafening thud. And the faithful saw the light, the light of Paradise, as when you open your eyes briefly while sound asleep in a silent summer's night, when you open your eyes toward a window and see the gentle

glow of the midsummer sun gleaming in the night sky, a brief interlude in a dream, then close them again. And the next morning when
you wake up there is only a faint memory left of something great and
mysterious. Love, perhaps.

* * *

After the funeral everyone was invited back to the house for coffee and
cakes. The mood was suddenly relaxed, almost exhilarated. Grandma
was with Jesus. Time to breathe again.

The only one not to thaw out was Isak. He prowled around in his
old preacher suit, and although it was a long time since he'd left the
straight and narrow, a few words over the coffin in praise of God had
been expected from him. A testimony from the prodigal son. Some
thought he might even have seen the light once again—greater things
than that had been witnessed at the funeral of a parent after all, a time
when one's own transience and mortality crept one generation closer to
home. The forefinger of God plunging like an iron rod into a hardened
heart and breaking the ice, messages from the Holy Ghost, confessions
of sins draining the penitent soul like the emptying of a brim-full
chamber pot, then forgiveness transforming it into a highly polished
Heavenly Chalice into which the Grace of God can fall like a summer
shower. But Isak had merely mumbled over the bier, softly, to himself.
Not even those in the front row had heard what he said.

Juice and buns were served up at the children's table. We had to eat
in shifts as there were so many of us. Niila looked uncomfortable in his
tightly buttoned Sunday shirt. While the old folk, clad in black, sat
around cackling away like crows, we youngsters wandered off outside.
The boys from Missouri followed us out. They were twins, aged about
eight, dressed in smart suits and ties. They spoke English to each other
while Niila and I conversed in Tornedalen Finnish; they kept yawning
because of jet lag, and were shivering noticeably. They both had crew
cuts and looked like miniature marines with ginger hair, like their Irish-

American father. You could see they were bewildered by being transplanted to the Old World and their mother's roots. It was May, the snow was melting after the long winter, but the river was still covered in ice. The birches were naked, and the previous year's grass was flat and yellow in the meadows where the snow had barely finished thawing away. They trod cautiously in their patent leather shoes, peering around uneasily on the lookout for Arctic predators.

I was curious and started chatting to them. They told us in sing-song Swedish-American that on their way to Sweden they'd broken their journey in London and seen the Beatles. I told them to cut out the fairytales. But they both swore blind the Beatles had driven past their hotel in a long, open Cadillac through rows of girls screeching and shrieking. It had all been filmed from a truck following close behind.

The twins had bought something as well. They produced a paper bag and took out a record with an English price tag.

"*Beatles*," I spelled out slowly. "*Roskn roll musis.*"

"'Rock 'n' Roll Music,'" they chorused, correcting my pronunciation with a grin. Then they handed the single over to Niila.

"It's a present. To our cousin."

Niila took hold of the record in both hands. Fascinated, he slowly slid out the circular piece of vinyl and stared at the hair-thin grooves. He held it so gingerly, as if afraid it would crack, like a wafer-thin disc of ice from a frozen waterbucket. Although this disc was black. Like sin.

"*Kiitos,*" he mumbled. "*Tack. Fenk yoo.*"

He sniffed at the plastic, then held it up toward the spring sun and watched the grooves glittering. The twins glanced at each other and smiled. They were already composing the story about their meeting with the natives that they'd recount for their buddies back home in Missouri as they all sat around chewing hamburgers and slurping colas.

Niila undid a few shirt buttons and hid the record under his clothes, next to his skin. He hesitated for a moment. Then he beckoned the twins, inviting them to follow him toward the road. Wondering what he had in mind, I accompanied them over the meadow, through the remains of the last, dirty snowdrifts.

We stopped when we came to the ditch. There was a culvert running underneath the road, made of large concrete tubes. If we bent down, we could see a white circle of light at the other end. Dirty grey melt-water was flowing through the culvert and splashing down at our feet, forming an oval-shaped pond. Next to it were the shrinking mountains of snow piled up by the snow plows, looking like heaps of filthy old bed linen. Niila pointed down into the murky depths.

"*Present,*" he said in English, with a smile to the twins.

They leaned forward. Just under the surface were some big, slimy lumps. From close up we could see there were little things moving inside. Tiny black embryos wriggling about. Some creatures had already forced their way out and were swimming around in the muddy water.

"*From cemetery,*" said Niila.

The twins eyed me skeptically as I endeavored to work out what Niila was trying to say.

"When the snow melts the water runs through the coffins," I elaborated in a low voice, "and the souls of the dead are washed along and end up here."

Niila found a rusty old coffee tin. The twins stared wide-eyed at the tadpoles in the pool.

"*Angels,*" Niila explained.

"If you rescue them they turn into angels and fly off to heaven," I added.

One of the twins took the coffee tin and started to unfasten his patent leather shoes. The other one hesitated, but soon followed suit. They quickly pulled off their socks and their immaculately creased trousers and stood barefoot at the edge of the pool in their baggy American boxer shorts. Then they waded into the mud with short, tentative steps. Within seconds they were going all out to rescue souls. The melted snow was up to their thighs. They were shivering with cold, but gripped by the excitement of the chase. Before long they were shouting with glee and holding up the coffee tin with a few tadpoles swimming around inside. Their lips had taken on a shade of blue.

Suddenly a dark, slimy mass slithered out of the culvert and dropped into the pool with a splash.

"*Grandma!*" exclaimed Niila.

One of the twins plunged his hands down into the mud, searching around for Grandma. Then he slipped and fell. His head disappeared under the slimy surface. His brother grabbed hold of him but lost his balance and was dragged down as well, flapping frantically with both arms. Spluttering and snorting they crawled back onto dry land, so cold by now that they could barely struggle to their feet. But the coffee tin was still standing in the grass, complete with tadpoles.

Niila and I were struck dumb by this display of bravery. The twins got dressed again, shivering so violently that we had to help them do up their shirt buttons. They pulled off their underpants and wrung them out, then removed the worst of the filth from their hair with their elegant tortoise-shell combs. Their eyes gleamed as they gazed into the coffee tin. A handful of little tadpoles were circling round and round, their tails wriggling from side to side. Eventually one of the brothers gave us a frozen-stiff but nevertheless hearty handshake.

"Thank you! *Tack! Keytoes!*"

Holding the coffee tin between them, they strode back toward the house, jabbering eagerly in American.

* * *

That same afternoon the arguments began over Grandma's estate. The family waited until the interment rituals were over and the neighbors and preachers had gone home, then all the house doors were closed to outsiders. The family's various branches, shoots and grafted-on stock assembled in the large kitchen. Documents were laid out on a table. Reading glasses were winkled out of handbags and perched on noses shiny with sweat. Throats were cleared. Lips were moistened with stiff, sharp tongues.

Then all Hell was let loose.

Grandma had actually written a will. It was in the notebook she'd left behind, and was comprehensive, to say the least. Detail after detail, page after page, in her shaky handwriting. This and that person should receive this and that under the following conditions. But as the old bird had been preparing her final exit for the last fifteen years or more, and was extremely capricious into the bargain, the pages teemed with alterations, crossings out, and additions in the margin, not to mention a loose sheet covered in cramped endnotes. Some relatives had been disinherited several times over, but then reinstated equally often. Others would only be allowed to inherit if certain conditions were fulfilled, such as declaring their allegiance to the Living Faith and renouncing the demon drink in the presence of the whole family, or begging all present plus Jesus Christ to forgive them a whole host of meticulously detailed sins they had committed over a number of years. The entire text had been signed and witnessed several times, but, alas, not the crucial loose page. Moreover, it was all written in Tornedalen Finnish.

Simply reading the document aloud in the stifling atmosphere of the kitchen took several hours. Every single word had to be translated into Swedish, standard Finnish, English, German, and Persian, since the daughter living in Växjö had married a Sunni Muslim immigrant. Not least the religious sections caused great difficulties. A fundamental requirement for inheriting was embracing the Living Faith, something most people from Tornedalen interpreted as meaning Laestadianism. After hearing the translation, there were protests from the Sunni Muslim, the son-in-law from New Zealand who was a Jew, and the daughter in Frankfurt who had become a Baptist: all of them argued in turn that their faith was just as much a Living Faith as that of anyone else there. Grandma's younger brother from Ullatti maintained noisily that as a West Laestadian he was the most Christian of all those present, whereupon an East Laestadian cousin, another one from the Assembly of Truth, and several fundamentalists protested strongly. An old biddy from a Finnish sect immediately went into a *liikutuksia* and started moaning and jumping around in ecstasy, sweat pouring off her. Others decided to play it safe and began confessing a multitude of sins while flailing their arms about, sobbing, embracing their neighbors and tripping over the rag carpets.

In the end Isak leapt to his feet and bellowed something about keeping traps shut, in both Swedish and Finnish. A drunken second cousin from Kainulasjärvi was caught red-handed adding a codicil of his own to the will, and was thrown out. A truce was declared and, after a series of protests and counteraccusations, a tense calm ensued. Several requested that the confessions they had just made, together with other proof of their allegiance to the Living Faith, should be recorded in the minutes, and this was accepted after a vote had been taken.

When the reading of the will was complete, the atmosphere was one of total and utter confusion. A laid-back engineer from Uppsala in the field of newfangled computing techniques suggested that the whole of the will should be put into a punched card program, so that with the aid of logic a just distribution of benefits could be achieved by running the program a number of times. Others immediately maintained that *ummikko*, a southerner, and in any case only a member of the family by marriage, would be well advised to keep his big mouth shut when important family matters were being discussed. Brothers and sisters, cousins and third cousins then huddled together in a series of small clusters to discuss tactics. The air was thick with whispers and mumblings. Feelers were put out, proposals made and rejected, alliances formed and dismantled, more or less hidden threats dispatched by messengers from one huddle to another. A few of the men withdrew for a pee in the garden and came back in suspiciously elevated spirits. Looks were exchanged. Sleeves were rolled up. The minutes-taker, a balding civil service clerk, tapped his coffee cup with a pencil and called the meeting to order. People thronged toward the kitchen table, jabbering in excitement and piously urging everybody else to be quiet.

"Hrm. Hrrruuuuummm…"

As far as the clerk could see, from his position as a neutral observer, the estate—that is, the total value of the smallholding and cottage, outbuildings, land, household goods, cash, bank accounts, and a small area of forest—should be divided into one hundred forty-three equal parts, apart from the spinning wheel, which had been specifically bequeathed to the next-door neighbor's wife.

A storm of agitated voices.

The official observer, a retired customs officer, requested that a reservation should be recorded in the minutes. In his view, admittedly not a very significant one although it was an opinion free of any partisan prejudice, the previous speaker had omitted to take into account the codicil on the loose sheet, paragraph three, about the evil and sinful nature of southern Sweden, and hence the smallholding, cottage, outbuildings, and household goods should go to the deceased's son Isak, while the remainder of the estate should be divided equally between those members of the family who were officially registered as domiciled within the constituency of Pajala.

The noise grew louder still.

The next-door neighbor's wife asked where the spinning wheel was, but was told in no uncertain terms to shut up.

A nephew who worked in the iron ore mines in Kiruna maintained that his home town could hardly be designated as southern Sweden, and, in any case, he had a summer cottage in nearby Sattajärvi and hence demanded to be categorized as a citizen of Pajala.

Another nephew from Kieksiäisvaara pointed out that the previous speaker had overlooked the paragraph on page fourteen in which the LKAB mines in Kiruna had been dismissed as the Babylon of the North, its employees condemned to the eternal fires of Hell, and that an illegally built property in Sattajärvi did nothing to alter that.

The drunken cousin started hammering on the door with a lump of firewood, demanding to be let in.

The Jew grabbed the Sunni Muslim by the collar, but was thrust back into the rocking chair. They shouted and cursed at each other while their wives stood by, translating. More and more of those present wanted to speak, and the clerk's pencil-tapping on his coffee cup was drowned in the uproar.

Then a fist was raised. A Sunday-scrubbed laborer's fist rising like a mushroom from the black-clothed fray. It swayed back and forth on its sturdy stalk, twisting around like the head of an owl. No doubt it was intended as a gesture, implying that enough was enough.

Immediately another identical mushroom sprung up. And another. A whole crop. People shouted each other down. Curses rang out in every conceivable language and dialect, threats swished through the air like whiplashes, and the house started shaking like the walls of Babylon.

Then all hell broke loose.

I shall stop at this point out of consideration for all those present. I shall desist from describing the punches, the bleeding lips, the scratches, the nosebleeds, the false teeth sent spinning though the air, the smashed spectacles, or the sly kicks and throttle-holds. I shall refrain from listing such weapons as frying pans, kitchen chairs, Wellington boots, shovels, dog bowls, and the Finnish family Bible. I shall omit all the un-Christian expressions, all the swearwords, especially the endless stream of those in Tornedalen Finnish, all the devastating accusations of stupidity, ugliness, obesity, inbreeding, senility, mental illness, or perverted sexual practices that were exchanged in overexcited voice registers.

I shall merely record that it was Gehenna.

CHAPTER 7

On rock music, its effect on the fair sex,
and the dangers of entering a room without knocking

It was getting dark when Niila came over to our house, his hand pressed against his shirt front. He was still wearing his best suit, but was a little shaken after the afternoon's encounters with his many relations. After a series of threats to call in the police and a long succession of counterthreats, they had considered the associated legal costs and decided to keep the matter within the family. The engineer from Uppsala had been given an opportunity to describe in detail the mechanics of punched card programming. A strict ban on any further consumption of alcohol within the boundaries of the smallholding had been announced. The Pajala cottage hospital had been required to dress the wounds of a surprisingly large number of people who had fallen and injured themselves. Running repairs on spectacles and false teeth had been made with insulating tape and superglue.

My sister was out, so we sneaked into her room. Niila unbuttoned his shirt and produced the lukewarm single. I solemnly placed it on the record player and lowered the pick-up arm. Turned up the volume. There was a faint scratching noise.

Then CRASH! A thunderclap. A powder keg exploded and blew up the room. All oxygen was sucked out, we were hurled against the walls, squashed into the wallpaper, and the whole house spun around at breakneck speed. We were like stamps on an envelope, all our blood rushed into our hearts, formed a gut-red clump—then suddenly everything changed direction, torrents raged into fingers and toes, red spurts of blood to every extremity of our bodies till we gaped cod-eyed.

An eternity later the spinning stopped. Air was sucked back in through the keyhole and we splatted down on the floor in tiny damp heaps.

Rock 'n' roll music.

Beatles.

It was too good to be true.

We couldn't speak for ages. We just lay there bleeding, drained, happy in the echoing silence. Then I stood up and played it one more time.

Same thing again. Incredible. This couldn't possibly be a human creation.

One more time.

In stormed Big Sister. She was furious, dug her talons into my arm and screeched so loud her chewing gum embedded itself in my eye. What the hell were we doing in her room? Fucking bastard kids, and she raised her ever-so-feminine arm to deliver a fatal karate blow.

Then she froze. The music beat her to it. It forced itself into her, swelled up like a prick inside her, spurted red all round. Magic! Three petrified mammals and a blaring portable gramophone.

When the record was finished, she was the one who started it again. That's the kind of music it was. You couldn't stop.

* * *

That night Niila and I biked to the River Torne. Out onto the bridge, high over the water, balanced on the narrow concrete thread stretched taut between the distant banks.

The whole river was still frozen, but the heat generated by the day had melted the snow of the endless forests, streams had started pumping through arteries under the icebound coffin lids enclosing the landscape, and the depths pulsated with new vigor. Muscles had swollen, and a thawed-out heart had started beating once more.

And now, at this very moment, the river breathes in and its rib-cage expands, pressing up against its three-feet-thick case, filling lungs and blood vessels like an escape artist intent on breaking out, digging in its heels, swelling up, slowly forcing up thousands upon thousands of icy tons, inch by inch. We don't see it, but it's going on all the time, subterranean, as tense as a dream, a surface buckling, a young man imprisoned but growing and growing until he fills the whole boiler with meat and muscles.

Another half inch.

We don't see it, we feel it. Maybe it's the air, the air pressure, a shudder in the sea of light stretching away towards Jupukka, the outline of a crow that suddenly turns back, or maybe it's something we feel in the pier of the bridge, through the concrete, a shimmering shriek of water.

Breathing in. Melted snow. The crow turns one more time, inexplicable.

Then it happens. Two terse crackling sounds. And then the snow-white surface splits asunder, cracking and splintering. A torrent of black water. A rumbling, new cracks, shattering axe-blows all over the mass of ice. Swelling blisters split open. Movement everywhere, everything starts moving. The whole of this incredible marble floor.

A minute later, and the river's risen more than two feet. Banks are flooded, black fingers of water probe their way forward. Enormous floes, a hundred tons, split wide open as everything round about forces its way in. They're thrust up on end, like glittering whales leaping then plunging back down into the sparkling deep. They're forced one over the other, like continents in the age of drift. They break up, low and bellow. Beat their foreheads on the bridge parapet, are crunched down

to clinking icicles. Noises you never hear otherwise, crashing and banging, creaking, sizzling, rustling, clanging, squeaking, it's non-stop music.
And we're in the midst of it.

Then the locals arrive. Park at the end of the bridge and come running out to join us, lining up along the iron railings; old men and old
women, young lads and young lasses and little girls and tiny tots held
tightly onto. Cousins and neighbors and old pals and even solitaries, as
if the river had gone around the village and bade them all to attend, as
if they'd all gotten the urge at the same time.

We just stand there. There's not much to add. We simply watch and
listen and feel the brittle concrete shuddering under our feet. Ice floes
hurtling past, one after another, there's no end to them, an endless
crashing, broken and chipped. And then we feel the bridge getting
dragged away from its foundations, it's melting away, it starts to swing
around upstream like a colossal icebreaker, we stand forward as it bat-
ters its way though the pack-ice, enormously powerful, at the start of a
long and adventurous journey.

"*Rock 'n' roll music!*" I yell to Niila.

He knows what I mean.

* * *

Once you've discovered the power the music has, there's no going back.
It's like the first time you tried wanking. You can't stop. You've opened
the bottle and the foam comes spurting out with such force that it rips
the door off its hinges and leaves a gaping hole behind. We all remember those films about submarines where the depth charges hit their
target and men covered in oil rush up to the watertight steel doors in
the bulkhead and try to close them, but they're thrown about like bits
of bark by the surging mass of water.

The College of Music at Nacka, on the other hand, was like practicing swimming on dry ground.

A bit like a spindly old schoolteacher teaching in primary school with wall charts and hands covered in chalk, trying to teach young lads how to masturbate. And to round it all off she sits at the harmonium and sings pedagogical wanking songs.

Niila started coming over much more often than he used to, and he always brought the record with him. As a result Sis suddenly turned into a human being and let us play it on her gramophone, as long as she could listen as well. Somehow or other, music brought us closer together, and it dawned on her that I wouldn't be a snotty-nosed kid for the rest of my life. Sometimes her friends were there as well. They sat on her bed, or on cushions on the floor: good-looking senior school girls who smelled nice of hair spray, chewing gum noisily. They wore tight jumpers, and had breasts. Mascara eyes. They got the measure of Niila and me—little brats—and tried to tease us and make us blush. Asked if we had girlfriends. If we'd ever kissed anybody. Described what to do with your tongue—it was pretty disgusting, enough to turn you on, although we were in our latency period and didn't really understand the point of the other sex.

One weekend night, when Mum and Dad had gone off to play car bingo at the local football ground, we marched into Sis's room without knocking. The girls screamed. There was a crate of beer in the middle of the floor. We backed out, but Sis dragged us in and locked the door. Then she threatened to thump us so hard if we squealed on her that our milk teeth would puncture what little brain we had, and she'd pull out so much of our hair that we'd go bald before we had a full mane, and then she'd scratch out our guts with her red-painted nails and slowly roast us with Dad's blowlamp that he used to wax our skis, and a lot more on the same theme.

I played the idiot in order to save my life—a good tactic in the Torne Valley context—and muttered something about how they were free to drink as much Tizer as they liked. Then the girls all burst out laughing and one of them said we had to taste a drop as well so that we were just as guilty as they were, that was the only way to seal our lips. She opened a bottle and came up close, and I felt her permanent wave on my cheek and her hair spray in my nostrils and her warm breath all over my face. She took hold of me by the cheeks, quite firmly, while another girl held the bottle over my mouth, and I opened it wide. She came so close that I could feel the softness of her tits, I leaned over backward like a suckling child waiting for its bottle, and I sucked and I drank and I sucked again, like at a woman's breast.

The beer tasted of straw. It stung my throat, bubbled and foamed. I lay back and gazed up into the girl's beautifully painted eyes: they were as blue as the river. She must have been at least fourteen, and she looked down at me so warmly, so tenderly. I wanted to stay there for the rest of my life, fall asleep in her embrace. Tears welled up in my eyes. She noticed, and took away the bottle. I'd drunk at least half of it. She zoomed in on me with her lipstick lips, and then she kissed me.

The girls all cheered. Sis smiled, her benevolence was unprecedented. I felt dizzy, and propped myself up against the wall. Niila was forced to drink the rest of the bottle. He did his best and was rewarded with applause. Panting for breath, he struggled for ages to unbutton his shirt, then produced the record. Then he sat down next to me, and Sis started the gramophone.

The girls went mad.

We must have played it at least twenty times.

I leaned against Niila and felt so happy, I thought I'd burst.

* * *

Afterward we found ourselves standing in the yard, shivering. The chill came tumbling down from the clear sky, it would be a bitterly cold night. Niila hung around, wanted to ask something, but didn't really dare. In the end he dragged me into the garage. Closed the door as quietly as he could, and then crept up close to my ear.

"What did she do?" he whispered.

I grabbed him by the shoulders.

"Stick out your tongue," I said. "No, not as much as that."

He pulled it back in so that just the tip was sticking out, round and wet and pink. I stuck mine out as well. We stood there without moving for a while. Then I leaned forward and kissed his salty, boyish mouth.

CHAPTER 8

*In which a piece of hardboard is carved, a mouth is opened,
and the stage is trodden for the first time*

The sixties were coming to an end, and in the big, wide world pop music was coming into its own. The Beatles went to India and learned to play the sitar, California was overwhelmed by Flower Power and psychedelic rock, and England bubbled over with bands like the Kinks, Procol Harum, The Who, Small Faces, and The Hollies.

Very little of all that reached as far out as Pajala. Sis did her best to keep up: she hung up a copper wire between a pair of pine trees in the garden as an antenna, and tuned in to Radio Luxembourg on our ancient steam radio. We occasionally went to Kiruna to see The Shanes from Tuolluvaara, who had appeared with the Beatles in 1966, or the Hep Stars when they happened to be passing through—but only after long, cautionary conversations with Mum behind closed doors.

It was a long way from Pajala to the rest of the world. And when Swedish Television eventually got around to broadcasting one of its rare pop concerts, it was a recording of an event several years earlier with Elvis Presley. You simply had to take whatever was on offer.

I sat down with great expectations. Sis opened the wood veneer doors shielding the screen from view, and switched it on quickly, in order to give the tube plenty of time to warm up. It matured like a loaf in the oven, and eventually produced a picture. The electrical signals were routed via the Kaknäs Tower in Stockholm and set off on their long, meandering journey over Sweden. The relay stations received the signals, and passed them on to the next, and the next, and eventually, just like one of those gigantic trains with neverending wagons laden with iron ore, they staggered as far as the Pajala TV mast on the top of Mount Jupukka, were duly transformed, and tumbled down like shelled peas into our black-and-white box.

And there he was. Elvis. Before he'd been sent to Germany as a GI, at the height of his career, a slim, virile young man with a wry smile, greasy hair, and legs as pliable as pipe-cleaners. Dad groaned and made a point of marching out to the garage. Mum pretended to knit, but she couldn't take her eyes off this sweaty stud in his black leather jacket. Sis bit her nails down to the quick, and wept into her pillow all night long. I wanted a guitar.

The next day, when school was over, I went down to the woodwork shop in the basement and made something looking like a guitar from a piece of hardboard. Nailed on a bit of wood to make a bridge. Stretched a few elastic bands to make strings. Attached a piece of string so that I could hang the thing over my shoulder.

The only place where I could count on having a bit of peace was the garage. I sneaked in when nobody was looking, spread my legs wide apart on the concrete floor, and looked out over the packed audience. I could hear the shrieks, and imagined the thousands and thousands of teenyboppers surging forward toward the stage. Then I launched into *Jailhouse Rock*, which I knew by heart, thanks to Sis's record. I tried wiggling my bottom. Felt the music pulsing through me, powerful and spicy. Then I grasped the toilet roll I was using as a microphone and opened my mouth. And started singing. But it was a song without words—I was only moving my lips, just as in the music lessons at school. I was miming to the music from deep down in my soul, wiggling my hips, bouncing about and belting out chords until the lump of hardboard trembled.

There was a sudden noise, and I froze in terror. Just for a moment I was convinced the roar of approval could be heard as far away as the church. But I was alone in the garage, and soon I was back into the make-believe. Absorbed by the acclaim, surrounded by lights and clamor. My hips were quivering, the stage was quaking, my body arched backward.

Then Niila materialized. He'd crept in as quietly as a lynx, and been studying me in silence, for God only knows how long. I stiffened in shame. Waited for the scornful smile, the splatter as I was squashed against the wall with a flyswatter.

Only once afterward have I ever felt as naked. That was on the train from Boden to Älvsbyn, in the toilet. I'd just had a crap, stood up, and was wiping my bottom with my trousers around my ankles when the door opened and the female conductor asked to see my ticket. She claimed she'd knocked first, but the hell she had.

Niila sat down on an upturned enamel bucket and scratched away thoughtfully at a scab. Eventually he asked me in a low voice what I was doing.

"Playing," I muttered, deeply embarrassed.

He sat in silence for what seemed an age, staring at my badly carved lump of hardboard.

"Can I have a go?" he asked at length.

At first I thought he was teasing me. But then I realized to my surprise that he was serious. Feeling increasingly relieved, I hung the board over his shoulder and showed him how to hold it. He started copying me, who'd in turn been copying Elvis. He swayed tentatively from side to side.

"You've got to get your legs working as well," I told him.

"Why?"

"For the girls, of course."

He suddenly looked shy.

"In that case you'll have to sing."

I nonchalantly raised the toilet roll to my lips and mimed silently, tossing my head from side to side. Niila looked disapprovingly at me.

"You must sing properly!"

"Bugger that!"

"Yes, you must."

"No, I can't."

"Yes, for the girls!" said Niila in Finnish. I burst out laughing, and a wave of warmth flowed between us.

That was how it all began, at home in the garage surrounded by skis and snow shovels and winter tyres. Niila played, and I opened my mouth and let my voice do its thing. Hoarse and shrill and bellowing. I crowed, I whined, it sounded worse than the dog, but for the first time in my life I dared to sing.

* * *

A few weeks later I happened to mention during recess that Niila and I had started a pop band. That's certainly how it felt. After all, we'd stood in the garage every day after school, and blown up each other's dream world into enormous, brightly colored balloons. And as I've always had far too low a sense of self-preservation, not to mention a tongue loose at both ends, it just slipped out.

The sensation spread like wildfire. This was Pajala in the sixties, remember: an earth-shattering piece of world news wasn't necessary. Niila and I were surrounded, it was the lunch break, and we were subjected to scorn and accusations of lying. The ring closed in on us, and in the end there was only one way out. We were forced to perform at the next Happy Hour.

Unfortunately our teacher agreed. She got the caretaker to dig out an old record player, and I borrowed Sis's record of *Jailhouse Rock* when she wasn't looking. We were going to mime, and I borrowed a girl's skipping rope to use as a microphone. I was going to sing into the handle. As early as the rehearsal at break, it was obvious it would be a disaster. The gramophone wouldn't work at 45 revs, it would only play at 33 or 78. The record sounded like either funeral bassoons in Tibet, or Donald Duck at the circus. We chose the latter.

The bell rang, and the class sat down at their desks. Niila was holding on to the hardboard guitar with a grip of iron, looking panic-stricken. The boys started throwing erasers at us even before we'd started. I picked up the skipping rope and thought about imminent death. Teacher was just about to introduce us, but I reckoned we might just as well get it over with, and slammed down the needle.

The music started off with a clatter. By God, but we jumped around! The floor sagged and the heavy needle pattered at the defenseless vinyl like a woodpecker's bill. Niila's nervousness made him so stiff-legged that he kept losing his balance, crashing into the teacher's desk, bumping against me, then staggering back into the blackboard and bending the chalk shelf. I threw myself wholeheartedly into the catastrophe, stopped miming, as the record sounded like a box of nails being shaken, and instead started yelling out in home-made English. I was bawling so frenetically that even the eraser-throwers lost the plot. I was trying simultaneously to prevent Niila jumping about so much he smashed the record player. As the needle was jumping back and forth, there was no sign of the song ever coming to an end. Niila tossed his head so violently that his shoulder strap came loose and the guitar flew into the wall map, making a deep dent close to Jyväskylä, and despite my bellowing I finally managed to hear Teacher shrieking. Niila got tangled up in the skipping rope and tumbled stiff-legged into me like a moose. We collapsed into the record player, the pickup arm fell off, and at last silence fell.

We lay there in a heap. Niila was winded and could only breathe in, not out, he was hiccuping and gasping as his lungs filled up to bursting point. My lip tasted of blood and salt. It was so quiet, you could have heard a mouse sneeze.

Then the girls started clapping. Hesitantly but approvingly. The boys were muttering enviously, and a big lump of eraser bounced off my head. And it dawned on me that it hadn't been a complete disaster after all.

* * *

The next few days were hectic. Niila was given a good hiding at home when it became known what he'd done, but he said bravely that it had been worth it. I was also threatened with a fate worse than death by my big sister when she saw her ruined record. I escaped by the skin of my teeth after agreeing to a Draconian installment plan by which she would take all my pocket money for the foreseeable future.

The reaction of the girls at school was more thought-provoking. Like most lads of my age I considered myself to be ugly and shy, with straggly hair and a potato of a nose and skinny forearms. But now, Niila and I started getting looks. Shy, fleeting glances in the lunchtime cafeteria line, quick smiles from clusters of girls outside the home ec room. We were invited to join their skipping games, and shyly agreed to do so. We were called ladykillers by the envious boys. It was all most bewildering and a bit frightening.

All the time we kept on practicing in the garage, tunes I'd heard on the radio then reproduced from memory. Niila jumped around with the piece of hardboard, and I sang. It sounded less awful than before as I'd learned not to strain my throat, but to sing from deeper down in my chest. My voice became steadier, and occasionally sounded a little bit like music. Niila started smiling inwardly and giving me friendly digs. We sometimes paused in between numbers, discussed the relationship between girls and rock music, drank lemonade, and felt nervous.

Things came to a head a few weeks later when a girl who lived in Strandvägen arranged a party. After sodas and popcorn, we played Consequences. Before Niila and I could get away, we'd been kissed to

death, and I got together with a girl for four days before I put an end
to it and gave her back the necklace and brass ring and the photograph
of her in her lace blouse and her Mum's lipstick.

Not long after that, it was all over. The girls found more exciting
things to do, and got together with boys from the big school. Niila and
I suddenly found ourselves in a backwater, and although we tried for
ages to fix a follow-up to our Happy Hour performance, our teacher
would have none of it. I had another go at the girl I'd turned down, but
didn't get anywhere. Life was a mystery.

CHAPTER 9

In which our heroes start at the big school and,
with considerable difficulty, learn fingering techniques

After three years at the Old School, most of us little brats could read and count, and it was time to proceed to the juniors at Pajala Central School, a yellow brick building looking as if it were made of Lego. The new school year started with a campaign to make us start brushing our teeth. There was a clear need for it, you might say: at my latest check-up I had ten cavities, and Niila had nine. The rest of the class fared just as badly, and the local authority had been forced to order a truckload of extra amalgam from Linköping. Now we all had to go in groups to the clinic and swallow a coloring tablet that turned the plaque an angry red, then look in a mirror and do some tooth-brushing gymnastics under the supervision of a stern-looking lady. Brush, brush, brush, at least ten times up and down in each place. I don't know if that's why, or if it was due to the fluoride rinse, but I didn't have any more cavities at all for the rest of my time at school.

Needless to say, the dentists soon noticed that they were doing fewer and fewer fillings, and started looking around for alternative sources of income. The answer was braces. Every week some poor soul was sent to

the clinic and came back with a mouth full of plastic and steel wire. As
soon as a tooth was the slightest little bit *klinkku*, it had to be corrected. For me it was a canine tooth that wasn't quite standing to attention,
and by God, I was sent to the National Dental Service like greased
lightning. The woman dentist had a permanent furrow in her brow,
reached for the pliers, and tightened the steel wire in the brace until the
whole of my skull ached. As soon as I got outside I loosened the wire
with the key for my bicycle lock, bringing relief until the next visit.
Sometimes the specialist traveled up, a bald fellow from Luleå. The
only difference was that he tightened the wires even harder, and that his
fingers tasted of cigarillo when he poked around inside my mouth.

Going to the junior school meant that puberty was getting closer.
You could see what was in store every break. Various couples from class
six wandering around holding hands and kissing. Girls having a smoke
behind the bike sheds. Makeup getting bolder and brasher, the higher
the class. It felt terrifying, we couldn't really understand it. Would I
change like that as well? Oh yes, it was there inside us all, we could feel
it, a seed. It was swelling already, and before long we'd lose control.

As it was considered useful to be able to speak several languages, we
started learning English, and our local Finnish dialect was heard less
frequently in the schoolyard. I started writing down English pop songs
by listening to Top Ten on the radio. We didn't have a tape recorder at
home then, so I had to write as quickly as I could while the program
was being broadcast. I still didn't understand the words, and had to
write phonetically, learn them by heart, and then sing for Niila in the
garage songs such as *Ollyu nidis lav* and *Owatter shayd ovpail*.

Niila was extremely impressed. Who had taught me English?

"I taught my self," I said, nonchalantly.

Niila thought about that for a while. Then he made his own bold
decision: He was going to learn to play the guitar.

I managed to borrow an acoustic guitar from an uncle who'd bought
it while on holiday in Bulgaria. There followed a hectic period, buying

some simplified sheet music from a shop in Luleå; first attempts at the mysterious art of tuning, short and stiff boyish fingers; figures and dots that were supposed to produce notes but didn't; more insight into the mysterious art of tuning; the culturally alien climate in Niila's house that forced him to practice in our garage until the winter cold set in and we had to move down into our boiler room, poking cotton wool under the strings so that my parents wouldn't hear and start telling tales; the first chord that was in fact E minor but sounded like somebody jumping up and down on a tin roof; the second that was A minor but sounded like two people jumping up and down on a tin roof, me singing to Niila's accompaniment with such neverending pauses when he needed to change chords that I ran out of breath; his total lack of humor in circumstances like this, which more than once led to an exchange of blows; my total inability to guess, even after eight attempts, the identity of the first tune Niila taught himself, and then having to dive and rescue the guitar a split second before it smashed onto the concrete floor.

The annoying thing was that I taught myself how to play in a fraction of the time. My fingers are long and supple, it's a family trait. My hand felt at home on the neck of the guitar, scampering up and down like a spider and spinning chords with an ease that astonished me. Before Niila had managed to produce his first clean chord, I had learned the whole of *The House of the Rising Sun*, and then succeeded by hook or by crook in getting my hands on a book about the acoustic jungle of barré-chords. Niila always left the guitar in the cellar, and as soon as he left for home I could let myself go.

Naturally, I couldn't let Niila know how good I was. He'd have been devastated. Even at his age he was starting to show signs of his pitch-black, self-deprecating depressions. In between, he was the best there was, completely deaf to how awful he sounded, cocky and big-headed and certain of his impending fame. I pretended to have a go at the guitar occasionally, and played badly on purpose, and I'd see him sniggering so hard through his nose that snot would start dripping down.

There were times when I very nearly gave the game away, it's true—there was a limit even to my patience. But I managed to restrain myself, hard though it was.

* * *

It was now in the junior school that a handful of boys in our class started to take snuff. You could see on their jeans the round marks of the lids of the tins, and during breaks there was a strong and telltale smell of tea in the air. Being unused to it, the boys became intoxicated and their pupils dilated. They'd sit around in corners shouting and yelling, then march down the corridors calling the girls whores and floozies. After PE they'd stand in the showers pulling back their foreskins for the others' delectation. Rumors started spreading about the ones who'd had it away. Those of us boys who were later developers or just shyer would look on in horror. The change had come suddenly. The old mates of yore were suddenly turned on by snuff and hormones. A bit like junkies, cantankerous, unpredictable. Instinctively, we kept in the background.

The more snuff they took, the more disgusting the girls thought it was. Snuff caught between their teeth and stained their fingers brown, and what looked like spit-covered used teabags stuck to the walls and in the washbasins. It was forbidden to take snuff in class, but they couldn't care less. Just squashed the wad a bit flatter when the bell rang for lessons.

On one occasion one of the snuff-takers was unexpectedly summoned to the front of the class. He was supposed to give an oral report on something he'd forgotten about. We all sat in expectation—the moment he opened his mouth he'd be found out and told off by the teacher, which was always exciting and interesting to watch. The boy was scared stiff, that was obvious. He turned white in the face, and was trembling. Then he started mumbling. The whole class stared at him, agog. He barely opened his mouth, and was exhorted by the teacher to speak up. He did as he was told, but held a piece of paper up in front of his mouth.

"You haven't been taking snuff, have you?" she asked.

A shake of the head.

"You know that's forbidden!"

A quick nod.

"Let me have a look!"

He stood rooted to the spot while the teacher lifted up his lip. A few seconds passed. Then to everybody's surprise, he was told to go and sit down. No shouting, no accusations, no threats of being reported and sent to the headmaster.

Everybody was disappointed and perplexed. When the next break came all the class gathered round the boy and asked what had happened. He was quite calm about it.

"I swallowed the snuff," he said casually.

He was talked about for ages afterward.

* * *

As early as in class six Niila's awkward relationship with girls started to become clear. It had nothing to do with his appearance, even if he was no beauty, with his typically Finnish potato of a nose, prominent cheekbones, and hair that was always greasy, no matter how often he washed it. He was lankier than I, and perhaps a bit jerky, fumbling in his movements. But he wasn't repulsive. On the contrary, he radiated a sort of energy that prowled around like a caged animal, looking for a way of escape. It would be an exaggeration to call it an inner fire, perhaps; but it was something warm and vulnerable. It rankled within him and the girls could sense it. He had will power, a root forming in his backbone.

Girls are different, of course. Many look for stability, they want boys who get up early in the morning, boys who know how to handle tools and weapons, who will build a house of their own on their parents' land in rural Anttis or Jarhois and prepare a potato bed with Uncle's Rotavator. That sort of pure-wool girl would be uncomfortable when she came up against Niila. I saw it happen several times over the years. He frightened them off with his silence and his restless eyes, or even worse, he gave the impression of being superior. I tried to teach him the basics of courtship—not that I knew much about it myself, but I wasn't quite as hopeless as he was. The fundamental rule was to pick girls who liked you. Incredible as it might seem there was always somebody with just a little bit of interest. That was the type to go for. Niila always did the opposite, and was always falling in love with girls who were bad for him. Girls who wouldn't even look at him, who made fun of him to their loudly giggling cronies, girls who were far too pretty or too cruel and who played with him like a cat with a young bird. It was painful to watch. All the time there were other girls in the background, not my type, it's true, but there nonetheless. Girls who were adventurous. Who were willing to take risks, cling to the edge of a precipice by their fingertips, who were willing to launch themselves into the night sky. Artistic girls, thoughtful girls who wrote poems for serious girls' magazines, who wondered about God and sado-masochism, girls who read books for adults, who sat listening in the kitchen when the men were talking politics. That was the type he needed. A mature, strong Communist from somewhere like Aareavaara.

This was before sex had really entered the scene, after all. The initial stages of puberty when the old pecking order and groups of chums began to be replaced by a new order, based on attractiveness. Nervous, hunchbacked little girls could suddenly turn into slim beauties with high cheekbones. Little boys with dimples and curly locks could turn into big-nosed baboons with prominent teeth. A morose young lad from Erkheikki could suddenly start talking and develop an understated but irresistible charm while a talkative lass from Pajala could sink into fits of inexplicable depression and gradually become somebody you no longer wanted anything to do with.

I was one of those children who grew uglier as I got older, but my charisma grew stronger. Niila became uglier to look at and less pleasant to be with as well, and music was probably his only lifeline.

I tried to teach him the trick of thinking about death whenever you came up against a girl. It's a trick I've used myself many times over the years, and it is surprisingly effective. Before so very many years have passed, I'm going to die. My body will decay and disappear for ever. The same will happen to the girl, we'll all be no more. In a thousand years our lives and all our sweetest dreams and worst fears will be nothing but dust and ashes. So what difference does it make if she turns you down or is snooty or laughs in your face? Thanks to that cynical attitude I've occasionally managed to achieve remarkable results when it comes to love—dared to be with lethally beautiful women, for instance, and sometimes even been allowed to play with them.

This was the only piece of advice Niila ever listened to. He started to think about death more than he did about girls. To be blunt, the kid became insufferable. He was going to need my help shortly, but neither of us knew anything about that as yet.

CHAPTER 10

*On an unwelcome nocturnal visit, an old skeleton
bearing gifts, and how to get out of tight corners*

A switch was thrown somewhere in my body, and the journey started
in earnest. Puberty. It was the spring term in class six, and nothing dramatic happened: I just became intensely aware that a change was taking
place. It wasn't anything in my body, no visible signs as yet, but it was
in my mind. Something was happening there, somebody was taking up
residence in there. Somebody reminiscent of me, but somebody else
even so. A certain whimsicality entered my life and I couldn't always
handle it. An impatience that I didn't understand. And an unexpected,
a really astonishingly intense interest in sex.

One afternoon at the end of the spring term when I was still in class
six, I was lying on my bed leafing through a copy of *Cute Chicks*. I'd
bought it furtively while on a visit to Luleå where nobody knew me
and so couldn't start badgering me. There was nothing worse than
getting knowing looks from middle-aged ladies with perms in the
local Co-op, who knew my mum and dad and whose pretty daughters
went to the same school as I did. Buying *Cute Chicks* was an admis-
sion that you were horny. That meant that you were exposed, you'd

put yourself at a disadvantage, and you might start blushing and stammering.

Suddenly, there he was in my room. I gave a start, dropped the magazine and raised my knees to conceal the bulge in my trousers.

"Bloody hell! I thought it was Mum!"

Niila didn't say a word. He had slipped into the room in his usual soundless way, and he was standing as motionless as a wall. I tried to cover up my embarrassment, and decided that attack was the best form of defense. Smirking loutishly I opened up the week's centerfold. Black lace bra, come-hither look, and red high-heeled boots.

"Why don't you stick her up on the wall at home?" I suggested crudely.

Niila recoiled at the impossible thought. But he couldn't take his eyes off the girl. He made no attempt to take the magazine, so I went through it for him, showing him picture after picture.

"How about that, she's tied him down! And look at that, rubber underwear! And I bet it was you who wrote this letter: *I lost my virginity at the Confirmation camp.*"

I could see Niila was trembling deep down. But at the same time he was stiff, negative, determined to maintain his dignity. His head was vibrating slightly, as if he were tensing his neck muscles as hard as he could. The more scared he became, the more my own shame died away, he could feel it instead of me. I pressed the rubbishy rag into his hands.

"Come on, choose a chick, Niila! One of these in the magazine, which one do you like?"

It was as if all the air went out of him. He flopped down onto a chair and sighed, leaned forward as if he felt ill—quite common behavior among shy residents of Tornedalen when they feel obliged to say something. He cleared his throat and swallowed in order to make room in his mouth for his voice.

"Grandma...," he said. Silence.

"Well, what about her?" I asked, trying to help him.

"She... she's dead..."

"Yes, I know. That was ages ago."

"But she's come back!"

And now that the blockage had cleared all the rest came rushing out, jerkily, one wheezy sentence after another. I listened to Niila baring his soul with a growing feeling of horror.

Grandma had started haunting them. Almost three years after her decease she'd returned to her old home. Although she'd been given a heroic burial in true Laestadian style she'd not found peace.

The first time he'd seen her she was just a blurred stain, a bit like the spots of light you can see in the outer edges of your eye. Then he started feeling a gentle breeze as well, as if somebody was breathing over him. As time passed she'd become more and more solid, filled out, and even started making noises. She gradually took back her old place in the family. She waddled stiff-hipped down the attic staircase, frail but substantial. Several nights she'd sat at the kitchen table, mixing mashed potatoes and carrots into what remained of the meat stew, then ladling the resulting gray goo into her mouth with loud sucking noises. She smelled something awful. Sweet old-woman's sweat mixed with odors from a fusty, subterranean world.

The odd thing was that only Niila seemed to notice her. Once, she'd sat down on the floor in the middle of the kitchen, catching flies then stirring them into the bowl of hash on the table. Everybody apart from Niila had gone on eating with undiminished appetite.

Niila shared an upstairs bedroom with his elder brother Johan. His brother had growing pains and therefore needed lots and lots of sleep. He slept like men do, deep and to the accompaniment of snores. Niila, on the other hand, was a very light sleeper.

One night quite recently Niila had been in the middle of a vivid dream. An extremely vivid dream, he repeated with a slight blush that made it clear what he was talking about. But his pleasure had been interrupted by an alarm bell, and he'd opened his eyes with a start.

Grandma was leaning over him. She was furious, her cheeks deeply wrinkled, her toothless mouth wide open and struggling to produce inaudible words, and a bitter liquid was dripping down onto his face. Niila had screamed so loudly that Johan had stopped snoring and turned over. But the ghost had disappeared by then.

And now, last night, he'd been woken up again. This time the old woman had wrapped her talons around his neck. They had felt as cold as iron. She'd started squeezing, but didn't have enough strength, and he'd managed, though panic-stricken, to kick himself free. He'd spent the rest of the night locked in the bathroom with the light on and armed with a sheath knife. He'd heard clicking noises coming from the bolt and seen luminous gas drifting in under the door, but it had disappeared when he'd splashed hot water on it.

Niila pulled back his shirt collar and I could see a purplish line across his neck, as if somebody had pulled a rope over it. It was reminiscent of frostbite, a fading furrow in his skin.

I'd grown increasingly horrified as Niila told his story. When he'd finished, I wanted to say something, try to console him a little, maybe cheer him up. But I couldn't. His expression was vacant, drained; he looked like an old man.

"This is too big," I mumbled.

Niila's head quivered even more. Then he produced the old Beatles EP and handed it to me. He wanted me to have it after he'd gone, he said curtly: he didn't own anything else of value.

I told him to shut up, but I could feel the repugnance rising inside me. Fear was running up my legs, and I stood up.

"You can sleep here with me."

"Sleep?" he whispered, as if the word had no meaning.

I told him it was the only chance he had. As soon as everybody had gone to bed, Niila should sneak out of the window, climb down the fire escape and spend the night in my room. He could go back at dawn, when the danger had passed. No need to tell any of our parents, as long as we were careful.

Then a couple of spades would be acquired, a grave in Pajala cemetery opened up, and a sharpened fir branch would be thrust with great
force through a twisted old biddy's heart.

Niila didn't have TV at home and therefore didn't have access to the
most basic of educational enlightenment, and couldn't agree. I could
see the problem, especially as spring nights were far too light.

That meant there was only one possible alternative. Both Niila and I
recognized that it had to be faced up to. One of us would be forced to
propose it sooner or later. I drew the short straw.

"We'll have to go to Russi-Jussi."

Niila turned pale. Closed his eyes. Grabbed hold of his neck as if he'd
placed it in a noose.

Russi-Jussi was one of Tornedalen's last itinerant peddlers of the old
school, and one of the most scary people for miles around. Crow-like,
hunched, as wrinkled as a seed potato, his old-man's cheeks were covered in moles. His nose was beak-like, his eyebrows joined, and his lips
were bloated and girlish, red and damp. He was aloof and sardonic,
malevolent and vindictive. Somebody to avoid if at all possible.

This scarecrow of a man would pedal his way round the forest villages on a lady's bicycle with a suitcase made of stiffened cardboard on
the luggage carrier. He would march into people's kitchens with the
audacity of a council official and pile on their tables shoelaces, zips, hair
lotion, linen handkerchiefs, razor blades, cotton reels, and mouse traps.
But concealed in the back of his case, in a special pocket, were the items
that made him welcome—one might even say sought after. Little jars
containing a gooey brown concoction called *nopat* in Tornedalen
Finnish. The substance was renowned for being able to arouse the sexual urge of the most decrepit old biddy and the most impotent of
drooping drips. They say the vital ingredients came from a mushroom
that Russi-Jussi harvested in the north of Finland, and, according to
witnesses, it must have contained the most remarkable of hallucino-
genic substances.

Jussi was born an illegitimate child at the end of the last century, in what was then the Russian province of Finland. His mother was a maid and had inculcated in him a hatred of the landed gentry and the rest of the upper classes, who had the privilege of taking advantage of their serving women with no threat of consequences, and in 1918 he had entered the Finnish civil war as a soldier for the reds. When they were defeated, like so many of his comrades he had moved to the workers' paradise in the newly created Soviet Union. But before long Stalin came to power, and since he was a foreigner and hence a spy, Jussi had been arrested and sent to a labor camp in Siberia. It became a center for Finnish and Tornedalen comrades who tried hard to convince themselves that they had been victims of a terrible mistake, and that in his infinite wisdom Uncle Joe would shortly realize this, and at any moment now release them, amid celebrations and rejoicings and an acknowledgement of mistakes made plus gratitude for heroic contributions to the new world order.

One of his fellow prisoners was an old Lapp from the Kola peninsula. Even when first captured he had been emaciated through lack of food as the old Sami villages had been replaced by kolkhozes, and no disrespect to Stalin, but at that time he was not a great fan of breeding reindeer. The old skeleton could feel that his end was nigh, and as he shared a bunk with Jussi he opened his heart to him. In a mixture of Sami, Finnish, and Russian, he mumbled on about mysterious powers and happenings. About abscesses healed, madnesses cured, herds of reindeer driven unharmed through wolf-infested country at dead of night. There were words. There were eyes that traveled through the air like a pair of testicles while their owner lay under a reindeer skin. There was blood that ran backward into a wound until there was nothing to be seen but a white mark. There was, in short, a possibility of escaping from the labor camp.

During the long, cold nights the old Lapp instructed Jussi on how he should get away, and how he could take the ancient wisdom with him into the unknown future, where it would doubtless be needed.

"When I die," wheezed the old man, "carry me out into a snowdrift. Wait until I'm frozen stiff, that won't take long, just wait until I'm stiff and hard. Then break off the little finger of my left hand. That's where I've collected all my powers. Break it off and swallow it before the guards see you."

The old man died shortly afterward. He was so thin that he rattled when Jussi shook him. Jussi did as he'd been told and put the body out in the Siberian deep freeze. He snapped off the dirty little finger at the knuckle, popped it into his mouth and swallowed it. And he was never the same again.

Jussi waited until an early spring night at the end of April. The snow had acquired a firm crust strong enough to walk on, so the time had come. The guards were in the middle of one of their gloomy, maudlin vodka parties, and Jussi went to the outhouse. There, he turned himself into a woman. She emerged and stood outside, dirty and in rags, but beautiful. She knocked discreetly on the door of the guards' hut. With coquettish charm she encouraged them to set upon one another until blood poured from mouths and fists, and the way of escape was open. Taking with her two dry crusts of bread and a broken-off knife blade, she started her long trek to Finland.

The next morning the men set out in chase, but when they caught up with her she changed their scent so that their own dogs turned on them and tore them to pieces. She cut as much meat off their bodies as she could carry, and strapped on a pair of skis taken from one of the dead soldiers, and it was only two months before she was clambering underneath the barbed wire at the Finnish border. For safety's sake she kept going all the way across Finland as well, skied through the endless forests until she came to the River Torne. She crossed over, and settled down on the far bank. In Swedish Tornedalen.

Now that safety had been reached at last, Russi-Jussi tried to turn himself back into a man, but he wasn't entirely successful. Too long a time had passed with him as a woman. So for the rest of his life he wore a skirt. Usually a long, thick one of coarse wool, but on Sundays and public holidays he would change into a more elegant black one. He also wore a head-scarf over his long, white hair, and when he was resting at home in his hut he would wear a home-made pinafore, but even in Tornedalen's roughest, toughest villages, not a soul dared even to grin. Instead people would look the other way and step aside when Russi-Jussi came cycling past, leaning forward and swaying from side to side, with piercing eyes and skirt flapping in the breeze. A bass-voiced witch, as burly as a lumberjack but with the all-conquering cunning of a woman.

* * *

We slunk out into the clear spring evening and hurried off to Niila's house. His big brother's three-wheel delivery moped was standing outside the barn. Niila wheeled it over the yellow grass to a path and, when we were out of earshot, kick-started it. Bluish-white fumes belched out of the exhaust pipe. I perched on the platform at the front where all the parcels were usually stacked, Niila engaged first gear and we headed somewhat uncertainly for the main road. We slowly gathered speed, and, amid the crunching of gears and clouds of two-stroke fumes, we put-putted our way through Pajala.

We took the old dirt road on the other side of the river as there was less traffic on it and less chance of being caught by the Gällivare police out on patrol. The sap was rising and it was just before summer delivered its green punch. The previous year's leaves were rotting in the moss, the birch trees were naked but had buds that were starting to grow plump, and on the sunny side of the ditches the heat had encouraged shoots of horsetails looking worryingly like rows of erect penises. The river was bluish black and unusually wide after the ice had melted. We rattled upstream along the narrow dirt road, up steep hills then down the other side following the outline of the wooded ridges, babbling brooks, spires of sedge at the edge of boggy pools. I was semirecumbent on the cargo platform, filling my young lungs with sap and spring resins. The evening chill was rising from their shady hollows and I could feel it seeping in through my long johns. Only once did we meet a car, a bloke chasing the land speed record in his souped-up Volvo Amazon on the straight stretch near Autio Bridge where normal laws didn't apply. Gravel was spattering against the bodywork as he roared toward us. I sat up uneasily, but he didn't even take his eye off the speedometer as he shot past us like a trumpet blast.

We crossed over the river when we came to the bridge and continued along the wider, asphalted Kiruna road. Erkheikki and Juhonpieti slipped past with their red-painted houses and grassy meadows, then we plunged into the forest once more. Here and there we caught glimpses of the river through the mass of trees, looking like a shiny strip of polished metal. It lay on its back gazing up into the spring-clear sky striped with its lines of migrating birds.

We eventually turned off onto a pock-marked forest track. We bumped and swayed down a slight incline as the trees began to thin out and it grew lighter. At last we came to the river, edged by one last strip of ice. Further up were a few barren meadows, once upon a time hacked out of the virgin forest but now dotted with little aspens and fir trees. A bit further up the hill, out of reach of the spring floods, was an ancient wooden cottage, gray with black windows. A lady's bike was leaning against the wall.

"He's at home," I muttered nervously, clambering down from the platform. My bottom ached after the long journey. Niila switched off the engine, and there was an eerie silence. We tip-toed unsteadily toward the steps leading up to the porch. A curtain moved in one of the windows. I knocked and tentatively opened the fragile-looking door. Then we went in.

Russi-Jussi was sitting at the kitchen table. He wore a dirty pinafore that had once been white, and around his head was a brownish, carelessly knotted head-scarf. Strands of gray, greasy hair dangled out and hung over his shoulders. The kitchen smelled strongly of old man, an acrid, choking stench, a mixture of burnt milk and rancid pork. There was also that typical smell you always find in Tornedalen cottages, a slightly musty tang of earth cellars and rag carpets, cold and old wool. The smell of poverty that seeped into the house walls and floors and never quite disappeared, no matter how often you renovated the place.

"*No nykkös tet tuletta.* So, you've turned up."

He pointed at the table where two steaming cups of coffee awaited us. He must have sensed that we were approaching. Peering out from under our bangs we started gulping down the coffee, which had a strange flavor of sour well water.

Russi-Jussi enquired gruffly what we wanted, and Niila came out with the whole tale, mumbling away in Finnish. He included everything from his grandmother's death three years earlier to her terrifying return and stealthy attempt to choke him with her hands round his throat. Russi-Jussi poked slowly at his stubble with a slender index finger. The nail was overgrown and had been carefully filed to form a sharp point. There were traces of red varnish on it.

When Niila had finished, the old man gave us a funny look. His eyes stared, glassy and hard. His face crumpled up and formed a knot, and in among all the wrinkles his pupils dilated and turned into black rifle muzzles. His left hand started trembling, and his little finger fluttered around in all directions like a pennant before coming to a sudden stop and pointing stiffly straight out. The skin of his face slowly softened and turned darkish blue and crisscrossed with veins. We didn't dare move a muscle.

"Well, there is a way," said a gentle and very beautiful voice in Finnish.

The old man's growl had disappeared. Instead we heard a surprisingly warm and mellow alto. And all at once we could see the woman. She'd been there all the time, hidden under the surface. Now she was leaning forward inside him, as if behind a darkened window pane, pressing up against the old man's wrinkles and smoothing them out from inside. She was a beauty. Thick womanly lips, a smooth, high forehead, arched eyebrows, bitter and very sorrowful eyes.

"There is a way...," she repeated hesitantly, turning half away. "The old girl must go back under the ground...; the old girl will disappear if you cut off her cock..."

She fell silent. A shudder ran through the whole of her tall body, like snow falling from an old fir tree. A chilly breeze blew out from between her lips and we shrunk back from her breath, which smelled of resin. Ever so slowly Russi-Jussi returned. He seemed exhausted and frozen stiff, hugging himself to keep warm.

"You'll be staying the night here, I expect," he said imploringly, and looked pitifully lonely.

We declined as politely as we could.

"You will bloody well stay the night!" he exclaimed angrily, knitting together his eyebrows to form an impenetrable thicket.

We thanked him and emptied our coffee cups, thanked him again, and then again as we backed toward the door. Russi-Jussi got to his feet and started following us. He smiled imploringly at us with his wet lips, and held out his arms as if to hug us. We wrenched the door open and raced toward the moped. Terror-stricken we leaped aboard. It wouldn't start. Niila fiddled with the choke and kicked hard, but nothing happened. The engine was stone dead. I tried push-starting it. Russi-Jussi strode down the steps in his slippers, gazing entreatingly at us.

"Just hold me a bit... just touch me..."

Suddenly I could feel his sharp-pointed nails on my back. They started tripping down toward my waist. Like claws.

"*Hiiri tullee...* Here comes the mouse..."

Down onto my bottom. Outraged, I turned round to face him. And his mouth was all over me in a flash, big and wet, dripping all over my face, and I felt as if I were drowning. Too wet, much too wet...

Slowly he caressed me, gazing into my eyes. Surely he could see! He must be able to see that I didn't want to!

I twisted and wriggled. He clung on to me. That hand seeking and searching.

But then it burst. The mask splintered. Tears gushed forth and streamed down his face. He made sure I saw that, stood there revealing his pain and waiting for me to rescue him. But I was no longer there. He hunched his shoulders, turned around, and shuffled back into the cottage.

Just then the engine started. In a turmoil, we accelerated away toward the forest track. The cottage disappeared behind the trees. The forest enveloped us in its placid darkness, the tree tops high above us glittered in the evening sun. I clung on for all I was worth, scared stiff of falling off as we raced through the woods. Felt the tension ease, the pain in my midriff fade away.

"We made it!" I yelled over the roar of the engine. Niila slowed down. I could still taste the old man and his musty coffee, and spat into the gravel as it rushed past. We slowed down still further, went slower and slower, and eventually ground to a halt. The engine cut out and everything fell silent. I looked questioningly at Niila. He was staring vacantly at the next bend.

"It's on fire," he said.

I didn't know what he was talking about. His jaw started moving as if he were eating, I could hear his teeth grinding.

"I expect we'll die," he said, his voice quivering. He got off the moped and staggered toward the ditch at the side of the road. Tip-toeing, swaying from side to side.

"Hang on!" I yelled, running after him. Then I realized how hard it was for me to reach down to the ground. It had sunk five inches, just out of range of my feet. I couldn't get any purchase when I tried to walk, and had to glide instead, with shaky skating movements. Niila had already disappeared into the forest. I thrust branches to one side and straddled a small birch sapling, almost falling over.

"Niila, stop!"

He was staring intensely at his left hand, as if it were some strange, unpleasant organism that had attached itself to his body.

"Red," he said.

Then I saw it as well. Angry red flames were bursting forth from his fingers. When he turned his hand over, bits of skin came loose and set fire to his clothes. I looked around in terror. Too late! The whole forest was burning. We were surrounded by a raging but totally silent forest fire. Niila had been right, we were going to die. And yet it was all so beautiful. Such bewildering beauty! Despite my fear I felt tears coming into my eyes, had an urge to embrace the nearest tree trunk as we were burned to death. The colors changed and merged. Butter yellow, flame yellow, meat red, and tiny violet arrowheads rained down from the treetops. I could feel myself rising even higher above the ground, and grabbed hold of Niila to stop myself flying away. I could feel that my head was lighter than the rest of my body, a balloon hoisting me upward. The fire was closing in on us from all sides. We stood there, black tubes in the midst of the glowing lava, waiting for the pain to hit us.

At that very moment Niila took out his knife. A shiny pocket knife, as flat as a little fish. He prized out the blade with his thumb nail. And when I looked up I could feel ice in my heart, a chill spreading out into all my limbs in spite of the fire licking my skin. I was an icicle in a pot of boiling meat stew, I screamed and bubbles rose to the surface.

There stood the old witch. Niila's grandma. Laughing scornfully with her toothless mouth, she came toward us, a shriveled specter with her arms held out as if to embrace us. At the end of them were her yellow strangler's hands. Niila stabbed at her, but she grabbed his wrist with the speed of a snake striking, held on tightly and slowly bent it back. And all the time she was laughing, and drips of sausagey fat rained down from her mouth into the fire. Niila flailed desperately with his free arm and grabbed hold of her bun. He tugged at the thick, gray

lump of hair with all his strength. She started shrieking and dug her
nails into his throat. Felt his pulse beating inside, a little pecking bird,
and squeezed. As if she were squashing an insect—pinch hard and out
come the juices. Niila tugged away at her hair, which resembled a mag-
pie's nest. I tried to prize her fingers away from his throat, but they were
clamped there like pincers. Niila went through the motions of opening
his mouth to scream, his eyes swelled up from lack of blood. One last
desperate wrench. *Craaatch!* The bunch of hair was ripped out like a
clump of grass from the soil. Bits of rotten scalp came away with the
roots. The old witch gave a roar, let go of Niila's neck, and groped after
her bun. Quick as a flash Niila ripped open her dress. She was naked
underneath. Two wrinkled old legs, with a black bush of hair between
them. And in the middle of the bush, something ghastly. A stalk. It was
alive. A wriggling serpent. It struck at Niila, spitting venom. He
grabbed it by its scraggy end, clung on tight, and with one swift blow
of his knife cut the penis off by its root.

As he did so the old woman opened her mouth wide. A rustling gust
of wind blew through the sea of fire, and the ground opened underneath her. As if somebody were pulling at her feet from below, the
monster was dragged down into the moss. To her waist, her chest, and
to her neck. But it was not until the whole of her hairless cranium had
disappeared from view that the horrific screams ceased.

Niila stood with the dripping penis in his hand. I touched it with a
shudder, felt the stiff black hairs. There was still life in the stump—it
was still struggling to break free. But he wouldn't let go.

And then it was all over, darkness fell. And the fire went out at last.

* * *

When we woke up, we were curled up in the moss, freezing cold. The
forest was all around us, gray and raw. The stained knife was visible in
the light of dawn, but there was no trace of the penis.

"The *nopat*," Niila groaned.

I shuddered and nodded. The old bastard had spiked our coffee. We drove home, frozen stiff. We had to stop several times and make little bonfires at the side of the road, longing to be in our warm beds.

The following week we got our first pubic hair.

CHAPTER 11

Where two pig-headed families are joined by marriage,
on which occasion muscles bulge and a sauna is taken

My old man was a silent type. He had three aims in life and he had accomplished all of them; he sometimes oozed a degree of self-satisfaction that annoyed me more and more, the older I grew. His first aim was to be strong, and his work as a lumberjack gave him bulging muscles. His second was to be financially self-supporting. And his third was to find a wife. As he had succeeded in all these, it was now my turn to follow suit, and I could feel the pressure on me growing by the day. Strumming a guitar was not an activity rated especially highly, no doubt about that. On the other hand, he liked to make me saw wood with the bluntest saw he could find, to build up my muscles. He would occasionally check to make sure I didn't cheat, thrusting out his clog-shaped jaw and adjusting the peak of his cap, which kept slipping down his low, sloping forehead. His facial hair was sparse and thin, something you often see in men from Tornedalen, and hence his cheeks were pale and pudgy, almost like a baby's. Sticking out of the middle of this doughy mass was his nose. It looked like a radish somebody had thrown, but it had landed at a slight angle. I always felt the urge to grab hold of it and straighten it up.

He used to stand there without speaking while I sawed away with sweat pouring off me. Eventually he would reach out and feel my biceps between his thumb and his index finger, and conclude that I ought to have been a girl.

Dad was broad-shouldered, just like his eight brothers; they all had the same rippling shoulder muscles and the same enormous bull neck jutting forward in a way that made them seem slightly hunch-backed. It's a pity I didn't inherit more of that trait, if only to avoid having to listen to the old bastards' comments when they got drunk at family gatherings. But no doubt most of the muscles were due to the hard manual labor they'd all been doing from the age of thirteen, just like my old man.

That was when they'd all started working in the forests. Chopping and sawing and dragging the logs through the snow to the frozen river in winter, spurred on by the piece-work rates. Then accompanying the logs downstream when the ice melted in spring, sorting out the log jams on the way. Their summers were spent haymaking in the fields and in the bogs, and digging ditches in order to qualify for state subsidies; in their spare time they chopped down enough trees to build themselves a cabin, and often worked all night long, hand-sawing planks. Drudgery like that made them as tough as Swedish wrought iron from Kengis.

My youngest uncle, Ville, had always been a bachelor, and many people thought he'd remain one for life. He'd often been to Finland to do some courting, but never managed to find himself a bride. He couldn't understand where he was going wrong. In the end a neighbor gave him a tip:

"You should buy a car."

Ville followed the advice and bought an old Volvo. Then he went to Finland again and got engaged straight away. He wondered why he hadn't thought of such an obvious ploy long ago.

The wedding took place in the middle of summer when everybody was on holiday, and the family home was flooded with relations. I was nearly thirteen, and was allowed to sit at the table with the grown-ups for the first time. A solid wall of silent men, shoulder to shoulder like huge blocks of stone, and here and there their pretty wives from Finland, like flowers on a cliff face. As was normal in our family, nobody said a word. Everyone was waiting for the food.

The first course was local crispbread and salmon. Every single one of the men turned his piece of crispbread upside down, so that the holes were underneath. That way they would save butter, just as their impecunious parents had taught them. Then on with the freshly cut slices of sweetly spiced gravadlax, prepared from salmon netted by poachers near Kardis. Ice-cold beer. No unnecessary comments. Only the newly-wed couple at the narrow end of the table urging everybody to take more. Crunching of crispbread in bull-like mouths, broad hunched backs, knitted eyebrows and concentration. The catering ladies in the kitchen lugged up barrels and bottles from the cellar. The bride's mother, who was from Finnish Kolari and so knew the local customs, said she'd never seen working men eat such tiny portions, whereupon everybody took a second helping.

Then came the pot of meat stew, steam rising as if it were on fire, tender lumps of reindeer meat that caressed the palate, golden turnips, sweetly spiced carrots and buttery yellow diced almond potatoes, the ones northerners dream about, in a rich broth tasting of sweat and forests, with circles of fat on the surface like rings made by nibbling char in a tarn one breezeless summer's night. A dish of newly cooked marrow bones was served up on the side. The ends had been cut off, and we poked out the gray, greasy fat inside with elongated toothpicks, the long strings of marrow so tender that they melted on the tongue. The men betrayed no trace of a smile, but their skin assumed a lighter hue and they emitted furtive sighs of relief at being served with food they recognized and appreciated, food that filled the belly and delivered nutritious juices as well as strength. On festive occasions, and not least at weddings, even the most reliable and sensible members of the fami-

ly were liable to get silly ideas into their heads about what was appropriate and what was classy enough, and start serving grass that they
called salad and sauces that tasted like soap, and they'd set out far too
many forks and serve up a drink called wine, something so sour and
bitter that your lips shriveled up and convinced you you'd pay a king's
ransom for a glass of buttermilk.

And so the slurping and gobbling got under way. The ladies in the
kitchen were inspired by the lip-smacking and slobbering. Guests
devoured the spicy stew, the meat reared and matured in Tornedalen
forests, the root vegetables nurtured and ripened in their native soil,
spitting out gristle and bones, sucking out marrow, fat dripping down
from their chins. The catering ladies scuttled around with bowls of
locally baked rieska bread, imbued with the smoke of the birchwood
that fired the ovens, still hot enough to melt lumps of butter, and made
from corn grown in northern fields, ripened in the northern wind and
sun and heavy rain—a full-bodied bread that made simple peasant
souls pause and worship, eyes uplifted to the heavens, while the serving
ladies exchanged justly proud looks, and smiled contentedly as they
clapped their hands to get rid of the flour still clinging to them.

Now was the right moment for the first schnapps. The bottle was
conveyed with due solemnity to the table by the old biddy who was the
least religious of those present. The men paused, swayed gently from
side to side, farted, brushed the debris from their chins, and followed
intently the progress of the relic. In accordance with instructions, it was
still sealed; but now in everyone's presence the cork was lifted and the
foil broken with an audible click so no one could doubt that they were
being served with the real thing and not moonshine, that no expense
had been spared. The bottle misted over and drops clinked into glasses
like pearls of ice breaking the devout silence. Broad thumbs and index
fingers caressed the frozen jewels before them. The bridegroom forgave
the sins of his brothers, whereupon they all leaned back and flung the
icy potion down into the depths of their being. A murmur rustled

through the congregation and the most loquacious of the brothers whispered Amen. The old biddy with the bottle shuffled around the table once again. The deep bass voice of the bride's mother was heard to declare indignantly that it was typical for her daughter to marry into the fussiest family in the whole of the Finnish-speaking land mass when it came to food, and that food was there to be shoveled down your throat in case nobody had realized that around here. Whereupon the serving ladies marched in with new sizzling pots of meat stew and dishes of marrow, and everybody took another helping.

The men took their second schnapps, and the women as well, apart from those who would have to drive. Sitting opposite me was a stunningly beautiful Finnish woman from near Kolari. She had brown, almost Arabian eyes, and raven hair; no doubt she came from a Lappish family, and she wore a large silver brooch on her neckband. She smiled with her sharp white teeth and slid her half-glass of schnapps over the table to me. Not a word, just a bold, frank look, as if she were challenging me. All the men paused, their soup spoons dripping. I could see my dad in the corner of my eye warning me not to touch it, but I was already holding the glass. The tips of the woman's fingers stroked the inside of my hand as gently as a butterfly's wing, it felt so good I almost spilled the precious contents.

And now at last the men started talking. For the first time all day something approximating a conversation broke out. No doubt it was the drink that had thawed out the frost in their tongues, and the first thing they discussed was whether the young whippersnapper would vomit or cough up the schnapps all over the table, in view of how puny and feeble he looked. Dad made to stand up and stop me, despite the expectant looks on the faces of his brothers, and I knew it was now or never.

I leaned quickly back and poured the whole lot down my throat, a bit like taking medicine. And it sunk down into my body like a jet of piss into snow, and the men grinned. I didn't even cough, I just felt a melting fire in my stomach and a desire to be sick that didn't show on the outside. The old man looked furious but realized that it was too late, while the brothers reckoned the lad was one of the family after all. Then they started to boast about how much drink our family could hold, and proceeded to justify the claims with a series of graphic tales and episodes. When the subject was exhausted, which took an awful long time, the conversation turned to how incredibly tolerant of saunas our family was, and equally comprehensive proof was provided. One of the men was sent out to start up the sauna in the yard outside, and consternation was expressed as to why such an obvious thing hadn't been thought of earlier. Someone mentioned the absolutely amazing capacity for hard work that was characteristic of our family and a matter for incredulous discussions on both sides of the border, and in order to prove that this was no mere boast or exaggeration, we were presented with an appropriate selection of the stories people told about us, whenever two or three were gathered together.

The bride's relations were starting to show signs of mild impatience. Some of the sturdier men had evident ambitions to loosen their tongues. Eventually one of the most talkative of them opened his cakehole for the first time that evening for a purpose other than eating. He delivered an astonishingly sarcastic address on families that are too big for their boots and blather on and on in public. Dad and his brothers ignored that contribution to the discussion and became engrossed in how one of their forefathers had carried on his back a hundred-pound sack of flour plus an iron stove and his rheumatic wife for all of thirty miles without even putting down his luggage when pausing for a pee.

Now the ladies marched in with gigantic trays containing mountains of home-made delicacies. Sugar buns as smooth as a maiden's cheek, crisp white Kangos biscuits, perfect Pajala puff pastries, succulent sponge cakes, glazed buns dusted with icing sugar, sponge rolls with stunning Arctic raspberry filling, to name but a few of the delights. And that wasn't all: bowls brimful of whipped cream and newly warmed cloudberry jam tasting of sun and gold. Masses of china cups were rattled onto the table and sooty black coffee poured from gigantic coffee kettles, any one of which could have serviced a major prayer meeting. Golden coffee-cheeses as big as winter tires were rolled out over the table, and then the *pièce de résistance* among all the sweetmeats: a hard, brown lump of dried reindeer meat. Salty slices were cut and placed in the coffee, chunks of coffee-cheese stirred in, and white sugar lumps were held between the lips. And then, fingers trembling, we all poured the coffee mixture into our saucers, and slurped our way to heaven.

The moment I got some coffee inside me, all traces of feeling sick melted away. It was like the sunshine after the storm. A misty cloud of rain evaporated and the beauty of the countryside was suddenly revealed. My eyes felt like warm balloons, the round, bull-like skulls of the men on all sides inflated and grew to enormous proportions. The coffee changed its taste inside my mouth, became blacker and more tarry. I had an irresistible urge to start boasting. Then I burst out laughing, I couldn't help it, it simply welled up inside me and couldn't be restrained. I caught sight of the wonderful Finnish woman and my mind filled with pussy, it just happened, her beauty was almost dream-like.

"*Mie uskon että poika on päissä.* I think the lad's pissed," she said in a deep, slightly hoarse voice.

Everybody roared with laughter, me as well, so much that I almost fell off my chair. Then I chewed some dried meat and coffee-cheese and spilled coffee from my saucer and thought Hey, I'm a racing driver. The bride's mum went on about all the shrinking violets around the table who didn't dare to eat properly, she couldn't understand how a clan so scared of filling their stomachs could manage to reproduce, and she'd never heard of such a disgraceful failure to live up to the hospitable reputation of Tornedalen since the King of Sweden declined a glass of schnapps in Vojakkala. Everybody immediately helped themselves to more. But the bride's mum complained that if that was the best they could do, pretending to be polite, they might as well stuff the cakes up a different orifice, as even her patience had its limits. Everybody was on the point of bursting by now, belts had been loosened to the last hole, but even so everybody took another helping. And more coffee, and still more. But in the end the limit was reached, the final limit. Absolutely impossible to force down a single crumb more.

Then more brandy was served. Most guests declined, apart from some of the Finnish women. However, if there were just possibly a drop more schnapps they wouldn't say no, as *kirkasta* had the remarkable quality of not taking up any room in one's stomach—indeed, on the contrary, it was good for the digestion and for one's general well-being, and helped to combat the lethargy that often overcame those who had just partaken of a good dinner. The bridegroom once again gave the nod to the least Christian of the serving ladies who disappeared into the kitchen with all the empty bottles. When she came back a miracle had taken place and they were all full again; but when I held out my glass I received a painful rap on the wrist from the old man.

Somebody suddenly remembered a topic of conversation that had been inadequately covered, and immediately all the brothers were at it again. Such as the time when Grandad's horse had gone lame on him, and he'd pulled the sledge laden with tree trunks all the way home himself, with the horse strapped on top. Or the cousin who was only eight when he punted the fifty-odd miles upstream from Matarenki to Kengis. Or Grandma's aunt who was confronted by a bear while picking berries in the forest, killed it with the axe she had with her for cutting firewood, butchered it, and carried the meat home on her back, wrapped in the knotted pelt. Or the twins who had to be tied down to their beds every evening in the lumberjacks' cabin to prevent them from chopping down all the trees in the Aareavaara forest. Or the cousin who was regarded as feeble-minded but had been taken on to help float the logs down-river at half wages; the very first night he had single-handedly broken up the hundred-yard-long log jam at Torinen. The fact of the matter was that our family had no rivals when it came to strong, persevering, persistent, patient, and, above all, modest workers, no one could match them in the whole of the Finnish-speaking world. The brothers drank noisily to that, then proceeded to recall all the gigantic boulders that had been shifted, the enormous areas of bog that had been dug out, the horrific endurance tests while doing national service, the truck that broke down and had to be pushed twenty-five miles from Pissiniemi to Ristimella, the endless meadows that had been scythed in record time, all the blood-curdling fights that had ended up in the family's favor, the five-inch nail that had been hammered home using only a bare fist, the skier who had overtaken the iron-ore train, and all the other unsurpassed exploits achieved with the aid of axe, pick, plow, handsaw, spade, fish-spear, and potato fork.

Then another toast was drunk. Not least to the women in the family and their amazing feats in hand-milking, butter-churning, berry-picking, weaving, bread-baking and hay-raking that had set similar unbreakable records in the field of women's activities. The likes of these staunch, willing wenches had never been seen outside this family of theirs. The men also congratulated themselves on being smart enough to pick wives from Finland, since they were as tough as oak trees, as patient as reindeer, and as pretty as birches by blue northern lakes, and they also had large backsides that enabled them to give birth to fine healthy babies easily and often.

The bride's male relatives had sat in silence, as Finns do, getting worked up while all this was going on. The biggest and baldest of them, Ismo, stood up now and declared that he'd never heard so much twaddle spoken in Finnish since the days of the Fascist Lappland Movement. My dad responded in aggressive fashion, totally out of character, claiming that everything the brothers had said was universally accepted fact, and that if some families felt envious or inferior as a result, he was the first to feel sorry for them.

Ismo insisted that nobody could cut so many acres of meadow in just one morning, nobody could pick a hundred liters of cloudberries

inside three hours, no creature of flesh and blood could fell a bull
moose with one punch then skin it and butcher it with the lid of a
snuff box. Uncle Einari, the eldest of the brothers, maintained frosti-
ly that felling bull moose was nothing compared with the other
matchless feats accomplished by the family's fists, especially at weddings, and especially when some big-mouthed pompous ass starts
throwing out accusations of lying. He'd have gone on to say more as
well, he was just getting into his stride, but his missus clamped her
hand over his mouth. Ismo responded by laying his arm on the table.
It was as thick as a telegraph pole. He maintained that fisticuffs was
risky and haphazard as a test of strength, but that arm wrestling always
produced rapid and reliable results.

There was a moment of complete silence. Then the brothers rose to
their feet as one man, Dad included, and surged forward like growling
bears. The preliminaries were over, the talking was finished, at last they
could get down to flexing and using their laborer's muscles. Einari was
first to the seat opposite Ismo: he took off his jacket, loosened his tie,
and rolled up his sleeve. His arm was almost as thick as his opponent's.
Coffee cups and schnapps glasses were hastily removed. The two men
grappled with each other, their hands closed like pincers. A sudden jerk
from both bodies, blood rushed into their faces, battle had commenced.

It was clear from the start that it could go either way. Their arms
swayed like two pythons with trembling heads, welded together.
Slight, almost imperceptible quakes were transmitted through the
kitchen table and into the pine floorboards. Their backs, broad as sta-
ble doors, were arched forward, their shoulder muscles swelled up like
rising pastry, their heads turned blood-red, criss-crossed with protrud-
ing black veins, sweat poured off them and dripped down from their
noses. The brothers crowded around, shouting and urging. At stake
was the family honor, dignity, pride: now was the time to put the
incomers in their place and earn the respect that was our family's due.
Their opponents echoed these sentiments. The fists trembled and

started to lean to the left. Yells and shouts. Then a fight-back, a leaning to the right. The lads were jumping up and down in excitement,
passing on advice, flexing their own muscles in the hope it would help.
When it became clear that this contest was going to go on for some
considerable time, their patience ran out. Hormones were pumping
and couldn't be restrained, lumberjack bodies demanded action. Soon
the whole table was covered in fat-veined tree trunks swaying back and
forth as if in a gale. Now and again one or two would come crashing
down, causing the table top to sag. The victor would grin contentedly, only to be challenged by the next in line. The women were also getting carried away, and started yelling and shouting. Some of them had
been on the schnapps after all, and the others were intoxicated by the
testosterone-laden atmosphere. Soon two of the elderly Finnish
women started finger-pulling, their middle fingers entwined, tugging
and jerking, each determined not to be the first to let go. All the time
they spat out ancient, almost forgotten curses. They dug their hook-
toed shoes into the wooden floor, groaning and grinding their false
teeth, and one of them peed herself but kept going even so, splashing
around in the pool under her wide skirts. Their fingers were speckled
brown and wrinkled, but as hard as pincers. The bride declared that
she had never seen stronger fingers, here were women hardened by
milking cows and men; her fellow-women chimed in, eager to pro-
nounce the superiority of women over men when it came to endurance,
dexterity, persistence, patience, thrift, berry-picking techniques, and
resistance to illness, all of which proved they were superior to the
good-for-nothing male sex. Then one of the women, Hilma, won with
a ferocious jerk and fell flat on her bottom, but managed not to break
her thigh bone, which everybody thought was lucky. Flushed with victory she started challenging the men, always assuming there were any
present, which seemed doubtful. Dad and the rest of them were now
busy huffing and puffing over a prestigious championship involving a
bewildering system of quarterfinals and semifinals with everybody get-

ting the results mixed up and shouting at each other. In the middle of it all sat Einari and Ismo clutching each other's hand, the match still undecided. Uncle Hååkani suggested the old woman should keep her mouth shut as that was the main role of women in this vale of tears, especially when men were present. That made Hilma even more furious, she thrust forward her colossal bust, sending Hååkani stumbling backward, and informed him he was welcome to suck her tits if he had nothing more sensible to say. The women cackled and guffawed in delight, while Hååkani blushed. Then he said he would only pull fingers with the old bitch if she had a drink first. She refused as she was a Christian. They argued and argued. In the end, shaking with fury, Hilma took a large glass of moonshine, emptied it in one gulp, then stretched out her long claw. Everyone fell silent and stared in horror at the old woman. Laestadius rotated twice in his grave in Pajala churchyard. Hååkani was shaken but threaded his plump middle finger into her hook in order to show who was boss, and raised his arm. She was sturdy but short and was lifted up like a Lappish glove but hung on to the finger, dangling in the air. Hååkani put her down again and started jerking from side to side instead. Hilma was hurled and twirled from wall to wall but still hung on. Hååkani was getting annoyed, and paused to think. The woman suddenly flung herself backward with all her weight and with a fierce wrench broke Hååkani's grip and fell back on her bottom once again. The women clapped and cheered till the walls shook. In the end they began to wonder if she really had broken her thigh bone this time, as the old girl hadn't been as quiet as this since she had the anaesthetic for her goitre operation. Then she turned her head to one side and spat out the schnapps in one long jet. To deafening applause she assured the assembly that she hadn't swallowed a single drop.

I started working my way through the throng, wondering how I could get more drunk without the old man noticing. I eventually saw a bottle with a few drops left in the bottom, picked it up together with several empties, and pretended to help the serving ladies clear away. Then I sneaked into the entrance hall. In the semi-darkness I nipped my nose and started to swill it down.

As I did so a pair of strong arms wrapped themselves round my chest. I dropped the bottle. Somebody was standing behind me, breathing down my neck. I was scared, twisted and turned, but couldn't break loose.

"Let me go," I gasped, "*päästä minut!*"

The nearest I got to an answer was to be picked up and shaken like a puppy. I felt something tickling my face. Hair. Long, dark hair. Then a giggle and I was dropped with a thud.

It was her. Soft as fur as near as this. Like a cat. I waited for the teeth biting my neck. She was breathing heavily, smiling with luminous lips. Then she tore open my shirt and stuck her hand inside. It happened so quickly I had no time to defend myself. I felt her warmth. Her caresses, the soft tips of her fingers stroking my nipples.

"Do you get horny when you're drunk?" she asked in Finnish, and kissed me before I could reply. She smelled of perfume and fresh underarm sweat, and her tongue tasted sausagey, of *lenkkimakkara*. Moaning softly she pressed herself up against me, it was amazing that a woman could be as strong as this.

"I'll give you a good hiding!" she whispered. "I'll kill you if you so much as mention a word of this!"

Then she opened my trousers and whipped out my erection before I could draw breath. Just as rapidly she lifted her skirt and pulled down her pants. I helped her, her pants were wet. Her skin was shimmering white, her thighs as long as a moose cow's, with a black tousled bush between. I knew that if I touched it, it would bite me. She stroked me and was just about to guide me in when the dam burst, the world split open and collapsed in a cascade of wet rags and became red and sore, and she swore and pulled down her skirt and disappeared into the kitchen.

I was still too young to produce sperm. My dick went limp and all that remained was a pounding memory, like when you've peed against an electric fence. I buttoned up my trousers and thought I didn't dare go back into the kitchen ever again.

The next moment the door burst open, and the entrance hall filled with men jostling and butting like a herd of reindeer. They were all drunk, staggering about and leaning against the walls. Last to arrive were Einari and Ismo, who had reluctantly agreed to a tie; their arms had been so closely intertwined that they had to be prized apart. The old man instructed me to come along, as the sauna hero was about to be selected. The front door was flung open and everybody surged expectantly down the steps. Within seconds the yard was inundated with dozens of serious streams of pee. Grandad kept going longest of all and was pilloried by his sons, who wondered if he was pissing snot, considering the rate at which it was emerging; or if the old bloke had caught foot and mouth disease after screwing the heifer; or if his last shot had got stuck in the barrel of his rifle, in which case they maybe ought to pierce it with a knitting needle. Grandad muttered bitterly something about it being all right to make fun of the old, but not of invalids, then declared that he would have done better to tar and feather his prick than to sire a generation of bastards like this one.

The sauna was made of wood, and was the old-fashioned type, a so-called "smoke sauna." As was the custom it was some way away from the main building, in case it ever caught fire. The wall over the door was black with soot. There was no chimney, the smoke from the stone-box had to find its way out through the smoke-holes in the walls. The men started to hang their clothes on nails, or put them on the wooden benches outside while the mosquitoes ran riot all over them. As head of the house and the sauna host, Grandad went in first and shoveled the remains of the embers into a tin bucket. Then he threw several scoops of water into the stone-box in order to clean the air. Steam bellowed forth, attached itself to the smoke particles and continued out through the door and the three smoke-holes. Finally he removed the sacks that had been protecting the benches from soot, and stuffed rags into the smoke-holes.

I slunk in with the bunch of men and was squeezed into the top corner. There was a pleasant smell of tarred wood, and whenever I brushed against the wall I got black marks. The benches, both the upper and lower ones, were filled to overflowing with heavy, white male bottoms. Some failed to find a seat and had to sit on the floor, complaining that it was a fate worse than being denied entry into Paradise. The mosquitoes hovered in the doorway like a gray curtain, but didn't dare come in. The last man in closed the door on the summer evening, and suddenly everything went black. And everyone fell silent, as if overcome by reverence.

Slowly our eyes grew used to the dark. The stove was glowing like an altar. The heat felt as if it were coming from a big, curled-up animal. Grandad took hold of the wooden scoop and started muttering to himself. The men settled themselves down, arching their backs as if preparing for whiplashes. The wooden benches creaked under the weight. Slowly Grandad dipped the scoop into the cold water from the well, then rapidly poured nine scoopfuls with uncanny accuracy into the stone-box, one in the center, one in every corner and one in the middle of each long and short side. A ferocious hissing noise climbed up toward us, followed by stinging heat. The men moaned with pleasure. Sweat broke out on shoulders, thighs, genitals, and bald heads, oozing salt and setting us itching. The bunch of birch twigs was taken out of the bucket where it had been in water, and used on the glowing stones. A smell of sun and summer filled the sauna, and the men started smiling inwardly and sighing longingly. The bridegroom grabbed the birch twigs and began beating himself all over his body, moaning ecstatically all the while. In a quivering voice he announced that it was better than sex, which made the rest start squirming impatiently. Grandad poured nine more scoops onto the stones, hitting precisely the places that hadn't been wet the first time around. The heat filled the sauna like an enjoyable good thrashing. The moaning and panting increased in volume, and there were several whimpering pleas for the bunch of birch twigs before all the itching made their skins burst open. The bridegroom reluctantly passed it on, saying that they ought to have the kitchen ladies there to whip their backs as nobody could handle a *vihta* with such ecstatic ruthlessness as an old harridan. The twigs pitter-pattered and showers of sweat rained down. Grandad kept scooping on more water, mumbling away, and clouds of steam floated around like spirits. Some voices were heard complaining about the cold, claiming they'd rarely had such a cold *löylyä*, which everybody knew meant that the sauna was approaching its maximum temperature. The steam was as merciless as a Laestadian sermon. The men crouched and grappled with the heat, pure pleasure. Their gums were starting to taste of blood. Ear lobes were stinging, pulses thundered like drums. Somebody gasped that you couldn't get closer to Eden than this, not this side of the grave.

Once the first sensual storms had died down, a discussion started on the various types of sauna. Everybody agreed that the "smoke sauna" was far and away the best, much better than the wood-burning type and the electric version. The last-mentioned was singled out for special scorn and dismissed as a toaster or a car heater. Some recalled with a shudder the dry, dusty airing cupboards they'd had to sit in on various visits to southern Sweden. Someone remembered a sauna he'd taken at the Mountain Hotel in Jormlien where the electric stove was Norwegian and looked like an old-fashioned spin-dryer. The stone-box was about the size of a teacup with only enough room for two pebbles, provided one of them was stood on end. Another had horror in his voice as he told us about a building contract he'd been involved in on the island of Gotland. It lasted three months, but not once had he been able to attend to his personal hygiene because sauna culture had not penetrated that far south. Instead, people there would lie and splash about in the filth they washed off themselves in something they called a bathtub.

Grandad left off scooping water onto the stones in order to point out that several of his sons had in fact installed electrically driven saunas in the houses they'd had built for themselves, thereby condemning Tornedalen culture to an early death. The sons concerned protested that their saunas had been made in Finland and hence were of unbeatable quality, just as good as the wood-burning variety, and that the Finnish sauna magazine *Saunalehti* had awarded them five out of five bundles of birch twigs in their ratings. Grandad maintained tetchily that electricity was the most ridiculous invention ever to come from southern Sweden, it pampered and spoiled man and beast alike, decreased the mass of muscle in working men and women as well, reduced your tolerance of the cold, spoiled people's night eyes, ruined the hearing of teenagers and made them incapable of eating rotten food, and was well on the way to eradicating the endurance and patience that were virtues of the Tornedalen people, since everything was done nowadays at breakneck speed by engines. Before long sexual intercourse would be replaced by electricity as it was a strenuous exercise and a sweaty one as well, and that kind of thing was regarded as old-fashioned now, as we all know.

Grandad started scooping water onto the stones again, ignoring his sons' protestations that they were still made of traditional Finnish hardwood. Instead he declared that they had all become idle layabouts, that Tornedalen had been conquered by *knapsut* and *ummikot* and that what he regretted most of all was not smacking them more often when they were little. But it was too late now. Nobody understood any more the feeling of sitting in a sauna where you'd been born, where your father had been born and his father before him, where the family's corpses had been washed and shrouded, where *kuppari*, the medicine men, had bled the sick, where children had been conceived and where generation after generation of the family had cleansed themselves after a week's work.

His voice broke and, with tears in his eyes, he announced that life, my boys, is cold and pain and lies and rubbish. Take just one example:

the revolution he'd been waiting for ever since the Pajala transport workers came out on strike for the first time in 1931, where the hell was it, had anybody seen any sign of it around here lately, well, had they? Only once had a spark of hope been lit, one day when he'd gone to Kolari to buy some provisions, and among the crowd of customers in Valinta Firberg's he'd caught a glimpse of Josef Stalin with a cart full of meat. But Uncle Joe had obviously decided it was a waste of time coming to Pajala.

A bottle was handed to Grandad as a crumb of comfort amidst all the heat, and he splashed a drop on the stones as well. A whiff of fusel oil drifted toward us. Grandad passed on the bottle, wiped his nose on his arm and said that life was a load of shit anyway and death wasn't far away. But he was still a Communist, he wanted to make that clear once and for all, and if on his deathbed he started rambling about seeking forgiveness for his sins and asking for Jesus, it would be no more than confusion and senility and they should stick a plaster over his cakehole. He wanted everybody to promise they'd do that, here and now, in the presence of his family and other witnesses. The fear of death was nothing compared to the fear of going gaga and talking twaddle at Pajala Cottage Hospital for anybody to hear.

Then he threw nine more scoops onto the stones and some of the lads started whimpering and climbed down saying they needed a pee, and only the very hardest remained behind, with blisters the size of one-krona coins on their shoulders. Grandad couldn't believe he was the father of all these milksops. Then he handed over the scoop and said they could sort out the final stages for themselves because he was fed up with tormenting them and having to smell their glands. He climbed down with dignity and started to wash himself in a bowl of hot water. He only soaped the three most important parts of the body, the way old men do: his bald head, his stomach, and his scrotum.

And so the grim final round was under way. This would be the ultimate test of strength for the two families. Einari took over the scooping of the water while the others complained of the cold. As always the struggle was largely psychological. Everybody used exaggerated body language to demonstrate how unaffected they were, how little the heat troubled them, how long they'd be able to put up with it, no problem. Einari emptied the bucket over the sizzling stones and had it filled again immediately. Another round of scooping, fiercer than ever. The first batch of the finalists staggered down and fell on the floor, panting. Grandad threw a bucket of cold water over them. The steam was whipping everyone's back, burning their lungs. Another one gave up. The others sat there like tree stumps, eyes glazed over. Somebody started swaying, nearly fell, and was helped down. More steam, more pain. Now Dad gave up, coughing as if he were about to choke. Only Einari was left, still scooping, and bald-headed Ismo, head dangling. The vanquished huddled together on the floor, determined to stay and see the outcome. Ismo looked near to passing out, but stayed on the bench even so, remarkably enough. With each new scoop he jerked back, like a defenseless boxer slowly being knocked out. Einari was gasping for breath, and his right arm shook as he poured on fresh scoops of water. His face was purple, his upper body swayed alarmingly. One more scoop. And another. Ismo started coughing, ready to choke, he was dribbling down his chin. Both of them were swaying violently now, and put their arms around each other to support themselves. Suddenly Einari shuddered and toppled stiffly toward Ismo, who also fell. They collapsed like slaughtered beasts, thudded down onto the lower bench, and stayed lying down, arms round each other.

"A draw!" shouted somebody.

Only now did I slither out of my dark corner on the upper bench, looking like a skinned rabbit. Everybody stared in amazement. Without a word I raised my fist in a victory salute.

As their applause and cheering rose to the soot-caked ceiling, I fell to my knees on the floor and vomited.

CHAPTER 12

*About a stomach-turning summer job, a poker that
went astray, and the perils that ensue from failing to do one's duty*

One gray and overcast day in May a slim, spry man came striding into
Pajala from the Korpilombolo direction. He was carrying an old-fashioned military rucksack, his head was weather-beaten and as worn as a
rune stone, topped by short, silvery gray hair. He stopped in
Naurisaho, gazed disapprovingly up at the leaden sky and took several
deep draughts from a water-bottle. Then he knocked on the door of the
nearest house. When the door opened he bade the stranger good day in
broken standard Finnish with an exotic accent. The man introduced
himself as Heinz, a German citizen, and he wondered if there might be
an empty cottage in the area available for renting over the summer.

A few telephone calls were made, and by that evening Heinz had
found a badly insulated little wooden cottage just outside the village.
The widow who used to live there had become feeble-minded over the
last few years, and had covered the whole of the floor with topsoil and
hay, so everything had to be scrubbed with soap and boiling water
before the German accepted it. He was provided with a mattress and
some china, some basic provisions were placed in the larder, curtains

were put up, and a truckload of firewood was dumped outside the front door. The electricity could be reconnected, although that would mean an increased rent. Heinz declined on the grounds that it was May already and electric lights would not be needed—after all, it wouldn't get dark again until well into August.

On the other hand he was keen to take a look at the sauna. It was on the edge of the forest, gray with age and covered in soot around the door. Heinz opened it. Breathed deeply. A melancholy smile spread over his face as he breathed in the scent of the smoke sauna.

"Sauna!" he whispered in his exotic foreign accent. "I haven't taken a sauna for over twenty years!"

That very night Niila and I lay concealed in our look-out post and watched him running naked down to the River Torne, saw him hurl himself into the water among the last of the lumps of ice drifting down-river and swim half-way across before turning back. Then he stood on the bank, blue with cold, leaping around with his shriveled penis wavering in the cold night air, before jogging back into the warmth of the cottage.

The next day he acquired an abandoned typewriter from the Customs' store of confiscated items, an ancient Halda made of cast iron. He set it up on the porch and sat there bashing away for hours on end, occasionally gazing over the meadows flush with shoots of fresh, green grass, listening to the curdling flute cadenzas of the curlew.

Who was this man, in fact? What was he doing here? Before long rumors were circulating to the effect that this mysterious stranger had been an SS officer in Finland during the war. That was where he had picked up his Finnish and learned about the sauna culture. In the later stages of the war his company had been forced to retreat as the Finnish army advanced, and they had withdrawn northward through Finnish Tornedalen, where the wild beauty of the landscape had made an indelible impression on him.

They had burned everything that stood in their path. Those were their orders, a scorched earth policy. Every single house and barn in village after village; even the churches had been drenched in gasoline and the whole area had become one vast, flaming ocean of fire. The whole of the north of Finland had been reduced to ashes. Heinz had been partly responsible. And now he had returned to record his memoirs.

That's what they said about him. Heinz kept his own council. Went for brisk walks in knee-length running shorts, followed a program of jerky military gymnastics outside the cottage every morning while the kids lay in the bushes and sniggered. Then filled page after page during his strictly regimented writing sessions.

The only thing that disturbed him was the mice.

The house was full of them. The widow had owned several cats, to be sure, but once she'd been taken away, the mice had run riot. They'd made themselves at home in all the mess, burrowed into the mattresses to make nests, made runs under the floorboards, and given birth to new generations. Heinz complained to his landlords, and was lent an old farm cat—but it ran back home at the first opportunity. Heinz rejected the offer of poison, on the grounds that lots of them would die under the floorboards and then stink the house out.

One evening in the first week of the summer holidays I was spying on Heinz as he sat out on his porch, bashing away at his typewriter. The noise was like that of an old-fashioned motor-bike. I crept along the house wall and got as far as the corner, carefully peered around it. I could see him in profile. A long, slightly curved and pointed nose, steel-framed glasses, and a few newly awakened mosquitoes swarming around his head, like a halo of old memories.

"*Tule tänne sinä!* Come here, my lad," he shouted in standard Finnish without pausing in his typing.

I stiffened, scared stiff.

"*Tule tänne!*" he shouted once more, and that was an order. He stopped typing, took off his glasses and turned his ice-gray eyes to focus on me.

I stepped forward, my knees trembling. Stood there like a conscript, ashamed, out-maneuvered.

"I'll give you fifty öre per tail," he said.

I didn't know what he was talking about. Felt stupid and afraid. "There are too many mice in this house," he went on. "Not easy to get to sleep with all that row at night."

He scrutinized me in order to gauge my reaction, got up from his creaking chair and came over to me. I didn't move a muscle, and it felt quite solemn despite my terror. He was the sort of man boys like to be praised by. With a flourish, he produced a brown wallet smelling of leather, and picked out a ten-kronor note. He dangled it in front of my nose, without a word, as if it had been a giant butterfly. The note was new and uncreased, something you didn't often see. How had it managed to find its way up here through the whole of Sweden without being damaged? The old king was contemplating me in profile. Silvery gray in color, fine and delicate lines, high-quality paper with a watermark that looked like a bruise when seen against the light. And behind it I suddenly noticed something else. An electric guitar. A real one, my very own electric guitar.

I accepted the note. I didn't crumple it up and put it in my pocket. I carried it home carefully between my finger and thumb, still without a single crease.

Like all village kids I was familiar with the technique for killing mice. You put a piece of raw potato peel at the side of the house wall, then stood nearby with a stick. You waited patiently without a sound until the mouse came creeping up. Then you battered it to death. If you found a fresh mouse hole in the ground you could pour in a few buckets of water. As the mouse started to drown it would come racing out of the hole and all you had to do was to bash it one.

The first day I killed three mice in this way, and two more the following day. Heinz duly paid up out of his leather wallet, but didn't seem happy. The methods seemed to him old-fashioned and inefficient. That same afternoon he bought eight spring traps at the ironmonger's in Pajala, with steel springs that broke the backs of the little creatures.

I learned how to bait them without cutting off my own fingers, using bits of bacon rind, crusts of cheese, and whatever else was at hand.

The next morning I found six dead bodies. The seventh trap was untouched and the eighth had gone off but the mouse had got away. I threw the woolly corpses away at the edge of the forest and reset the traps. When I went to check that evening, I found four more dead bodies. Heinz checked the cut-off tails and was pleased with my efforts, paid up on the spot, and encouraged me to keep it up.

The rest of the week I checked both morning and evening, and the daily catch amounted to about ten. I kept moving the traps, putting them in the pantry, in the food cellar, in the attic, but also outdoors under the porch steps or round at the back near the wood pile. The bodies were strangely flaccid, soft little fur bags with a snapped spine and crushed ribs. Sometimes the sharp steel spring ripped open the skin so that their intestines spilled out over the trap like violet-colored algae. That meant I had to grit my teeth and clean up the mess. The job had to be done, even if it was nauseating.

And sure enough, things quieted down in the house at night. But it was never completely silent. No matter how many mice were killed, more and more kept coming, new litters were born, new guests moved in the moment the old ones had disappeared.

Moreover the dead bodies started to be a problem. The fox ate as many as he could, but the remainder soon started to smell. Before long the edge of the forest was swarming with crows. They would come especially at dawn, screaming and croaking as they asserted their pecking order, and disturbing Heinz's sleep even more than the mice had done. He gave me a spade from out of the shed and got me to dig a hole out of earshot in the forest into which I was to start emptying the bodies.

It was high summer by now. Skylarks hovered up in the air like frayed propellers, starlings whistled and told tall tales in the aspens, pied wagtails pulled juicy worms out of the potato beds, and house martins sat on the overhead wires plucking lice from their wing feathers. And under the ground, the mice multiplied at a mind-boggling rate.

As time went by I became more and more of an expert on mouse behavior. Many people think mice are chaotic little furry creatures who scamper around at random and frightened to death. But as I messed about with the traps outside the house I'd noticed all kinds of mouse paths. They were often difficult to see, meandering like little tunnels through the dry grass from the last year, closest to the ground. Mice have their own paths just as ants do, and I soon discovered that placing traps along these routes nearly always produced results. The best way of preventing new mice from colonizing the house, therefore, was to mine their approach roads.

The tactic was only partially successful, however. Conventional mouse traps have a basic constructional fault in that once they have gone off, they are harmless until they've been re-set. Meanwhile, there is nothing to stop mice proceeding past unhindered. I thought about this problem for a while, then submitted a plan to Heinz. He approved wholeheartedly.

We borrowed a few dented zinc-plated buckets from a neighbor. I dug them down at strategic points in the middle of the mice paths, so that the edge was level with the ground. Then I poured in water until they were half full. I placed a thin layer of grass and leaves over the top, and tried to make everything seem as natural as possible.

The next morning I went to check. Six mice had fallen into the first bucket. They'd swum round and round without being able to either touch the bottom or scramble up the sides, grown weaker and weaker, and eventually drowned. There were five dead bodies in the second bucket. Another seven in the third. The last bucket had a hole in it and the water had leaked out: two terrified souls were running round at the bottom, and I trampled them to death with my heel. Twenty dead mice! A fantastic score! There were four more in the spring traps, so when I snipped off the tails and presented them to Heinz, he was most impressed and handed over twelve whole kronor. His narrow mouth showed signs of a smile, a most unusual sight, like a wolf trying to laugh. I threw the dead bodies into the hole in the forest, changed the leaking bucket, and dug down some more buckets and tubs in suitable places.

The next few weeks produced very satisfactory profits. The mice fell into the traps in hordes, scratched desperately at the sides of the bucket until they were exhausted, then drowned. The bodies were much more attractive than those from the spring traps. At first the sheer numbers made the job repulsive, several pounds of them to cart away every day. But you got used to it. And it helped to think about the coins dropping into the tin back at home, money that was growing rapidly into an electric guitar.

Now at last Heinz could see that the war was being won. Only occasionally could he hear the soft pitter-patter of some valiant little warrior who had managed to thread his way through the minefield. But generally speaking the poor chap found himself caught in a spring trap soon afterward. Heinz was sleeping soundly now, his typewriter clattered away like an old-fashioned machine gun and the whole of the porch smelled of insect spray as the mosquito plague had started in earnest. Sometimes he would pull a sheet of paper out of the typewriter and read it aloud in his high Wagnerian voice, to test the rhythm of the language. Austere, powerful prose describing hardships and troop movements, vivid pictures of war during the Finnish winter, frost and sharp pine needles inside the blankets, here and there some crude military humor, sexual deprivation in foul-smelling camps, and now and then romantic sections with nubile Finnish beauties feeding bandaged war heroes, or caressing a German military cheek in the evening in a blacked-out canteen.

In the meantime I continued to rationalize the business. For instance, I noticed it wasn't necessary to cover the buckets with grass. The mice fell in even so. They didn't seem to have time to slow down as they hurtled along the paths, but they just dropped down even though the chasm was in full view. But on the other hand, the mice paths stopped being used as the mice died off. New ones were inaugurated elsewhere, so I had to keep my eyes peeled and keep moving the buckets.

The grave in the forest filled up before one could blink. I topped it up with soil and dug a new one. That was also full before we knew where we were. The foxes kept digging up the rotting carcasses and dragging them off in all directions. Before long their dead bellies were full of maggots burrowing under their skin. The heat made things worse, and whenever the wind was blowing in from the forest there was no mistaking—despite the distance—the disgusting sweet-and-sour stench.

Heinz had an idea. He found an old petrol can and filled it up. At regular intervals I had to lug it out into the forest and empty it into the hole. Then I threw a lit match after it. With a deep sigh the heap of corpses caught fire and kept on burning with a barely visible glow. There was a damp crackling noise as fur charred, whiskers drooped then melted, ants came scuttling out of the eye sockets and shriveled up, legs flailing, maggots wriggled their way up but were fried and liquified, pupae burst and half-formed, blind bluebottles squirmed helplessly. The smoke was black and greasy, stinking of wool and burned blood, and clung to my clothes if I stood too close. It spread out among the treetops like a menacing specter, a war god, a swelling harbinger of death that slowly moved away and then dispersed, leaving nothing behind but the taste of fatty ash in my mouth. When the pyre had burned itself out I filled in the hole with soil and moss and piled heavy stones on top of it until not even the foxes would think it was worth the trouble.

Think of the money. If I did that, it became more bearable. Count up the tails, collect them in a bundle and then cash them in with the dapper gentleman who was spending the evening on his porch, sipping coffee. It was a summer job, that's all. No worse than scrubbing clean the outdoor toilets at Pajala camping site.

After the evening check I generally sat in my room and played the old open-reel tape recorder on which I'd saved some of the best tunes from the Top Ten program on the radio. With a series of sensual shudders I would listen to the remarkable, fantastic sounds an electric guitar could produce, spiky meows, wolf-like howls, dentist's drills or the roar of a souped-up moped careering through the village. I imitated them inadequately on my old acoustic guitar. At the same time, back at the cottage, the first mouse was tumbling into the water. Starting to swim. And swim. And swim.

* * *

One morning in mid-July I stumbled upon a mouse-path that was wider than any I'd ever seen before. It ran from the forest to the potato bed alongside a green ditch, well hidden by straggly brushwood. Here and there it was joined by paths from the house and the outdoor toilet, becoming even wider, an impressive main road. A well-trampled mouse run, a major road for mice. I followed it in a state of increasing excitement. Past the old barn that was half-full of old hay. I paused here. A new path led from the barn. Almost as wide. I was certain it hadn't been there before. And there, a few feet short of the potato plot, the two paths joined. Came together to form a multilane highway.

I realized it was the potatoes they were after. The tops were tall and green, the widow's relatives had continued growing them there even after she'd been put away, and underneath, inside the mounds, the tubers were growing fat, nicely tender and yellow. The mice were flocking over to binge on potatoes all night long. Gnawing and munching, then staggering back home to their hideaways, choc-a-bloc.

There was no time to lose. Before half an hour had passed I'd got hold of a rusty gasoline drum, and then spent a large part of the afternoon sawing it in two with a hack-saw. Then it was just a matter of digging it down. In the middle of the autobahn. I loaded the earth into a wheelbarrow and tipped it out in the forest. After a lot of sweat and toil, I was ready to sink the drum into the ground and fill in the gaps round the rim. Then I lugged bucket after bucket of water from the well until it was more or less half full.

It was evening by now. The typewriter had fallen silent. The porch steps were deserted. I knocked on the door with the day's collection of mouse-tails in my hand, and found Heinz busy packing. His rucksack was in the middle of the floor, and clothes were draped over chair backs and on the table. Heinz dug out the money he owed me while darting around, and explained that he was going to Finland for about a week to dig out some information from various archives. He needed to establish the precise location of some houses in a village before they were burned down, and to scour the lists of local residents. As a writer he was very meticulous about details, like every true author ought to be— although in his view a lot of them were very cavalier on this point, especially the new wave of prose writers. Meanwhile, perhaps, I might be so kind as to keep an eye on the house?

I promised I would, and was told where to find the key. It was about then that I started to feel queasy. I had a bit of a headache, and there was a feeling of stiffness in my armholes. Perhaps a thunderstorm was on the way. I went out onto the porch, and sure enough, an ominous bank of clouds was approaching from Finland. It looked like the mushroom of smoke from the cremation pit, but it was bigger, more ominous. There was a dull rumble, as if from Russian tanks. Heinz came out and stood beside me. I was surprised when he put his arm round my shoulders, almost like a father. The air became more oppressive, harder to breathe. Beads of sweat broke out on my brow. In the darkness under the mass of clouds there were flashes of lightning, like darting fish.

"There!" exclaimed Heinz, pointing.

A column of smoke was rising several miles away. A tree, a copse? Or a house? Was it a house on fire? And just for a moment the storm clouds were turned into smoke from a fire, the whole of Finland was in flames, being destroyed by a blazing inferno. Heinz was motionless. His icy gray eyes were gaping, transfixed on something far distant. They looked like coins. Then he stroked his moustache with his fingertips. One of the hairs came loose. He held it between his thumb and his forefinger, and he came back down to earth. The hair was stiff, and drooping like a used match. He twirled it around, then let go. Dropped it in among his memories.

* * *

As the rain started to fall, I had the first fit of shivers. I biked back home and collapsed onto the kitchen sofa. When the storm began, Mum closed all the windows and doors and pulled all the electric plugs out of their sockets. The bank of clouds enveloped us in its creepy twilight. The rain pattered down onto the roofing felt, pouring grey curtains down outside the windows. More rumbling. I pulled the quilt and blankets over my head, sweating and freezing in turn. Mum came with a glass of water and a sachet of Samarin, since the healing power of Samarin was uncanny and went far beyond what the packet said it could do. Even so, my temperature rose in step with the thunderstorm. The weather clamped its wet foot down on the village until my head was on the point of bursting. All kinds of strange images were pressed out of it, witches luminescent round the edges launching themselves gently into the air. They all had knives and were cutting pieces out of each other, as flat as cardboard cut-outs. Dancing around in slow motion, they mutilated one another then merged with the bite they'd cut away, constantly changing, mixing flesh. The vision made me feel sick, disgusted, but there was nothing I could do to stop it. It was as if somebody else was thinking with my brain, as if I'd been invaded.

Mum tried to keep calm, but her unease was obvious. She tried to hide it behind a stern expression, pouting and sticking her lower lip out so far that the mucous membrane was in full view. She had reached an age when the skin on her face had started to sag, like a sweater that's a bit on the big side. When she laughed, her face collapsed into a mass of wrinkles that made her look like a chopping block—and that was about the limit of her facial expressions. The beautiful thing about her was her hair, ginger in color and dense, extending down toward the top of her spine. When she had brushed it and let a lock tumble down over one of her eyes, she could be reminiscent of a film star.

I was so cold, I couldn't stop shivering. Mum lit a fire in the living room, even though we were in the middle of summer. I could hear her ripping up pieces of birch bark and prodding around with the poker. Then everything went strangely quiet.

The kitchen was lit up. As if the sun had broken through the clouds. But it was still pouring down outside. I made a big effort and sat up. Peered around in bewilderment, and realized that the light was coming from the living room.

"What's going on?" I shouted. No answer. I staggered out on legs made wobbly by the fever. Mum was standing in front of the open fire like a fencer, the poker stretched out in front of her. The light was coming down the chimney. Yellowish-white, sharp.

"Back off, Mum!" I shouted.

Mum took a step back, still holding the poker, but the light followed her. A glowing globe had emerged from the chimney and was hovering in the hearth. Sparkling like white-hot iron straight out of the furnace, bobbing up and down as if floating in the air. A marked tremor, then it came to a halt, on the end of the poker. I could see Mum lighting up. A blue glow around her head. Her hair stood on end and started sticking out in all directions.

"Let go! Let go of the poker!"

But she seemed to be in a trance. Backed off one step at a time, the poker swaying from side to side. The fireball followed her all the way. She waved the poker more violently, but the fireball seemed to stick to the end of it, as if drawn by a magnet.

"Let go of it, Mum, for God's sake!"

Instead she started spinning around with the poker. Rotating like a hammer-thrower in an attempt to shake off the unwanted guest. But it persisted. She spun faster and faster. There was a swishing noise. Sparks were flying from the handle. But the fireball was still stuck fast to the end of the poker. She was panting now, gasping and spinning around faster and faster. Soon she was surrounded by a ring, a halo, a circle of electricity. She couldn't stop. Spun round and round, the swishing sound grew louder and louder, burst into song. The whole room was filled with blue sparks. Faster. Still faster. To the very limit.

Then she let go. The poker and the fireball were launched into space. Hurtled into the wall, *smaaaash!* A deafening crash, and wood splinters showered down over us. Then silence.

I'd been knocked over and was lying on the floor. Dazed, I slowly raised my head and shook out the bits in my hair. Mum was flat on her bottom, legs akimbo and her mouth spelling out a little "o." It dawned on us that we'd survived. We staggered unsteadily to our feet and stumbled over toward the wall.

There was a hole in it. A gaping hole through all the layers, as if somebody had delivered a punch and pierced the whole caboodle. There was no sign of the poker. It wasn't inside the house, nor on the lawn outside, and we thought for ages that it had simply disintegrated.

But we were surprised to come across it that autumn. Hidden among the neighbor's blackcurrant bushes, two blocks down the road, rusty and twisted like a corkscrew.

I carefully measured the distance. A hundred and ten yards. A women's world record for throwing the hammer.

* * *

The storm receded, but I was still laid up. The fever continued for two whole days, then developed into a migraine-like headache. My joints were stiff, my eyes over-sensitive to light, and my throat felt loose and furry. My body seemed to be as heavy as an iron hull, torpedoed, slowly sinking down into the depths of the ocean. I could barely lift an arm, and had difficulty in swallowing. As was the norm in Tornedalen, we avoided going to the doctor for as long as possible, as that was the surest way of getting an early burial. Instead Dad went over to a neighbor who had a medical book in Finnish, and diagnosed me as having meningitis, measles, urticaria, brain cancer, mumps, and juvenile diabetes. Then came the coughing and the runny nose, and it became obvious I had gastric influenza. A really nasty attack with painful sinuses, but all in all, nothing serious. Niila came to call on me, but went back out almost before he'd come in through the door, the moment he noticed the smell of the plague.

Outside, the heat of high summer had arrived. The thunders had created a warm front, clearing the way for a mass of hot air drifting in from Siberia. A ridge of high pressure towered up over us like a gigantic circus tent with a blue, blue roof and static heat. Millions of mosquitoes hatched out in the swamps, the cable ferry was going back and forth non-stop over the river to the bathing beach at Esisaari, and Altenburg's Carnival had pitched their red and yellow saloon in the meadow with shooting galleries, one-armed bandits, and no end of other temptations aimed at the local kids' pocket money. The carnival manager strutted around shirtless, as hairy as an old he-bear, with a cowboy hat over his mane of gray hair, shouting:

"Lottery tickets, ten for a fiver! Ten fivers for Lotta!"

But I was stuck at home in bed, sweating buckets, and had to ask for a jug of water by my bed. I drank and drank, but could only manage a few dark yellow drops of pee. My face was swollen and puffed up with green slime, and I had to blow my nose so much it was covered in sores. I occasionally tried to pass the time by playing the guitar, but it only made me sweat more and feel dizzy. So I dozed instead. Listened to the bumble bee that had found its way into the house but couldn't get out again, banging up against the mosquito netting in the windows, buzzing away, while the mosquitoes on the other side stuck their proboscises through the holes.

The cold slowly got better. Early one morning, when the sun was starting to heat up, I sat up in bed and groped for the water jug. I drank greedily, wiping the drops from the corner of my mouth.

And then I remembered. The thing that had been in the back of my mind all the time, but kept there by the high temperatures and all that coughing.

I gave a shudder, and got dressed. Heard Dad snoring in the bedroom. I crept out quietly and emerged into the bright morning light. I tried to work out how long I'd been ill in bed, how many days had gone by. With a nasty premonition of what lay in store, I cycled off to the German's cottage.

You could smell the stench from as far away as the main road. Sickly. Acidic. It grew stronger the closer I came. Sweeter and more disgusting. I put my hand over my nose and mouth. Saw the potato patch with the tall greenery. The barn and the mouse path. The gasoline drum.

At a hundred feet away I was on the point of choking. I took a deep breath and raced like mad over the final stretch.

Gray porridge. So many that they'd died one on top of the other.

I bent down and my shadow fell over the surface. A flash of light. A thick cloud of flies whirled up. I recoiled with a start. You could see the movement down below. Billowing like a sea. A swaying carpet of larvae.

In a state of shock I staggered away into the grass. A nauseous shudder ran right up my body. I heaved, and ran until I collapsed. Spat into a bed of dandelions, tried to be sick but couldn't.

I eventually managed to get control of myself and kicked off my shoes. Pulled off my socks, which were damp with sweat. Then I bound them over my nose and mouth. The smell was bad but at least it was my own. Spurred on by desperation I scrambled to my feet.

I found the wheelbarrow and started to fill it with soil. I'd fill in the mass grave where it lay. It was the only way. Cover up the whole thing. Spread soil over the top and try to forget all about it.

When the barrow was full I took a deep breath, tied the socks on tighter and moved forward. Get it over with, not think about it. Just do it, as quickly as possible.

If it hadn't been for one thing.

The money.

That was the problem after all, if you tried to look at it rationally, which wasn't easy, it's true. The drum was full of money. It contained pile upon pile of fifty-öre pieces. And I was about to bury them.

I put the wheelbarrow down. Hesitated. Then grit my teeth and with determination born of desperation went to the shed and found a rake. Took a deep breath and returned to the drum. Stuck the rake down into the sludge, making the flies shift out of the way. Fished around and managed to bring up a few dead bodies. The skin had split and white maggots dripped into the grass like rain. Retching violently I drew back in order to breathe. Brought the shears and pulled on a pair of old working gloves. Then forced myself to rush back.

I could see all the details when I got close up. No, it wasn't possible. It was asking too much.

I lay flat on my face at the edge of the forest and could feel my fever returning. Money! You have to think about the money! There were at least seventy bodies. Maybe even eighty. That meant forty shiny, silvery kronor.

It was only a job after all. That was the way to look at it, a summer job.

Rush back again. Snip, fifty öre. Snip, one krona. Drop the bodies into the slop-pail, then withdraw in order to breathe.

One krona. A whole bloody krona. Bloody hell, a whole krona.

Down with the rake once more. Snip, one-fifty.

It was getting into my mouth. I could taste it.

Snip, two kronor. Two-fifty.

If only it weren't for the stench.

Four kronor. Five. Six-fifty.

No, that's enough, must stop now, bloody hell…

It went incredibly slowly. Some were more recent, still stiff. Others fell apart. Little paws with claws spread, shiny yellow teeth. In among the mice were a few voles as well, as big as cats and grotesquely swollen. They were floating around, distorted and stiff after their horrific struggle with death.

A large chunk of the morning had passed before the first slop-pail was full. In a series of short rushes I carried it into the forest. The contents were bubbling and slopping around. I tipped the sludge into the mass grave. Went back to the drum.

There were fewer victims in the smaller water traps, but they were just as rotten. The bodies in the spring traps had been almost entirely eaten by ants and had already started drying out. I struggled on for most of the rest of the day, and could feel my clothes getting sticky from all the splashes. Emptied the slop-pail into the hole in among the trees. Another bucket. Back again. Snip, snip. There was a chilly tickling feeling inside my gloves and I emptied out a few maggots. Flies were swarming around my face, settling all over me. If only I'd had a hat. Bucketful after bucketful. Pull back and breathe. Deeper and deeper down into the drum.

In the end there was nothing but grey, slushy death juices at the bottom. I raked through it, and it was lucky I did because there were four tails there that had fallen off, two kronor, and when I looked more closely I noticed another one, fifty öre—it obviously paid to be meticulous.

To round things off I pushed the wheelbarrow up to the rum, tipped the soil into it and flattened the surface down with a spade. There was barely a trace left of the massacre. Just a bare patch of earth that would soon be covered in grass.

My fever came back, though, when I stumbled off in a daze to fetch the gasoline can. Only the final act left to complete now.

The grave in the forest was overfull. The last bucketfuls had spilled over onto the parched brushwood. Flies flew up in thick clouds but soon settled again like a shaggy blanket, injecting eggs into the sunwarmed mass of decay. The stench was worse than I could ever have imagined, a fermenting dough of death with millions of microbes swelling up and reproducing.

I had to run back again in order to get some fresh air. Unscrewed the lid of the can and sniffed at it. The gas cleared out my nose, sweet and strong. I pulled myself together and prepared for the final act, the only thing still left to do before it was all over. Before I could relax and forget it.

In a dream I sprayed gas over the dead bodies, gave them a good splashing, a good soak. It felt like a religious act, as if trying to atone for something, to put things right. I struck a match, and dropped it onto the pile. There was a deep, sad cough as it burst into flames. A barely visible flame shot up stiffly, cracking. The nearest bushes were scorched, the brushwood caught fire. I stamped out the flames. Then I realized I'd splashed my trouser legs with gas, and flames were creeping up toward my kneecaps. I screamed, flung myself to the ground and ripped off my trousers. They got stuck around my shoes, which were also burning. I frantically kicked my shoes off and put out the fires by flapping with my hands.

Back at the grave, the fire had caught hold in the parched under-growth. The nearest bushes were already ablaze. I broke off a leafy branch and tried to beat out the flames, but everything was so dry that they continued to spread. Before long they'd reached the nearest tree. I tried desperately to prevent catastrophe. There was a sudden breath of air through the forest, a gentle breeze closing in on the hearth. The fire was sucking all the oxygen from the surrounding area, the fire's own breathing, a wind getting stronger and stronger as the flames worked their way up through the branches. And at the heart of it all, at the center of destruction, the crematorium was bubbling away.

I was petrified. The flames spread through the forest with astonishing speed, throwing their torches from tree to tree. I started beating again with my leafy branch, flailing around in terror, but the catastrophe grew worse by the minute.

"The fire brigade!" I thought, and wanted to run for help. But I couldn't, something was holding me back, I carried on beating, my eyes stinging. The fire spread inexorably toward the edge of the forest, a raging battle front. The hay barn started smoldering and would soon be beyond rescue. And the wind was blowing toward the cottage. The sparks rained down thicker and thicker. Sharp nails of fire cascaded down. And soon they had taken hold of the roofing felt.

It was war. A wild animal had been aroused and could no longer be restrained. And I was the one responsible. It was my fault.

At that point Heinz materialized. Eyes staring. Panic.

"The manuscript!" he bellowed, wrenching open the front door. The roof was alight and belching thick smoke, but he crouched down under it. He had to get inside, and surged forward. Tears poured from his eyes as he was forced to retreat, empty-handed. Another swift attempt, and now there were flames, not just smoke—there was a yellow glow inside the cottage. And this time he came storming out clutching a bundle of papers. He held them close to his chest, as if they were a child, embraced them passionately, then collapsed into the grass, coughing.

I went up to him. Covered in soot, stinking, wearing nothing but my underpants. In my hand was the string tied round the decaying tails. They were bundled together in tens, to make counting easy. Easier to check.

"One hundred and eighty-four," I stammered. "Ninety-two kronor."

Heinz stared vacantly at me. Then he grabbed hold of the string with the stinking tails and hurled them into the raging fire.

"It was all your fault!"

No brown leather wallet. No money. No electric guitar.

Heartbroken, I reached for his bundle of papers and flung them into the fire. Then ran for it, for all I was worth.

Heinz leaped to his feet with a roar. He tried to force his way in, but this time he was driven back.

When the fire brigade finally arrived, he was sitting on the lid of the well, the old soldier, sobbing.

CHAPTER 13

In which we acquire a music teacher with a thumb in the middle of his hand, and get to know an unexpected talent from Kihlanki

In class seven we got a new music teacher. His name was Greger and he came from Skåne, a tall, thick-lipped farmer's boy who had lost all the fingers of his right hand in a piece of farm machinery. Only the thumb was left, as big as a fluted almond potato. After his accident he had retrained, and landed in Pajala immediately after graduating as a music master. It was difficult to understand what he said. Apart from that, he was a cheerful fellow with an odd sense of humor. I'll never forget the very first lesson he gave, when he bounced in with his hand hidden in his pocket, and announced in his typical Skanian burr:

"Good morrrning! Now you've got a teacherrr with a thumb in the middle of his hand!"

With precise timing to maximize the shock effect, he whipped out his deformed hand. We gasped with horror. He turned his hand around, and we noticed that from a certain angle his thumb and hairy knuckles looked like a male sexual organ. Only bonier and more frightening, and supernaturally mobile.

Greger brought with him to Pajala an unusual novelty: a twelve-gear racing bicycle. It was among the most outrageous and useless things we'd ever seen, with a rock-hard leather saddle and tires no broader than cigars; it didn't even have mudguards or a luggage carrier. It looked almost improper, completely naked. He started whizzing like a rocket along our roads in a red tracksuit, frightening the living daylights out of old ladies and local kids, and gave rise to several reports of UFOs in the *Haparanda Daily News*. He also made dogs go mad. It must have had something to do with his scent, something Skanian in his intestinal flora. As soon as he came swishing past, they went berserk. They would break loose and race after him for mile after mile, barking for all they were worth in flocks that got bigger and bigger. One day he returned from a practice run to Korpilombolo followed by two Norrbotten spitzes, a Swedish foxhound, a Jämtland wolfhound, two Norwegian elkhounds, plus a few more of mixed race. They were all white-eyed and intent on murder. Greger pulled up outside the police station and was immediately attacked by the pitch-black labrador that had taken on a leadership role in the hysterical pack. Greger waited for the right moment, then calmly kicked it on the snout with his fancy cycling shoe, whereupon the cur staggered back to his friends yelping and whining. Then he strolled with dignity into the police station. The duty officer had to chain them all up, apart from the labrador—it needed veterinary attention. For the rest of the day silent peasants from the surrounding villages came driving up in their cars to collect their Fido. From then on Greger was much talked about locally.

Another topic of discussion was just how fast you can ride on a contraption like his. One evening Staffan, from class nine, claimed he'd just tested his newly-souped-up moped to see how fast it would go, on the road to Kengis. He'd bent forward low over the handlebars and maintained the moped had clocked forty-two miles per hour. Just then Greger had come swishing past. Pedalling away vigorously and effortlessly, he'd soon disappeared over the crown of the hill ahead.

One of the lads from Vittulajänkkä with a penchant for making money arranged an unusual wager. Greger would race against the school bus from Pajala to Kaunisvaara. The bus wasn't exactly renowned for its scandalously high speeds, but even so. The lad fiddled the odds and took a shamelessly high percentage for himself, but nevertheless persuaded people to place bets and also got Greger to take up the challenge.

The race took place one Wednesday at the end of September. The bus stopped as usual at the back of Central School, and the pupils filed aboard. The driver, who knew nothing about the challenge, pulled away and noticed a creature dressed in red shoot past him on the outside.

The next time the man in red was seen was in Mukkakangas. He was standing at attention next to a Gällivare Police patrol car when the bus drove past. One of the officers was making notes in a book, and the other was beating off an aggressive Jämtland wolfhound with his baton.

By the time we came to Jupukka, Greger had caught us up again. The bus was going at a fair lick, but the man in red was in our slipstream and belting along. As the bus was going downhill shortly afterward, he surged past to the excited approval of the pupils. The driver blew his nose in astonishment and couldn't believe his eyes.

Five miles further on the man in red was crouched at the side of the road changing a tire on his back wheel. He occasionally had to hit out at a snarling fox with his bicycle pump.

But there was no sign of him after that. The pupils crowded around the back window, staring out through the dirt. But the road was deserted. Bogs and woods flashed past, Kaunisvaara was getting closer and closer. In the end the signpost appeared some way ahead, and everybody began to realize it was too late now.

Then a little dot came into view. A figure in red. A vehicle catching up on us, but not quickly enough. Just then a tractor appeared in front of the bus, chugging along. It was being driven by an aged pensioner wearing a peaked cap. Slap bang in the middle of the road. The bus slowed down and sounded its horn. The tractor pulled in very slightly. The bus started to overtake, with only a couple of inches to spare. The road was completely blocked by the two vehicles. The man in red was getting nearer and nearer.

The tractor chugged along.

"Greger will never make it!"

There was the sign: Kaunisvaara. And the road was blocked, it was impossible to overtake.

"There!" yelled Tommy from class seven.

Down in the ditch at the side of the road. Something red was lurching its way forward. Through all the gravel and undergrowth. Along the side of the bus. Then past, just as we came to the road sign.

Just for a moment everybody sat there as if paralyzed. Trying to take in what they'd just witnessed.

"The guy from Skåne did it!"

A fat Lapland hound knocked over an old biddie picking berries and raced after the man in red, barking like mad.

* * *

Greger had another remarkable talent. He could speak Tornedalen Finnish. As he was from Skåne, everybody had taken it for granted that he was an *ummikko*, in other words, ignorant of the mother tongue of glory and heroism; but confirmation of the fact came from several neutral observers. Old men and women swore blind they had conducted long and informative conversations in *meän kieli* with this outsider with the burr.

Greger was a cheerful soul, and, like southerners do, he had an abnormally developed need to make contact with people. After scorching along on his racing bike for a few dozen silent miles, he used to get off and chat with the locals. Startled men and women in Anttis, Kardis, Pissiniemi, Saittarova, Kivijärvi, or Kolari might suddenly be hailed for no reason at all. They'd look up and find in front of them a sweaty man from Mars, babbling away with spit spraying around like rain. They didn't recognize the words, but to be on the safe side they would reply in Finnish that they didn't want to buy anything.

Then it dawned on them that, strangely enough, they could understand what he was saying. It was unreal. This double Dutch full of sounds that only a drunk could possibly produce! And when they replied with *joo varmasti*, or said *niinkö*, this stranger understood exactly what they meant.

The mystery was solved by a retired customs officer who'd been stationed for some years in Helsingborg when he was a young man. As a result he was one of the few people in Tornedalen who understood both Tornedalen Finnish and the dialect of Skåne. He happened to be passing Conrad Mäki's country store in Juhonpieti one day when Greger was standing outside jabbering away with some pensioners. The customs officer stopped a couple of yards away and listened discreetly but carefully. Afterward he reported his conclusions in an objective and detailed way for anybody who was interested. By force of habit he also recorded his testimony; I've seen and read it: It was duly signed by himself in accordance with the regulations, and witnessed by two independent observers.

What was clear was that converser G (Greger, that is) spoke a Skanian dialect strikingly muddy in character throughout the conversation, with the exception of a small number of Tornedalen emphatic expressions (see appendix one), usually incorrectly pronounced. Conversers A, B, and C (two old men and an old lady) had equally obviously spoken Tornedalen Finnish the entire time. The strange thing was that the conversation had followed a totally logical course with both parties apparently understanding everything the other said. The topics of conversation were, in chronological order:

1. The latest spells of rain and cold weather.
2. The progress made by potatoes in late summer, the taste advantages enjoyed by almond potatoes in comparison with

round ones, and to what extent all the rain would cause potato rot.

3. The summer's hay harvest, the number and quality of the drying racks for hay, and to what extent the late spring has affected the nourishment content of the hay.

4. The number of animals on farms owned by local villagers, the foddering of milch cows nowadays and some years ago, the mechanization of farming and whether tractors were cheaper on the Swedish or Finnish side of the border.

5. A number of recently pulled-up deformed carrots that looked like penises, and to what extent that was a whim of nature or a warning sent by the Creator regarding dances arranged by young people.

6. Hopes regarding improvements in the weather, and good-bye phrases.

In the interests of science the customs officer had hailed Greger just before he pedaled off, and in a neutral tone asked him for the time in Finnish:

"*Mitäs kello on?*"

"And the same to you," Greger had replied in a friendly tone.

The customs officer drew the following conclusions:

Greger knew no Finnish (apart from the incorrectly pronounced swearwords, appendix one as mentioned above). Similarly, the pensioners couldn't understand a word of the Skåne dialect. The mysterious understanding between the parties could be ascribed to two causes: Greger's body-language, which was strikingly exaggerated and clear, and also his extraordinarily comprehensive knowledge of agriculture.

The customs officer's son was studying linguistics at the University of Umeå, and started a thesis entitled *Bilingual Understanding in a Northern Scandinavian Multicultural Environment*. But he turned to drink and never finished it.

Greger himself just laughed whenever the subject was broached. They're like that, people from Skåne. They laugh a lot.

* * *

On the very first day of term Greger took stock of the music cupboard, with its class set of birch drumsticks; two tamborines, of which one was split; two triangles; a wooden xylophone with F sharp and A out of action; a maraca leaking seeds; a guitar with three strings; and a broken felt-tipped mallet. There was also a class set of *Let's Sing, Book I*, and a few copies of *Patriotic Songs* by Olof Söderhjelm.

"Bloody hell, what a disaster!" muttered Greger.

And before we knew where we were he'd gripped the powers that be and squeezed money out of the school budget that nobody'd even suspected was there, and bought a set of drums, an electric bass, an electric guitar, and an amplifier. Plus a state-of-the-art record player. The next lesson, he demonstrated that he was an unexpectedly good guitar player. His enormous (and whole) left hand scuttled up and down the fretboard like a hairy South American bird spider, while his lonely right thumb strummed diminished and augmented chords, not to mention flageolet imitations, as easy as pie. Then he went over to blues, and pretended to sing like a black man—which was easy for him as he came from Skåne. He played us a sorrowful guitar solo using his thumb nail as a pick. The class gaped in astonishment.

When the bell rang, Niila and I stayed behind.

"I'll never be able to play like that," said Niila gloomily.

Greger put the guitar down.

"Hold your hands up!" he said.

Niila did as he was told. Greger did the same, and looked hard at his fingers.

"Count 'em," he said.

And Niila did so. Six fingers.

"And how many have you got?"

"Ten."

Well, no need to say any more.

Now that Greger had realized we were interested, we were given permission to have jam sessions during the breaks. Niila stroked the electric guitar, wide-eyed, and was amazed how easy it was to press down the strings. I went for the bass. It felt surprisingly heavy, hanging from its shoulder strap like a Mauser. Then I switched on the two amplifiers. Niila was a bit worried in case he got an electric shock in his fingers. I told him there was no need to flap as the strings were insulated.

Then we started playing. It felt nerve-wracking but wonderful, and it sounded awful. But from then on our playing was somehow more real. We'd started off with a home-made piece of hardboard, via a discordant acoustic guitar in the cellar, and here we were now with the real McCoy. Shiny lacquer, chrome pegs, and buttons, a loudspeaker membrane humming softly. This was serious stuff. This was big time.

Our first problem was to keep time. Individually, to start with, which was bad enough. Then together, which was much worse. The next problem was changing chords. At the same time. Still keeping in step. And then changing back again.

Those of you who play yourselves will understand what it was like. It was some time before we produced anything that could be called music.

Greger listened to us sometimes and gave us some friendly advice. His biggest asset was his enormous patience. Like that lunchtime when he taught us how to start off at the same time. He counted us in over and over again, but I would always start on three and Niila on four. For a while it was the other way round. In the end, when we were both starting on four, Greger told us we ought to start on one. The second one. The one that's never spoken out loud.

"One, two, three, fourrr—(now!)."

Niila said he'd never been what you might call a math genius. Greger then held up his deformed hand and asked Niila to count his stumps.

"Fourrr fingers are missing, and that's when you are quiet," Greger explained helpfully. "And then the music starts with the thumb!"

Strangely enough, it worked. For the first time we started correctly.

Even today when I count in a tune, I can still see Greger's finger stumps in my mind's eye.

We had jam sessions the whole autumn. Made the most of every free minute. Breaks, free periods, and after school. And at last, one lunch break, we managed to complete a blues number reasonably well.

Greger was listening, and nodded in approval.

"Keep it up," he urged.

Then he opened the hall door. In came a shy-looking lad with a cherubic face and a long fringe hanging over his forehead. He didn't look at us. Just opened up the oblong case he had with him. The inside was lined with red plush. With his long fingers he took out a red and white electric guitar, plugged it into one of the amplifiers and turned up the volume. Then he played a solo over our backing that almost tore our hearts from our chests, a screaming solo full of harrowing sorrow. The window panes rattled in sympathy. The sound was quite different from anything we were used to, fractured, heart-rending, wailing. Like a heartbroken woman. He adjusted a little box on the guitar and the lament became even worse. Then he played another solo. A crunching, bellowing guitar solo, manly in a beastly way, inconceivable coming from this delicate thirteen-year-old. His fingers flew from string to string, the pick plucked out violent cascades of notes, your ear couldn't keep up with it, only your heart, your body, your skin. In the end he did something I'd never seen before. He released his grip on the guitar and held it against the loudspeaker: soon it started to play all by itself, tragic whistles, wolf howls, and flutes simultaneously.

Then he smiled. Gently, almost girlishly. He stroked back his bangs and switched off. His face looked very Finnish, with ice-blue eyes.

"Jimi Hendrix," he said abruptly.

We opened up the curtains. A dozen or so pupils had their noses pressed against the window, tightly packed, shoulder to shoulder. The sound had been audible all over the school.

Greger gave us a faraway look.
"Now you'rrre getting somewhere, lads! This is Holgerrri."
I turned to Niila and muttered a gruesome premonition:
"By God, but he's going to get beaten up."
"What?" said Greger.
"Oh, nothing."

* * *

It was in the senior school that the bullying started to get serious. Pajala Central School was an awful place to be at that time, if you stood out from the crowd in the wrong way. You wouldn't have expected it if you were from somewhere else in Sweden—a country school in a quiet village, only a couple of hundred pupils. The atmosphere in the corridors was calm, almost shy, you might think.

The fact was that some of the pupils were dangerous. They had started causing trouble before, but it was only now that things really came to a head. Perhaps it had to do with puberty. Too much horniness, too much angst.

Some of them found it amusing to inflict bruises on their fellow-pupils in dark corners of the corridors, ramming bony knees into thighs or buttocks. Tender parts. When you turned around, in agony from the pain, they would be grinning at you. Sometimes they had sewing needles hidden in their hands, and would stick them through your clothes and into your skin as you passed. It was also common to punch the muscles in other pupils' upper arms, which hurt for hours afterward.

The bullies could sniff out the vulnerable. They knew right away when somebody was different, and they would pick on loners, artistic boys or girls, anybody who was too intelligent. One of their victims was a quiet little lad called Hans, who liked going around with girls. His persecutors succeeded in controlling the whole of his life, making him so scared that he no longer dared to walk alone in the corridors. He always tried to be with friends, hiding himself in the herd like a weak antelope. It wasn't until several years later that he was able to move to Stockholm and come out as a homosexual.

Another of the victims was Mikael. He was also shy and introverted, incapable of hitting back. He was different, that was obvious; he thought deep down that he was something special. On one occasion the gang surrounded him in the metalwork shop while the teacher was out of the room. With the class's sadist, Uffe, in the lead, they tried out various strangleholds on Mikael. Uffe slowly squeezed harder and harder with his snuff-stained fingers round Mikael's slender throat until he started croaking like a frog. His classmates stood by watching, but nobody protested. Instead they watched it all with something approaching curiosity. Is that how you strangle somebody? Just look how swollen his eyes are! Before long several of the other lads were so intrigued, they wanted a go as well. They didn't even need to hold their victim down, he just sat there, paralyzed with fear. Oh look, he's going to be sick, better let go now. Anybody else want a try? Come on, have a go! Just look at the idiot, he's scared to death! Squeeze there, a bit further down, it's more effective there. Cough, cough, uuuhhhuuurhhh… You have a try, he'll never dare to tell anybody! There's his throat, bloody hell, it's amazing how thin it is!

The teachers had a good idea of what was going on in the corridors, but they didn't dare to intervene. Several of them were badly treated themselves. One woman teacher from the south of Sweden was taunted systematically, and time and time again she'd go running out of the classroom in tears. The pupils just sneered at her no matter what she said, refused to fill in her stencils, hid her books, made sexual allusions because she was unmarried, put pornographic pictures in her bag, and things like that. More and more pupils joined in when they saw the opportunity. Perfectly normal boys and girls. Classmates. So frenzied they were trembling inside. There were times when the air in the classroom was unbreathable.

* * *

The moment I heard Holgeri's solo, I knew he was vulnerable. He was precisely the sort the bullies picked on, delicate little boys who drew too much attention to themselves. I'd seen him before in the corridors, but had never taken any notice of him. He was evasive but not unfriendly. One of those quiet lads from the outlying villages who prefer to keep to themselves, who stand around in corners in little groups, mumbling to each other in Finnish. They never felt at home in Pajala itself. Holgeri told me how difficult it was for the first few weeks every autumn term. He'd been speaking Finnish for the whole of the long summer holidays, and all of a sudden his brain needed to readjust to Swedish. It took several weeks, he couldn't think of the right word and made linguistic mistakes, and so it was safest to keep quiet.

Holgeri came from Kihlanki, and we used to chat while he was waiting for the school bus. We usually talked about music. I wondered how he'd learned to play the guitar, and he said it was his dad who'd taught him. His dad had been dead for several years, and Holgeri never wanted to say exactly what had happened. What he remembered best from his childhood was sitting on his dad's knee while he played traditional Liikavaara tunes, singing quietly in the euphoric stage of intoxication; how he would wipe the spit from his moustache, which he used to trim with nail scissors, and then slip his son a throat pastille. When his father died, his guitar was left hanging from its hook. Holgeri had taken it down, started fingering the strings, and imagined he could hear his father's voice, coming from somewhere in the depths of the forests where he now was.

His mother retired early on account of her nervous state, and her son was all she had left. And when Holgeri asked for an electric guitar with amplifiers, that's what he got, even though she could scarcely afford to buy shoes and clothes.

Just like me, he'd sat by the radio. He made up the fingering himself and played solos to the background accompaniment, and in his fantasy world he had been the big star, the genius, the one who dumbfounded his audience single-handedly. This caused quite a few problems for the band. Niila was working hard on rhythm guitar, but he still found it difficult to change chords. Holgeri was much more skillful from a purely technical point of view, but there again, he seemed to be deaf to what the rest of us were doing. His contributions came too soon or too late, and seldom fit in with the tunes we were playing. I tried to tell him this in a friendly way, but he either didn't listen or just smiled distantly. Holgeri was one of those people who find it hard to be simple. He sort of made lace frills for the music. If you wanted a note he would come out with a chord, if you went along with the chord he would come up with a riff, if you liked the riff it would be transformed into a solo or into variations in another key. It was impossible to pin him down. Niila hated Holgeri at first, largely because he was jealous of course, but at the same time he recognized that we couldn't do without him.

In the evenings Holgeri would sometimes sit on the sofabed back home in Kihlanki and get out his father's old guitar. His teenager's fingers caressed the strings to produce chords like large butterflies. They fluttered off over wooden chairs and rag carpets, rose up over the stove where the potatoes were cooking, swerved past the wall calendar, the clock, the woven Norwegian wall hanging, dived down over the potty and the broom, brushed past the school satchel and the Wellington boots, up again toward Mum in the rocking chair, circled around her clicking knitting needles and the Lapp mittens and the ball of wool, then off toward the potted plants, the begonias and sanchezias, up inside the window panes, a brief glimpse of grassy meadows, birches, and nipple-warm evening sunshine, past the treadle sewing machine, the teak-veneered radio, the wardrobe with the door that wouldn't close, then back into the guitar, into the murky sound hole where other butterflies were clamoring to get out.

His mum never used to say anything, never praised him but never disturbed him either. Just sat there in body, providing body warmth.

CHAPTER 14

*On a mind-blowing contest in the Pajala sewage treatment works,
and how we unexpectedly acquired another band member*

Despite the admonitions of Laestadius, despite the warnings issued by medical science and despite many frightening examples among family and friends, several of my schoolmates started drinking themselves silly on the weekends. Tornedalen is part of the vodka belt stretching all the way across Finland and deep into Russia, and in the senior school one of the most popular spare-time activities was getting drunk. There were many tyro alcoholics who had seen the light and at every break preached the gospel according to 40-percent proof; where one had trodden, others were keen to follow in his footsteps.

It was around this time that the lads from Kaunisvaara started spreading the rumor that they could hold more drink than anybody else throughout the whole of Norrbotten. The proof was indisputable. Over the past year they had traveled to Gällivare and Kiruna and drunk under the table legions of miners' sons from alcohol-soaked laborers' families, and if the likes of them were unable to compete, who else could?

The Kaunis boys were getting too big for their boots, in fact. When others expressed doubt, they offered to challenge all comers. After a little consultation, two brothers from Paskajänkkä intervened. As they considered themselves to have not only a degree of insight into the subject but also a talent for organizing things, they announced their intention of arranging a Regional Boozing Championship.

News spread rapidly through the local boys' gangs. The rules were simple: it was to be a young people's contest and you had to be in class nine or lower. The message was passed on via school buses, cousins, poker schools, and, not least, sports clubs. As every district was allowed to nominate only one representative, ruthlessly tough preliminary rounds took place throughout the region. Eventually, one Friday evening at the beginning of October, it was time for the championship finals.

The contest was to be held in the old Pajala sewage treatment works. In those days it was situated on the steep river bank not far from the church, and was a red-brick building enveloped in a faint but unmistakable smell of shit. For that very reason it had become the main location for the making of mash. The lads had discovered a way into the top floor through a hatch in the roof and found a quiet corner where the tubs could bubble away undisturbed, with the yeasty smells being masked by the sewage odors.

As I knew the Paskajänkkä brothers I was allowed to help with the preparations, and in return Niila and I would be able to watch the contest. We fetched and carried some big buckets and filled them with water, while the actual potion was mixed by those who knew more about the recipe than we did. It involved baking yeast and sugar, and some of the containers also had potatoes and raisins added. It all had to mature for a few weeks, to acquire the right strength and aroma. The Paskajänkkä boys wanted nothing to do with distilling. It was true that three of them had produced HiLaGu schnapps, the name being composed from the first names of the lads involved. It had its own homemade label and looked authentic, but the level of fusel oil was such that drinking it made the hairs on the back of your neck stand on end. The elder brother, who was more technically inclined, had also had a go, using equipment he'd welded together in the workshop at the local College of Technology when nobody was looking. He'd stood it on a hotplate in the garage, but the connections had not been tight enough, leaking ethanol fumes had caught fire, and the whole caboodle had blown up. At the community hospital he explained away the extensive burns by claiming that a pot of boiling potatoes had been knocked off the stove, and that the smell of yeast in his clothes came from his mother's yeast liquid for baking bread that he'd poured over himself in an attempt to cool the burns down. In memory of that he'd been known as Breadloaf ever since, and had a blotchy red and hairless lower arm.

After this incident the brothers had agreed that distilling was for fools, a fiddly and unnecessary procedure that both spoiled the taste and resulted in the loss of valuable amounts of vitamin B. A real man should be able to drink mash, and it was on that basis that contestants were invited to take part.

We waited until evening, when the sewage workers had gone home in blissful ignorance of what was going on. It was dark by the time a dozen or so boys climbed in through the roof hatch and gathered in the storeroom upstairs, a dirty and untidy room smelling of sewage. All the competitors sat down on the floor in a circle. They started assessing the opposition while waiting for proceedings to start.

The boy from Korpilombolo had a freckled forehead and a melancholy air, with an unruly black fringe. The Junosuando boy grinned non-stop, his lower lip projecting alarmingly—a characteristic of people from that area. The young hopeful from Tärendö had a cleft chin and a dripping potato-nose. The Muodoslompolo youth had a curly brown sheep-hairstyle and was so nervous he couldn't stop spitting. Pajala's representative was Breadloaf, with his low forehead and ice-blue, slightly squinting eyes. There were also a few boys from the outlying villages. The aspirant from Lainio was pale and looked pious, with large, shy, doe-like eyes. The Torinen boy had enormous lumberjack-hands stuck on the end of his puny teenage forearms, and a nose with so many blackheads it appeared to be covered in gnats. The contestant from Kaunisvaara, the alleged favorite, was one of the village's agile long-distance cross-country skiers, a thin-lipped, stooping giant of a youth who had already, at the age of fourteen, managed to finish eleventh in the Malmloppet ski race and had lungs with the capacity of fully inflated tractor tires. And there were also a few supporters present to see fair play.

Breadloaf's younger brother, whose name was Erkki and was in class eight, opened the first tub with a ceremonial flourish. He was short but sturdy, known for his foolhardy fighting technique. The sight of the bubbling mash inspired him to request permission to join in the contest as a late entry. Everybody objected as Pajala had already filled its quota. Erkki then began to go into detail about his roots as a forest Sami and listed rank upon rank of ancestors while urging Breadloaf in an increasingly provocative tone to confirm the validity of his origins. In the end a compromise was agreed. Erkki would be allowed to take part as a representative of Sattajärvi's Forest Samis, and his duties as competition steward would be taken over by Niila and me.

We started sharing out the mash without delay: I poured and Niila handed out the mugs. All the contestants emptied them quickly, in solid silence. The next round followed immediately. Eager slurping and gulping. Mug number three. When that was emptied a pause was declared for belching and recharging of snuff. They all glanced furtively at everybody else and muttered something about never having tasted insipid maiden's water like this before, and that where they came from it was the kind of thing you put into babies' bottles. Supporters and observers begged for a drop to taste, and their wish was granted. I knocked back a mouthful and almost choked on a raw potato. It tasted of baking mix and was hellishly strong.

I was reminded of the job I was supposed to be doing, for Christ's sake, so I opened the next container. In the interests of justice I did my best to ensure that all the mugs contained the same amount, and Niila checked

that everybody drank the whole lot. The mood was getting more excited, of course. Then all of a sudden, everybody started babbling away in
Tornedalen Finnish. Happiest was probably Erkki, who had only been
allowed to take part as a favor after all, and he started shaking hands with
all present and thanking them until Breadloaf told him to shut his trap
and stop disturbing the concentration of the other contestants.

As always, the intoxication brought about the most astonishing per-
sonality changes. The Korpilombolo boy's face had lit up like a sun and
he started telling obscene jokes about substitute teachers. Junosuando
was frowning grimly and started going on about the large number of
Nazis in the 1930s in certain villages not a thousand miles away from
here, until the penny dropped for the lad from Tärendö, who became
aggressive and started to recall the statistics with regard to village idiots
in Junosuando. Lainio suddenly lost all his shyness and piety and proposed a game of poker at one krona a shot. Kaunisvaara wondered caus-
tically when Lainio Laestadians had acquired an interest in that kind of
thing. A conspiratorial expression came over Muodoslompolo's face as
he hinted at being descended from eighteenth-century French royals
traveling clandestinely. Torinen maintained that as far as he was aware
the Muodoslompolo area was better known for the feuding and blood-
shed among local families, and for turning inbreeding into an art form.
Breadloaf once again suggested that everybody shut their traps, whereupon they all commented sarcastically about the *Pajalan piksipojat* and
such newfangled nonsense as merging local authorities into bigger units
so that people living in the biggest place, like the aforementioned Pajala
peacock, suffered delusions of grandeur.

After two more mugs the atmosphere turned even more cantankerous. At the same time the arguments became less lively and less precisely articulated. The only one in a good mood was Korpilombolo,
who suddenly rose to his feet. He apologized profusely, but he would
have to break off now as he was feeling extremely horny and did we
know any depraved Pajala women? Erkki described in great detail how

to get to the home of a recently retired math teacher and with a sly wink wished him the best of luck. The rest had decided now was the time to start a fight, but first they all needed a pee and a couple of minutes to get worked up. After the pee, however, everyone was so plagued by a lack of fluid that Niila and I were required to put that right immediately.

Eyelids were now at half mast. Tongues were growing bigger. The air was growing even smellier thanks to all the farting brought on by the mash. Junosuando and Tärendö exchanged a few slurred punches, then fell into each other's arms and collapsed in a heap. Muodoslompolo laughed so much at the sight that he had to grab the nearest empty mash bucket to throw up in. He demanded in a loud voice to be allowed to get on with the contest even so, then passed out, sitting down with his head dangling. Kaunisvaara snorted in disgust at all this beginners' incompetence.

A few new rounds followed. Lainio seemed surprised that he'd kept up with the rest for so long as the whole of his family were very religious, and he'd only started drinking so recently that he hadn't really got used to it yet. Torinen was calmly confident on grounds of heredity and started counting all the alcoholics in his family. He got to a dozen then fell sideways and remained slumped on the floor.

Niila produced yet another bucket. Breadloaf and Kaunisvaara glared at each other like punch-drunk boxers and emptied their mugs in unison. Laino was hanging on in there, as was Erkki, who didn't feel under pressure and was still drinking the stuff because he liked it. Breadloaf was now having trouble speaking whole sentences and came out instead with a string of vowels. Kaunisvaara was having problems with his eyes and kept missing his mug unless he covered one eye. But he exploited his verbal superiority and started singing the Pajala strike anthem, with scarcely a slurred consonant. That provoked Lainio into suggesting that every Communist should go back home to the inviting Siberian winter, and he went so far as to suggest that Lenin and Stalin had been sexual partners, and that Marx would doubtless have joined in as well were it not for the fact that he was already dead and buried. Then he stressed once again, with a degree of astonishment, how good it felt to be a sinner, and that if only he'd known, he'd have started long ago. Then, satisfied with his input, he leaned back against the wall and fell asleep without saying his prayers.

It was clear to the supporters that the end was now nigh, and they started chanting their encouragement. Three of them were from Kaunisvaara, descendants of strikers and Stalinists. They never said a word when sober, but were now keen to declare that Communist drinking habits helped to stir up revolution and sharpen arguments, and that the most amusing drunks in the whole world were the ones at Red Youth parties. One of the Pajala supporters was from Naurisaho and another from Paskajänkkä, and when they both announced that they were Social Democrats, the temperature rose noticeably. While Breadloaf and Kaunisvaara emptied yet another mug, the Kaunisvaara boys announced their intention of beating the living daylights out of all comers, first in beautiful Tornedalen Finnish similes, then spelled out in words of one syllable, and finally to the accompaniment of threatening gestures and aggressive stares. Social Fascists would be pissing blood after a few revolutionary hammer-blows. The Pajala lads wondered sarcastically what these revolutionaries had ever contributed to local history, apart from wrecking a bus not far from Kengis and waving a few revolvers about in remote cottages out in the forests. The Kaunisvaara boys went on about how only idiots who had spent too much time licking upper-class assholes could say things like that, and that working class action was just as much justified now as it had been then. At the last moment Erkki placed himself between the warring factions and explained somewhat haltingly but craftily that he'd always felt drawn toward Communism, but that he'd also been impressed by the Young Socialists, especially as they served up buns and juice at their meetings, and hence he hadn't yet made up his mind where he stood politically. Both sides immediately homed in on him with missionary zeal, while I assiduously refilled all their mugs.

Breadloaf was forced to lean against the wall in order not to fall down. Kaunisvaara was seeing double in the one eye he was still using, and was also compelled to hold his eyelids up with his forefingers. Both had fallen silent. The pain barrier had been passed, and the poison offered nothing more than death and paralysis. Kaunisvaara's arm collapsed, and his eyelid closed. Silence. But just when everybody had concluded it was all over, he announced that since his arm no longer did what he told it, somebody would have to help him. One of his mates raised the lad's mug to his lips, and emptied it into the void. Breadloaf wasn't answering questions as his powers of hearing had now failed him, but he still understood sign language. He could still raise his mug, but was unable to swallow and hence was forced to pour the stuff out slowly and let it find its own way down his throat. I proposed that the match should be declared a draw. The Kaunisvaara supporters were quick to declare vociferously that such cowardice was unthinkable, and besides, no Pajala upstart was going to rob them of the championship that was so obviously theirs.

I filled the mugs yet again. They were duly emptied as before. I was really worried now, and insisted that as they were both unconscious, the championship should be shared. The Kaunis supporters reacted by lifting the eyelids of their hero and demonstrating that his pupils were not fixed, but were in fact eager to continue with the contest. Somebody yelled into Breadloaf's ear and asked if he wanted to keep going, in which case he should open his mouth. This he did, and another mug was poured in.

But now the last signs of life had faded away. Heavy-handed attempts were made from both sides to revive them. Breadloaf slumped at what looked like an uncomfortable angle, and the lad from Kaunisvaara started drooling with his tongue hanging out. As a result of my urging they were both laid down on their sides with their tongues hanging out, whereupon it was discovered that they had both wet themselves.

Erkki inshishted on having another mug. Like his brother, he found it hardest to speak when he was drunk—but even so, I gathered what he wanted and served him up another round. He emptied his mug, and then announced in Finnish, with more than a few intrusive consonants, that the champion boozer of Pajala and district was the representative of the Sattarjärvi Forest Sami.

Supporters of both Kaunisvaara and Pajala stared at me. I stared in turn at Niila. He nodded and said that it was right. Erkki had drunk one more mug than all the others. Erkki grinned and stammered in a hoarse voice something about this having been the most he'd ever drunk in his life. And whether or not he was a Social Democrat or a Communist, that was worth thinking about, but what he most needed now was a pee.

* * *

Niila and I helped Erkki out through the hatch in the roof. The Kaunisvaara supporters were thunderstruck and stayed put, started drinking to drown their sorrow and talked about the latest case of suicide that autumn. The Pajala boys realized that Breadloaf had thrown up and cleaned out his mouth to make sure he didn't choke. A sweet and sour smell indicated that mash diarrhea had already arrived. The fallen Kaunisvaara hero looked worryingly pale, but it was assumed his strong skier's heart would see him through. The others were snoring like pigs, their eyes either open or closed, blissfully unaware of the morrow.

Outside the sewage treatment works Erkki proceeded to paint the autumn night with steaming brush strokes. I congratulated him heartily, and then had a sudden idea. I explained solemnly that as he was now the youth champion, Erkki would receive the surprise award, namely a position as drummer in the most promising local rock band.

Niila opened his mouth but said nothing after I'd given him a nudge. Erkki said he'd barely even seen a photo of a drum. I assured him that if he could hold his willy and paint pictures in pee as he was doing now, he should be able to handle a drumstick. Erkki laughed so much the brush strokes broke in several places, and it was agreed.

* * *

And so the following Monday during lunch, the rock band was formed. It was a memorable day for several reasons. Although it was two days since the contest took place, Erkki was still hung over. But that was nothing compared to the state of his brother, Breadloaf, who signed the pledge over and over again in between fits of nausea, and actually stuck to it for a few weeks. The Kaunisvaara lad fought his attacks of sickness by means of a ruthlessly hard training program: running through the biggest swamps he could find, wearing his father's Wellington boots with stones packed into the legs to make them heavier; chopping up several truckloads of firewood, alternately using his left and right arms; and bicycling to school in Pajala with no saddle so that he couldn't cheat by resting, and breathing only every other time to strengthen his lungs.

At first Erkki wanted to back out when he discovered that playing the drums involved using two drumsticks. That was twice as many as he'd expected. In the end, however, he reluctantly sat down behind the school's drum set, grasped hold of the sticks as if they were hatchets, and started to chop down the set. It fell over as if struck by a tornado— the stand, the cymbals, the lot. Erkki remained seated. Stared into space for a while. Then claimed his hangover was getting better already. Duly impressed, he picked everything up and set it all to rights, then tried again with similarly disastrous results. And now his headache had gone more or less completely. Very remarkable. If he played for a few more minutes, no doubt the shaking and sweating would stop as well.

I tried to get a beat going with the bass to Erkki's non-existent rhythm, Niila and Holgeri filled in the holes with their guitars. We didn't mention the word "key," we hadn't reached that level yet. Erkki seemed to be totally unaware of the rest of us, was going cross-eyed, sticking his tongue out, and twisting his mouth into strange shapes. Already he had mastered the imbecilic look that lots of drummers assume when they're playing, even though they look normal in other circumstances.

All of a sudden, in the middle of Holgeri's guitar solo, Erkki stopped and loosened his belt. We lost the thread and stopped playing as well. Erkki said this rock music lark was the most enjoyable thing he'd ever tried, including getting drunk and masturbating. He was unable to compare it with sexual intercourse because he hadn't yet had that experience, but no doubt it would be irrelevant because he'd always suspected that sex is overrated anyway.

I asked him to try again, but this time attempt to hit the drum with regular intervals between each contact. Erkki was doubtful, but set off again. The result was even worse, a hellish row. Splinters of wood flew off the drumsticks, the skin was pockmarked, the screws in the stand worked loose and the whole thing collapsed again. I looked at Niila. He shook his head. We had never been anywhere near such an unrhythmical and infernal commotion as this. Holgeri had already unplugged his guitar and was packing up. Niila did the same. I wondered how we could get rid of Erkki without making him angry. Perhaps tell him the award had only been for one day. That would be best. He was mistaken if he'd thought anything else.

But Erkki beat us all to it. He stood up before I could get around to saying anything, and marched out of the door with a cheery "So long."

The next second I heard jeering coming from outside. Quiet but triumphant. I looked out of the door and saw that Erkki was being held down by Uffe and his mate Jouko. Several of their underlings were standing by, watching. Suddenly a couple of them jumped on Holgeri and forced him down to his knees in a neck-lock.

"Now, you bloody pansies!" they snarled.

I was terrified. My stomach turned inside out, my blood vessels contracted in preparation for the attack. Uncertainty was always the worst.

Never knowing how far they would go this time. How many bruises? How much pain? How long before Greger turned up?

There were screams from outside. Shrill and piercing. What the hell were they doing to Erkki? Surely they weren't using knives?

I felt as if I were going to die. Then I noticed them crawling on the ground. Jouko was blinking over and over again with blood pouring from his skinned, split eyebrows. Uffe was drooling and collecting the remains of his front teeth.

The underlings backed away, white with terror. Erkki limped back into the hall with blood trickling down his chin from his lower lip.

"They won't bother us again," he said calmly.

CHAPTER 15

In which tongues are loosened after the Saturday sauna,
and what every young man ought to know

In our family we used to have a sauna every Saturday evening, a tradition that no doubt went back to prehistoric times. As time went by my sister wanted to be alone in the sauna—that was when she'd started to grow titties; when she'd finished, Mum and Dad and I would go in. We'd sweat all the dirt out of us, then wash ourselves with soap and scratch away old bits of skin and scrub one another's backs until we were as red as skinned rabbits. The only thing you needed to think about when you were in the sauna was not to fart. That was also something that had been handed down from generation to generation, and it was best not to if you wanted to avoid being thrown out.

Last of all we'd create a final head of steam so that the remaining bits of soap dissolved, and when we finally rinsed everything away with cold water, we were cleaner than it was really possible to be.

On this particular night, though, everything was different. I realized afterward that Dad had planned it all; there was something in the air. Nervousness. We sat down in the changing room, where the washing machine was standing in one corner. Mum was in a hurry to get away:

it was obvious she wanted to leave us on our own. There was a fire burning and crackling away in the stove, making it cozy. A fir log occasionally spit lumps of charcoal out onto the floor, and Dad put them out with his bare feet. We each grilled a sausage or two and really enjoyed them—we were hungry after all that sweating that had drained us of salt. Dad finished off his post-sauna beer, then went over to grog: Koskenkorva schnapps and lemonade. He hadn't said a word from start to finish.

I would normally have gone and left Dad in peace. I knew he liked to be on his own, and enjoyed sitting for hours, looking at the flames and filling his Ugrian brain with melancholy thoughts. On this occasion, though, I had a feeling that something was up. There was that intuitive contact that often develops between father and son when you're not chattering away all the time. You turn into a couple of bucks, smelling the scent of each other's sweat, listening to each other breathing. You tense your muscles, then you relax and listen to the soft messages relayed through skin and blood by your digestive systems. You become organic. Strip yourselves naked. Iron out the wrinkled everyday phrases from your brows.

Dad cleared his throat, but then said nothing for several minutes. Cleared his throat once more, to soften up his tongue. Drank. I put another lump of wood on the fire. Watched the condensation trickling down the cold glass.

"Anyway, now that you're not a little lad any more..." he eventually started, speaking in Finnish.

I didn't reply. Thought how I hadn't yet grown a beard, but on the other hand had started to get a bit cheeky and my feet were getting bigger every day, some of the first signs of puberty.

"I expect you've sometimes wondered... asked yourself all sorts of questions..."

I glanced at him in astonishment, and could see his jaw muscles throbbing.

"Asked yourself... about life... about people.... Now that you've grown a bit older you ought to know..."

He paused, took another swig, and avoided looking at me. He's going to go on about the birds and the bees, I thought. Condoms.

"What I'm going to say is just between you and me. Confidential. Man to man."

Now he looked at me for the first time, bleary-eyed. I nodded. He stared back at the fire.

"My father, your grandad that is, was a real stallion when he was a young man. That's why I have two half sisters," he said abruptly. "They're my age, and have children of their own. That means that around here, in the Pajala area, you have five first cousins you didn't know about: three of them are girls, and you ought to know who they are so as to avoid in-breeding."

He spelled out who they were. One of them was in my year at school, and was pretty.

"Anyway, another thing. There are two families in this district that have caused us a lot of harm, and you're going to have to hate them for ever and a day. In one case it all goes back to a perjury suit in 1929, and in the other it's got to do with some grazing rights that a neighbor cheated your grandad's father out of in 1902, and both these injustices have to be avenged at all costs, whenever you get the chance; and you must keep going until them bastards have confessed and paid, and also gone down on their bare knees to beg for forgiveness."

Dad summarized what had happened over the years. There were summonses and countersummonses, false witness, bribery and corruption, fisticuffs, threatening letters, damage to property, attempted blackmail, and on one occasion the kidnapping of a promising elkhound that had its ears branded with a knife, like a reindeer. There was no limit to the outrages these madmen had perpetrated on us, and although we'd exacted as much revenge as we could, we were still a long way in debit. The worst thing was that these families were spreading false propaganda about us, and were greatly exaggerating the modest little counterattacks we'd managed to pull off. The upshot was that I'd better be on my guard when I went to dance halls and other public gatherings where vengeance could suddenly leap out of the bushes or from dark corners, with the most terrible consequences.

He named the families, and spelled out all their offshoots and all those who'd married and sometimes changed their last names as a result, but whose blood was nevertheless the same poisonous sort as before. Once again I was given the name of a fellow pupil, a skinny little chap from one of the outlying small villages who didn't seem to have paid me any attention at all so far. Dad said that was just a front: they appeared to be quite harmless and instilled a false sense of security, and then your back was exposed. More than one of our relatives had been made to regret bitterly his gullibility by being stabbed or having bones broken, Dad could assure me of that all right.

I committed all this to memory, then Dad tested me on it as it was important that nothing be forgotten or forgiven through sheer carelessness. He took another swig or two and did a bit of ranting, then got me to grunt and snort and help him to work out a few crafty plots. He suggested I might like to make a career for myself in local government, because that put you in a position where you could create merry hell and, even better, they couldn't sack you; if you played your cards right you could exploit a bit of nepotism and get the rest of the clan into positions of authority until it was impossible for these perjurers and land thieves to stay around.

Dad polished off the lemonade and resorted to swigging schnapps straight from the bottle. Then he went over to passing on information of a more general kind. As I would soon be a fully grown working man, I ought to know who had been strike-breakers during the road-building strike of 1931 and the log-floating strike at Alanen Kihlankijoki in 1933; also all those who had supported the Nazis, mainly in Tärendö and Anttis, although there were some in Pajala as well; not to mention informers during the Second World War, among whom were several who still called themselves Social Democrats but who had sent Communist workmates to the concentration camp at Storsien to be shot the moment Hitler set foot in Sweden. I was also informed which of them had apologized afterward, and which of them had not, and instructed that relatives of the latter should be reminded of the fact whenever an opportunity arose.

There was another mass of families to keep an eye on, and once again some of my schoolmates were involved. Dad reckoned we ought to review all the names, which we duly did with great thoroughness. Then he continued with a more general history of the labor movement, including explanations of why socialists with long memories still avoid reading newspapers such as the *Haparanda Daily News* and the *Norrbotten Courier*, why one should shop at the Co-op and not at Spar, and why customs officers, foresters, primary school teachers, and religious revivalists of the Laestadian persuasion should be regarded with suspicion even today.

This led him to an account of weird goings-on, and he rehearsed the history of the Laestadian sect involving disciples of the Finnish preacher Korpela. Having recited the names of all the families concerned, he leaned forward and guffawed over the way in which they were awaiting the arrival of a crystal ark, how they painted each other's pussies and assholes, how they would curse worse than a gang of lumberjacks, and said "eat" instead of "screw," and played silly games wearing reindeer antlers, and rode each other like horses, and drank so much distiller's mash they used to shit themselves when they were driven off in police cars, and basically had as much fun as it was possible to have given the limited opportunities of life in a remote backwater.

I just gaped in astonishment and suggested he must be putting me on—this was the first time I'd ever heard about such things. Dad said he was only giving me a cleaned-up version of what they got up to, and he'd tell me the rest when I'd reached a sexually more mature age.

The whole of Tornedalen seemed to be transformed before my very eyes. The place where I'd grown up was apparently criss-crossed by a mass of threads enmeshing all who lived there. A vast and powerful spider's web of hatred, lust, fear, memories. A four-dimensional web whose sticky strands extended both backward and forward through time, down to the dead bodies buried under the earth and up to the as-yet-unborn in the heavens, and it was going to envelop me with its field of force whether I liked it or not. It was powerful, it was beautiful, and it scared me to no end. I had been a child, and Dad had now taught me how to see. Roots, culture, whatever you'd like to call it—it was mine.

Dad finally got around to accounting for the inherent weaknesses in our own family. There were drinkers among us. That's why he wasn't going to offer me anything just now: I ought to wait until I came of age before getting involved with the poison known as alcohol, since the art of intoxication was a complicated one and needed a degree of maturity. When that time came, if I started to acquire a taste for the stuff I'd better be very careful. The nature of alcohol was such that it spread warmth and good cheer throughout one's body even though ordinary folk found its taste bitter and unpleasant. Nevertheless, Dad had heard many alcoholics actually claiming to like the taste of it, which is no doubt why it brought about their downfall.

Moreover, some members of our family used to get violent when they were drunk. That was something impossible to predict until you'd actually tried it, but it was important to be aware of it, as an inability to hold your liquor would lead inevitably to fines and knife wounds that never healed properly, not to mention spells in the clink in Haparanda. And so, to be on the safe side, the first time I got drunk ought to be when I was all alone and locked up in the safety of my own room. If I felt an irresistible urge to start fighting, I should always shun strong drink while in the company of others. The only option was getting used, at an early age, to going to dances in a sober state, which was extremely difficult to achieve, but not impossible.

Then he started going through a list of all the family idiots. I'd already met some of them: one was in the psychiatric hospital in Gällivare, and another in Piteå. In medical jargon it was called schizophrenia, and it seemed to run in the family. It would appear when you reached the age of eighteen or so, and was due to certain causes. Frustrated love was one, and Dad begged me to be very wary of getting involved with complicated women who were scared of sex. Dad urged me never to be too persistent with the fair sex if they declined to open their legs, but rather to follow his own example and find myself an unabashed peasant girl with a big ass.

The other cause of lunacy was brooding. Dad strongly advised me never to start thinking too much, but to do as little as possible of it, since thinking was a menace that only got worse the more of it you did. He could recommend hard manual labor as an antidote: shoveling snow, chopping firewood, skiing cross-country, and that kind of thing, because thinking usually affected people when they were lolling about on the sofa or sitting back to rest in some other way. Getting up early was also recommended, especially on weekends and when you had a hangover, because all kinds of nasty thoughts could worm their way into your mind then.

It was particularly important not to brood about religion. God and death and the meaning of life were all extremely dangerous topics for a young and vulnerable mind, a dense forest in which you could easily get lost and end up with acute attacks of madness. You could confidently leave that kind of stuff until your old age, because by then you would be hardened and tougher, and wouldn't have much else to do. Confirmation classes should be regarded as a purely theoretical exercise: a few texts and rituals to memorize, but certainly not anything to start worrying about.

The most dangerous thing of all, and something he wanted to warn me about above all else, the one thing that had consigned whole regiments of unfortunate young people to the twilight world of insanity, was reading books. This objectionable practice had increased among the younger generation, and Dad was more pleased than he could say to note that I had not yet displayed any such tendencies. Lunatic asylums were overflowing with folk who'd been reading too much. Once upon a time they'd been just like you and me, physically strong, straightforward, cheerful, and well balanced. Then they'd started reading. Most often by chance. A bout of flu perhaps, with a few days in bed. An attractive book cover that had aroused some curiosity. And suddenly the bad habit had taken hold. The first book had led to another. Then another, and another, all links in a chain that led straight down into the eternal night of mental illness. It was impossible to stop. It was worse than drugs.

It might just be possible, if you were very careful, to look at the occasional book that could teach you something, such as encyclopedias or repair manuals. The most dangerous kind of book was fiction—that's where all the brooding was sparked and encouraged. Damnit all! Addictive and risky products like that should only be available in state-regulated monopoly stores, rationed and sold only to those with a license, and mature in age.

At that point Mum shouted down the stairs that it was time to eat. We wrapped ourselves in towels and made our way up. Dad was swaying a bit, and stubbed his big toe, but he didn't seem to feel the pain.

As for me, I was no longer a boy.

CHAPTER 16

In which a bad man becomes acquainted with crusted snow,
after which his wife is treated to a cold drink

Niila's old man, Isak, tried to put a stop to his sons' puberty by beating them. The bigger they grew, the more he beat them. Isak's bouts of drunkenness became more frequent and lasted longer. When sober he was moody, touchy and melancholy. He spent his time setting up rules and regulations for how to behave in every corner of the house, then methodically dealing out punishment every time he caught a sinner.

Isak regarded himself as extremely fair. He would often complain, as dictators always do, about how onerous his duties were, how ungrateful his family was, and what catastrophes would befall the house when he was gone, which would probably be quite soon. Like all alcoholics he used to think a lot about death. He longed for it, threatened to kill himself, but feared death above all else. Such thoughts grew stronger the seedier he became. He would often cover the kitchen table with sheets of newspaper and sit there cleaning his old moose rifle. He'd check the mechanism, dismantle and oil it, lift the barrel to his eye, and follow the spiraling rifled grooves into infinity. If relatives dropped by he liked to inform them about how he intended to distribute his estate, which was his favorite hymn, which Biblical quotation he thought would be most appropriate for his obituary notice. The children tried to get used to the thought, but it remained pretty awful. If he was out for longer than usual, they would find an excuse to go down into the cellar, out to the garage, or up into the loft. They wanted to know if he'd achieved his aim, but they never mentioned it to one another. Whenever he slapped them with the palm of his hand or lashed them with his belt, his eyes would disappear, they would turn black like holes in a skull. He was not of this world, he was already partially decomposed, already half with God, or Satan. His sense of duty and justice was so strong that he could carry out a beating and weep at the same time, belt his children with tears rolling down his cheeks, hit them with a confused passion that he called love.

When he was drinking he came closer to real life. He had more color in his cheeks, the dried-out river beds filled with moisture and started to flow again. He could laugh, enjoy the first few glasses, and lust after women, food, and money. But jealousy grew at the same rate. It was directed primarily at his sons, and was stronger the more grown-up they became. He treated Johan worst, his eldest son, who was closest to adulthood. Isak was jealous of the fact that Johan would soon have women of his own, delicious young lovers, and that the hard stuff hadn't damaged his young body, that Johan would soon be earning money and be able to live his own life and enjoy all the temptations the world had to offer, while he himself would be eaten up by unfeeling maggots. In Isak's dreams Johan would walk up to him, force his mouth open, and press his decayed teeth one by one until they sunk right down into his rotten gums. The boy would keep on going until only the bare gums remained, flat and bloody like the hands of Christ disfigured by nails.

Puberty was stronger than death. It was a plant that could grow through asphalt, a rib cage that could burst through shirts, a rush of blood that was more potent than vodka. Deep down, Isak wanted to kill his sons. But such a thought was so forbidden that he re-jigged it and turned it into beatings, into many beatings, into a long, drawn-out execution. But they kept on growing even so.

One Saturday in early spring when Johan was sixteen and Niila thirteen, they were instructed to accompany their father into the forest. They would have to shift some piles of timber to a forest road while the hard crust of snow lasted, before the midday sun—Isak had struck a good deal on some cheap wood he could use for his stoves back home. He had borrowed a snowmobile and raced off into the wilderness, weaving his way around tree stumps and tufts of grass, while his sons bumped around in the trailer, rubbing away at their cheeks to stave off the cold caused by the slipstream. You could see they were muttering away to each other and repeatedly looking at his back, but you couldn't hear a word of what they were saying over the roar of the engine.

It was a sunny day. Light seeped in through the tops of the fir trees, glittering and gleaming in the mirror-prisms of the snow. The spring winds had blown down lumps of beard lichen and flakes of bark that gradually melted into the crust of snow. The night frost had hardened the surface into a solid floor that could be pierced with your thumbs and lifted up in large sheets. Underneath, the snow was soft and powdery, so loose that you could sink into it right up to your thighs.

Isak kicked at the piles of logs covered in snow, produced a spade, and ordered Johan to start shoveling. And he'd better get a move on as well: if they hadn't finished before the midday thaw came because the two boys had been wasting time, it would be no joke, no laughing matter at all.

Without a word Johan took the spade and leaned it carefully against the wood-pile. Then he took off his gloves and delivered a vicious punch that landed just over his father's right eyebrow. Isak lost his balance and fell flat on his back. His bellowing echoed in the vast silence. Johan continued punching him, on the nose, his chin, his cheekbones. Niila flung himself over his father's legs, as they'd planned, and pummelled away at his midriff. No weapons were used, just clenched fists with boney knuckles, strong, hard, boys' fists that punched and punched. Isak wriggled like a crocodile, screaming all the while. His body was pressed through the hard crust and sunk down into the powdery snow. He was flailing his arms around, his mouth filled with snow. Blood was flowing freely, red and viscid, his eyes swelled and closed. But still the boys punched. Isak kicked at them, defended himself as best he could, fighting for his life now. He grabbed hold of Niila's throat and squeezed hard. Johan bent his father's little finger back until he screamed and was forced to let go. He disappeared down through the hard crust, floundering like a drowning man in the cold, white foam. More punches, harder and harder, a slab of iron under heavy hammers, a red-hot lump that glowed less red with every blow, became darker, greyer, stiffer.

Eventually the old man was no longer moving. The boys got to their feet, panting, and scrambled up onto the hard crust. The old man lay down at the bottom of his snow hole, looking at his sons outlined against the sky above. They peered down as if into a grave, whispering to each other like two priests. Flakes of snow melted and chilled the old man's death mask.

"Do you give up?" shouted Johan in the piping squeal of a lad whose voice is breaking.

"Go to hell!" wheezed Isak, spitting blood.

They jumped back down into the hole. Started again. They punched their father until the sweat poured off them, pounded that old alcohol-sodden face out of shape, beating the life out of the wreck, finished him off once and for all.

"Do you give up?"

And now their father burst out crying. He sobbed and sniveled deep down in his grave, no longer capable of moving. His sons climbed back up, made a fire, and melted some snow in the sooty saucepan. And when the coffee had boiled and the dregs sunk down to the bottom, and the smell spread, inducing Siberian jays to fly up and peer around the tree trunks, they lifted the old bloke up and lay him down on a reindeer skin. They pushed a lump of sugar between his battered lips and handed him a steaming mug. And as their father slurped pitifully at his coffee, Johan explained to him quietly that the next time he laid a hand on any member of the family, they would beat him to death.

For the next few days they were expecting revenge at any minute. They locked their bedroom door at night in order to avoid being surprised in their sleep, they hid the bolt of the moose gun and they made sure no knives were left lying around. Their mother tended her husband when he was in bed, feeding him with sour milk and blueberry soup and changing his plasters. She questioned her sons with her eyes but not with her voice, and noticed how they avoided entering the room. Isak himself said nothing. He stared at the cracks in the white-painted ceiling, a confusion of thin, black lines meandering along, branching off, coming to a sudden stop. They formed roads through remote, unknown landscapes. In his torment he started walking down those roads. He passed by houses and farms, got to know the local population and the names of villages. He wandered alongside rivers and tried his luck at fishing, trekked through forests teeming with game and berries, climbed low mountains and admired the views. Eventually he came across a spot where he'd like to live, and made himself a house out of fir logs he chopped down himself. He moved in to lead a solitary life. There was plenty of meat and fish, lots of wood to make fires with. The winters were long but he was used to that, the summers shimmeringly light. Only two things were different from the old world. First, there were no mosquitoes here. Not even around the enormous swamps where cloudberries hung down like yellow fists, not a single mosquito, no gnats, no gadflies, no clegs, no horseflies: a strange forest world completely devoid of bites or stings.

Second, there were no sins here.

Isak was shaken deep down in his soul when he realized that. He had found Paradise at last. No matter how hard he searched, he could find no evil. Nature gave birth and nourished, ate and was eaten in a never-ending round of hunger and death. But it was an innocent struggle, uncorrupted. Nature breathed all around him, inside him, through him. He could abandon despair. Stop his desperate fight to keep his head above water. Just open himself up like a cavity and let the good, verdant air blow through him.

And in this unexpected way, for the second time in his life, Isak found God.

* * *

As time passed he recovered, and turned nasty again. Anything else would have been too much to expect. But he stopped talking about suicide. And he stopped beating everybody, as he took the threats from his sons seriously. Instead he now started to see some point in growing old. Years later, when the sons had flown the nest, he tried to revive the tradition of beating his wife, but discovered that she had changed so much, she hit him back.

Instead, he devoted his time to harassing the garbage collectors, telling off the mechanics running the official car roadworthiness tests, and adjusting the borders of his plot, not to mention protests and various claims for damages to every authority in sight. But he was never much good as an agitator, and officials took no notice of his ranting.

There was a continental shift that affected the whole family. The landscape crumpled and assumed new contours. Niila's mother had devoted her whole life to diversionary maneuvers, but suddenly found herself with breathing space. Unused to this, she became depressed. She felt isolated and undervalued. Her children could manage for themselves, without needing her as a punching bag or go-between. Now that the war was over, how was she going to get by?

With time to think about her own welfare, she was suddenly overwhelmed by aches and pains. Her voice was nowadays heard in the house, unpracticed and hesitant, monotonously squeaky like an old wheel. The moment she opened her mouth, the house was filled with big, tired lumps of fluff that piled up to waist height and made it difficult to move around. The younger children, the girls and baby brother, became unruly. At last they dared to start growing up, and distanced themselves more and more from the stifling atmosphere of home. Their mother breathed her grey membranes over her children, but they thrust them aside and stuck their tongues out at life. She changed tactics and told them they were making her ill, that it was their fault that she was suffering. She kept on saying it over and over again, day in and day out, until they couldn't fight it any longer. The spider's web wrapped itself round them strand by strand, until every move they made was strenuous and treacly. They struggled and bit with their milk teeth, but they couldn't break loose.

Johan was now something of a head of household, but he couldn't understand what was happening. Isak refused to have anything to do with the hysterical little brats, claiming that people get like that if they are not properly punished for original sin. The whole house seemed to be decaying and falling to pieces. The lust for life trickled down between the floorboards and gradually rotted away. Things had gotten so bad, everybody wanted to be beaten again. First a beating, then God's grace.

In the end Johan marched up to his mother.

"It's time you got yourself a job," he said.

She turned white, and wondered why he wanted to send her to her death, given her agonized and exhausted state.

"It's time you got yourself a job!" he said again.

She refused, she'd become a laughing stock, who would want to employ an old woman with no qualifications?

"Meals on wheels," he said. "School dinners, old folks' homes."

She didn't reply, just slumped down onto the kitchen sofa, panting and wheezing from an attack of asthma. The children stopped squabbling on the floor, Isak froze in the rocking chair. Mum squirmed and wriggled, unable to breathe. Niila ran to phone for an ambulance, but Johan stopped him. Without saying a word he fetched a bottle of milk from the fridge. Walked over to his mother and emptied it all over her. A white flood flowed down her face, over her bust, down her skirt and her wrinkled stockings. A copious milky mess. And cold.

His mother flailed around like a suckling, then suddenly recovered her strength and got to her feet, furious. Then she hit Johan for the first time in her life, a fierce, resounding box on the ear.

"It's time you got yourself a job," he said for the third time.

She could feel the violent blow pulsating through her hand, could still feel the force flowing through her arm and her shoulder, and into the muscles of her back. She twisted her body back and forth in astonishment, and looked around, red in the face. The pain had gone.

CHAPTER 17

*In which May bonfires are lit, weapons are acquired, and
a bounty is placed on the heads of two young forest guerrillas*

They older we grew, the more we understood the way Pajala worked. It
transpired that the village was made up of several districts, each with its
own unofficial name—such as Naurisaho, Strandvägen, or Centrum. A
new housing estate was dubbed Texas, appropriately for a wild west set-
tlement; the area around the old sewage treatment works was called
Paskajänkkä, which translates from Finnish as "Shitmire," and, as mentioned before, the block where I lived was known as Vittulajänkkä,
"Cuntsmire."

In every district the boys formed their own gang, each with its leader.
Relations between the gangs could be anything from friendly cooperation
to competition, from saber rattling to open warfare, depending on when
you looked. A delicate balance of power, if you like. Sometimes two gangs
combined to fight a third party. Sometimes it was a free-for-all.

Having been born into one of the districts where there were most
children, you soon got used to challenges between the various gangs.
You just weighed in and did your bit. It might be prestigious ice hockey matches in the road some winter evening. You stuck to the brightest

parts, under a street lamp. Heaps of snow as goal posts, piles of snow, produced by the plows, at the sides of the road as touch lines, left- or right-handed sticks you bought in the hardware shop or borrowed from your elder brother, a tennis ball or an ancient puck, no protective clothing, no referee, but ten to fifteen snotty-nosed kids inspired by a prodigious determination to win.

Everything went fairly smoothly as far as 2–2. Energetic forechecking, hair-raising solo dashes, a gesture in the direction of passing but more often than not a rocket of a shot, then ages spent searching for the puck in the snowdrifts. We all played our heroes in the national ice-hockey team—Uffe Sterner, or Stisse, or Lillprosten. Or maybe Phil Esposito, who'd hit the puck so hard on Canadian television that it pierced a sheet of iron.

It's about now we see the first kid get his lips split. A center forward with a stick so long that the handle sticks out a few feet behind him manages to smash somebody in the face. Milk teeth still there, but oceans of blood. A dramatic vote is taken: send him off.

Then a foul tackle with no attempt to hide it. A dive into the snow. Shortly afterward, another one to get his own back. Excited discussions. A goal that's disallowed because somebody's shifted the goalposts. Protests. Counter-protests. A puck blasted into somebody's crotch. Tears. Penalty, another blast. Misses somebody's face by a hair's breadth. Elbowing. Shoulder-charge into a snowdrift. Trip. Punch on the nose.

Then before you know where you are, ten boys sprawled half-hidden in the piles made by the plows, mouths crammed full of snow, and one lonely kid at the far goal tapping the puck to and fro over the goal line: his team wins a hundred to three and he trudges home all alone through the glittering galaxy of snow.

* * *

Another thing the gangs did was to gather firewood and stuff for the traditional bonfires lit on the last day of April, and kept burning into May.

This task started immediately after New Year when the Christmas trees were thrown out. The village was suddenly full of little boys with enormous piles of fir needles on their kick-sleds. The main competition was between Paskajänkkä and Strandvägen as both districts were alongside the river, and so the bonfires could be as big as you liked. That was the aim, in fact—to make the biggest fire.

On top of the dead Christmas trees went practically anything that would burn: empty cardboard boxes from the shops, wood from buildings that had been demolished, car tires, plastic buckets, furniture, empty milk cartons, broken skis, sheets of hardboard, shoes, and even school books. Now and then a spy would be sent to the neighboring fire to compare and report on progress.

Stuff was occasionally pinched from somebody else's fire.

Violence also occurred, but not as often as in the hockey matches. The preferred methods of intimidation were implied threats, pigheadedness, or cunning.

For instance, you could make your bonfire look bigger than it really was by piling the material up high. In extreme cases this could lead to murder-fires that could collapse like swaying skyscrapers and burn to death twenty of the nearest spectators. Uncomprehending adults used to pull the tower down before it was lit, however, and pile it up more sensibly.

On one occasion some boys who were hopelessly far behind their rivals set fire to the opposition's superior effort a few days in advance. But that was regarded as being so dastardly nobody admired the winning fires.

Then everybody would stand in the snow around these burning rubbish heaps throwing firecrackers, and watching several months' work go up in smoke. That was the reward. Plus the two rockets the gang had managed to save up for, which were let off toward the end when the sky had become as dark as possible. They soared up like glowing flower stems, then each blossomed forth with its own glittering blooms. And then it was spring. Spring had come at last.

* * *

When you were a bit older, the macho thing to do was to acquire an air rifle. I nagged at my old man for months until he bought me one, second hand and a bit battered. It leaked, so that your hair would blow about whenever you shot, and there was hardly enough power for the pellet to exit from the muzzle. Results improved after the application of some electrical insulation tape and tightening of the spring, but it never became what you might call a killer gun. After school I used to practice shooting at a target on the garage wall. The sight couldn't be adjusted, so you always had to aim above and to the left. My old man had a go once, but he got cross when he could never hit the target and muttered something about being long-sighted.

Air rifles made the gangs both wilder and noisier. Boys would wander about in hordes: sweaty, excited teenagers with dirty trouser-knees. They would have peeing competitions, draw willies on shed walls, learn new swearwords and cause as much trouble as possible. It was fun to be in a group. You felt strong. And when you finally bumped into another gang, just as excited and also armed to the teeth, there could only be one outcome: air rifle war.

In order to prevent adults from intervening, the wars would be conducted in the extensive forests on the other side of the river. I badly wanted to join in, but wasn't sure if I was up to it. I'd just started class seven and was called a rabbit by the older pupils: I didn't have a moped, and my air rifle was nothing to shout about. On the other hand, Niila had managed to borrow from one of his cousins an East German pump-action rifle that was frighteningly powerful. It could shoot a hole straight through a sheet of hardboard, whereas my rifle barely made a mark.

One afternoon we decided to visit the front line. We got on our bikes with our guns slung over our shoulders, and set off over the old bridge. The river and village had soon disappeared behind us, and we entered a pine forest with thick undergrowth on all sides. We passed the saw mill, turned off onto a rough forest track and hid our bikes in a thicket. The forest was spookily silent. War was being waged not far away, but everything seemed to be calm and still. There was a smell of autumn. Sticky mushrooms were wearing their big, brown hats, weighed down by maggots. I picked a few overripe blueberries and sucked at the watery juice.

Suddenly there was a sharp crack, and Niila's cap fell off his head. Before the sniper had time to reload, I yelled out that we'd come to join up, for Christ's sake. A boy came scrambling down from a tree muttering something about being sorry that his finger had slipped, and that the main force was a bit further on. We followed him along a narrow path and soon came to a camp fire where a group of about ten boys were drinking coffee and taking snuff. Most of them were a year or two older than us, some were wearing camouflage clothing and legionnaire hats. They spat out a brown mess, and scrutinized us critically. The General, a burly fellow from Paskajänkkä with a fluffy moustache, pointed at a cone-laden pine branch about thirty feet away. I aimed above and to the left. The cone fell down first go. Niila hadn't had time to practice, and missed with his first attempt. And his second. And his third. The lads grinned and told him to go to hell. Niila missed with his fourth shot as well. Started sweating. The General was annoyed by this time and told him to run along back home to Mummy. Niila didn't say a word, but re-loaded. Pumped away. Pumped still more, ignoring all the jeers. Then he shot into the fire. There was a clang. Two jets of brown liquid spurted out from the pierced coffee kettle.

The lads gaped askance. Stared at Niila's rifle. At the coffee sizzling down into the embers. Then one of the boys threatened to beat the living daylights out of him, but hesitated as Niila had already reloaded and was busy pumping.

"I'll bring you a new kettle tomorrow," said Niila calmly.

The General spat into the fire. Then nodded. We had enlisted.

Then we lay concealed in the bushes on the river bank, the whole lot
of us, silent and motionless with our eyes skinned. They came in two
boats—long, thin craft specially designed to cope with the Tornedalen
rapids. Six lads in one, seven in the other. They were all armed, scanning
the edge of the forest, apart from the two in charge of the engines. They
hadn't noticed the ambush, but they were on the alert, just in case.
Gliding closer and closer to us. Slowed down, watching out for rocks.

The only rule was not to shoot at faces. Bottoms and thighs were the
preferred targets. That's where it hurt most, and you could make lovely big bruises. We glanced at the General. He was still lying motionless.
The enemy were now so close that we could read the logos on their
caps. The outboard motors were switched off, the boats glided increasingly slowly toward the river bank. The boy in the bow stood up to take
the impact with his foot.

That was when the General shot. Slap bang into the boy's thigh muscle. The rest of us blasted away the first salvo. A swarm of lead-heavy
wasps shot out from the bushes and landed painfully on their targets.
The victims screamed out in fear and pain, by Hell but we gave them
a good peppering! They shot back without having time to take aim,
then eventually they managed to get the engines going again. Salvo
after salvo. Stinging snake-bites all over their bodies. They lay prone at
the bottom of the boats, trying to hide. Slowly, the boats moved out
into the river, slid away. And we started laughing, roared so much we
had to roll around in the moss.

They landed a few hundred feet further upstream. Several were limp-
ing. We guffawed even louder, then withdrew into the trees to prepare
fresh attacks.

We had a sort of strategy—at first, at least. But soon it was just a
matter of hit and run, and in between, crouch down as low as possible
in the wild rosemary. I tried to stick close to Niila. Felt protected to
some extent by the power of his rifle. But he aimed like a bleary-eyed
old dodderer and hardly ever hit, which might have been just as well,

in fact. We lay there panting after withdrawing at the double, with our hands over our mouths to deaden the sounds. Wondered where our friends had got to. Peered into the dark depths of the forest, where we could hear somebody running and shooting. There were screams coming from the other direction, people moving around.

"Let's go over there," I whispered.

Just then Niila nudged me in the back. Only a couple of paces away were four of the enemy grinning, their rifles aimed straight at us as we scrambled to our feet. I dropped my rifle in the moss. Niila hung on to his.

"Drop your gun or we'll shoot your cocks off!" barked the tallest of them.

Niila was white-eyed with terror. His lower jaw was chewing at nothing. I carefully loosened his desperate grip on the butt of his rifle. Then I heard him whisper:

"You shoot then…"

"Drop that gun!" yelled the tall boy in his puberty-stricken voice—he'd seen a lot of American police films on television.

I nodded obediently. Bent slowly down with Niila's rifle in my hands. And then, before he could react, I shot the warbling berk in the thigh.

He roared like a bull. Slumped to the ground. Shots stuttered all around us as we zig-zagged away at high speed. I felt a sharp pain in my bottom. Niila, who'd managed to rescue my rifle, screamed and clutched at his shoulder. But we were free, we crowed in triumph and raced off between the trees with branches whipping our faces.

After this, the level of respect they had for us increased considerably. The boy with the breaking voice had to remove the pellet with the tip of a sheath knife. A bounty was placed on the heads of both me and Niila. A ten-pack of Finnish cigarettes to whoever succeeded in capturing us.

Taking prisoners was one of the greatest pleasures in our war games, but also probably the hardest. Niila and I once managed to creep up on one of the Strandvägen kids when he was squatting down and having a crap. The reputation of Niila's pump-action rifle was widespread, and Niila made it convincingly clear that the bloke would get one up the back passage if he didn't give himself up. Pale and trembling, the poor lad pulled up his trousers without bothering to wipe himself. Then we escorted him back to HQ. The applause was deafening. We used his own shoelaces to tie him against a pine tree, then embarked on the obligatory torture. This consisted of the General waving a penknife under his nose and scaring him to death with all sorts of threats. It was a matter of dicks being abbreviated and anthills being provided with victuals and other niceties he'd read about in the comics. If we could reduce the prisoner to tears, that was a plus. Things rarely went any further than that. Let's face it, you might find yourself in the same position one of these days...

We once captured the enemy leader. We tied his hands over his head and flung the rope over a stout branch. Then we pulled it taut until he was standing on his toes with a sweaty sock stuffed in his mouth. I suppose we thought he'd work himself loose eventually. But he didn't. When night fell his mum began to wonder where he was. After a few telephone calls his friends put two and two together. It was already starting to be very dark. Contact was made with our gang, directions were provided, and eventually a group of his friends set out with torches.

The difficulty was in finding the place. It was hard to work out where you were in the gathering autumnal gloom, and, anyway, the bloke couldn't shout out directions because of the smelly sock in his mouth. All the trees looked the same, paths were rubbed out, and the contours melted away. A wind got up, and the soughing and sighing drowned out all other noises. Then, to top it all off, it started raining.

It was several hours before they found him. His trousers were soaked in pee. When they untied the rope, he collapsed in a heap. The first thing he did when the gag was removed was to pass a death sentence on a number of named teenagers.

A temporary truce was declared for the next few days, to let feelings cool down a bit. Then I got caught in a crafty ambush. I was split off from the flock like an antelope, and was peppered with shots in my bottom until I flung aside my rifle and gave myself up. My God, but it hurt! Nasty purple bruises all over my thigh. But I refused to cry even so, while the lads who'd caught me argued about who was going to get the ten-pack of cigarettes. Their leader forced me onto the ground and announced that I was now going to get the same treatment he'd had. Grinning broadly, he slung a rope up over a sturdy pine branch. The he pulled off one of my socks and peed all over it until it was soaked through. My throat felt dry, I was dizzy with fear. Tried to prepare myself for the torture to come. Whatever they did to me, I mustn't start crying. I had to resist, no matter how much pain I felt. Be tough. But for Hell's sake, what would happen if I couldn't manage it?

Just then we all heard a shouting and screaming not far away. One of the look-outs yelled that we were being attacked. The leader hesitated, then listened to the sound of the battle approaching.

"Run for it!" he barked, and raised his rifle to take aim at me. All the others did the same. I held my breath in anticipation of the pain, then ran for it. I raced for all I was worth, zig-zagging from side to side. Pellets thudded into my body, hurting like third-degree burns.

"You missed, you missed!" I scoffed, with tears welling up as I glanced back in terror.

At that point their leader shot: I fell. Collapsed completely. Landed on my back in the moss. When I tried to open my eyes, I realized I was blind.

"Stop shooting!" somebody yelled.

The attack crumbled. Footsteps approached. My head was pounding like a drum. Pain, darkness. I felt my face. Warm and wet.

"Fucking hell!" somebody yelled. "Some water, quick!"

They all gathered round me, I could hear them panting after all their efforts.

"I'm blind," I said, and felt like throwing up.

"You hit him in the eye! Jesus Christ, there's blood everywhere!"

Somebody handed me a soaking wet bit of cloth, and I tried to wipe away the blood. Sat up, and could feel it dripping. Gave it another wipe. Ran my fingers over my eyes.

Panic-stricken, I blinked wildly: but everything was in a fog. I rubbed harder. Found I could see a bit clearer. I wrung out the cloth over my face, and the water streamed down, washing and cleansing. I blinked. Put my hand over one eye. Then the other. What a relief, I could see! Mind you, I could feel a sort of bulge under the skin.

The pellet had hit me right between the eyes. What had blinded me was the blood.

War was called off for the rest of the day. Niila managed to prize out the pellet with a red-hot needle, and when I got home I told them I'd been hit by a stone flung up by a passing truck. The wound healed eventually, but I still have the scar.

That marked the end of my participation in the air rifle war.

CHAPTER 18

*On messing about making music
and other more or less manly activities*

Our first public performance took place during morning assembly in the Pajala school hall one bleak, chilly day in February. The aims of morning assembly were high-flown, namely that for twenty minutes every Friday morning the senior school would be crammed together in order to inculcate morality, raise the spiritual tone, and reinforce the feelings of camaraderie among pupils. It was no doubt an idea from southern Sweden that had spread up to the far north as a result of some school principals' conference, but which over time had turned into something more like a *seura*, a prayer meeting. The role of preacher was played by the well-combed and anxious-looking careers counselor Henrik Pekkari or the velvet-eyed principal Sven-Erik Klippmark, who tried to convert all the sinners who had scrawled graffiti, spat out snuff, kicked in cupboards, smashed bottles, carved on desk lids, or raised the bill for local taxpayers in some other way. They would no doubt have had more effect if they'd used their Tornedalen Finnish and threatened the young devils with a good hiding and injuries that would be with them for the rest of their lives, which was the way most of them had been brought up.

There would occasionally be a musical interlude. The church organist and choirmaster, Göran Thornberg, had pluckily played a Bach prelude on the piano, apparently oblivious to the fact that his audience's concentration had left much to be desired. The school's girls' choir had sung a canon with their silver-haired conductor Birgitta Söderberg trying to ignore the sexy wolf whistles from class nine's special needs group. A lad from Peräjävaara had played the trumpet with the elan of a man bent on suicide, and he'd made so many mistakes that even the teachers joined in the laughter. But he survived, and eventually became a music teacher.

Friday came around, the village boys from class nine yawned, sat down in the back row, burped loudly, and started flicking erasers around. The rest of the pupils filled up the space in front. The stage was hidden by a curtain. Greger had received permission from the Head to arrange the morning assembly however he liked, having submitted a proposed theme based on responsibility and creativity in young people. It was only when you stood close to the curtain that you heard a strange, low, electrical hum.

The pupils prepared to sit it through or heckle, according to their temperament and reserves of courage. The teachers squeezed themselves into strategic seats. The brave, close-cropped history teacher Gunnar Lindfors took up his position on the back row and switched on his radar eyes, ready to lift up by the scruff of their neck anybody who transgressed.

Greger climbed up onto the stage with a solemn expression on his face and stood in front of the curtain. Nobody took any notice. The teachers called for silence. The chattering and giggling continued as if it had been rehearsed. Teachers glared threateningly at the most active pockets of resistance. New defiant laughter, fits of coughing, an empty bottle rolling down the aisle, a sheet of paper being torn over and over again, very loudly.

Greger raised his deformed hand. Waved with his thumb without saying a word, then disappeared into the wings.

That was our cue to start.

"Djuss letmi eersumutha rokunroal muzzeek!"

The ones in the front row were flung back in their seats. The rest stared uncomprehendingly at the closed curtain. It was swaying and bulging like the lid of a tin of fermented Baltic herring.

"Rokunroal muzzeek! If yoo wonner lav vitmi!"

We bashed away like madmen in the half-darkness behind it. Erkki got stage fright and started hitting out at everything that moved until the speed of the song was doubled. Niila was playing his chords in the wrong key, and Holgeri's acoustic feedback sounded like the last trumpet. And in front of it all. At the floor microphone. Was me.

I wasn't singing, I was bellowing. The call of a moose in heat. The death shriek of a lemming. I was doing my own damn thing. Without realizing it, we had invented punk several years too soon. The tune decomposed, more or less; "ended" would be the wrong word, as Erkki was still pummeling away and flashing the whites of his eyes. So I stooped over the mike once again:

"Djuss letmi eersumutha rokunroal muzzeek!"

For the second time. The curtain was still drawn. I tried to follow the bass drum, but Erkki's playing had now turned into something more like an epileptic fit. Niila eventually found the right key, but came in two bars too late. Holgeri played the solo for the second tune, not having realized that we were repeating the first one.

"Djuss letmi eersumuth…"

The same song for the third time. Greger was fiddling feverishly in the dark, tugging at ropes and bits of cloth. Erkki was bashing the drums so deafeningly loudly that I could no longer hear my own voice. Then suddenly the curtain shot up and the spotlights dazzled us. There they sat, the whole bloody school, and I leaned forward and bellowed out *Djuss letmi eersumutha* for the fourth time.

The inconceivable happened, and Niila came in at the right time. He followed Erkki, and Holgeri and I tagged on as well. Like a runaway train we stormed through the song on the rails all the way, and when we came to the final chord we pulled Erkki back onto his chair so hard that he fell over.

Silence.

I staggered as far toward the side of the stage as the guitar cord would let me, and felt an overwhelming urge to emigrate. My skull felt like a maraca. Greger grabbed hold of my shoulders. Turned me round. Said something, but I'd been deafened by Erkki's cymbals.

Then I saw. They were applauding. The whole chock-a-block hall. They were clapping their hands, apparently voluntarily, and some of the girls who'd been to pop concerts in Luleå and hence knew what to do were screaming and shouting for an encore.

Eventually the audience trooped out, but we stood transfixed, not really understanding what had happened. Already, after our first concert, we were possessed by the emptiness one feels after every performance, a sort of introverted sorrow. Erkki claimed his mind was a blank, but said his body felt as hot as it was after a sauna. Greger muttered something about the curtain rope needing to be marked with fluorescent paint. In a daze, we started carrying our things back to the music room.

* * *

Reactions afterward were varied. One could hardly call it a success, but we had certainly left an indelible impression. The Laestadian pupils had left the hall the moment we started, but the kids in the back row had immediately stopped throwing balls of paper at the math teacher's bald head. Some of our pals gave us the highest praise you will ever hear from the mouth of a Tornedalen citizen:

"You weren't too bad, really."

Others assured us that it was the biggest load of rubbish they'd heard at morning assembly since the lady accordion player from Sion, and said they'd cut the strings if we ever tried it again. It was also a little worrying that some claimed the second number was best. Others preferred the third, and some even placed the first one at the top. On the other hand, nobody seemed to prefer the fourth number, which was the only time we'd played the song properly. We didn't have the courage to tell them it was the same song all four times, in various stages of panic. A few girls in class eight started making eyes at Erkki, as he'd had the biggest stage presence, and others ogled Holgeri, as he was the most handsome. Greger, on the other hand, was severely criticized at a rancorous staff meeting for his artistic irresponsibility.

On the whole, then, we survived with no more damage than sheer fright.

* * *

In Tornedalen creativity has generally been linked with survival. You could respect, and even admire, the skilled wood-carver who could turn a bit of a tree into anything from a butter knife to a grandfather clock; or the lumberjack whose engine conked out but drove his snowmobile for six miles on a mixture of heart medicine and moonshine; or the old lady who picked fifty pounds of cloudberries and, not having a bucket, carried them home in her ingeniously knotted knickers; or the bachelor who brought back a whole year's supply of cigarettes in his brother's coffin, seeing as he'd happened to die on the Finnish side of the border; or the smuggler-widow who cut a horse up into small pieces so skillfully that her sons were able to get it through customs into Sweden and fasten it together again as good as new, then sell it at a considerable profit. Mind you, that last incident took place in the forties, before I was born.

An example of Tornedalen creativity is the fish fanatics. All those men who live for drilling holes through the ice and lying on reindeer skins and jigging their tiny rods and pulling up all those Arctic char, who spend all winter tying salmon flies, whose pockets are stuffed full of dragonflies and blind reptiles, who prefer fishing to sexual intercourse, who have mastered fourteen ways of tying a fly but only the missionary position, who pay a thousand kronor for every pound of salmon they catch instead of buying it from the Co-op for a fraction of the price, who would rather stand around in leaking waders than celebrate midsummer with their families, who abandon a good night's sleep, ruin their marriage, get the sack, pay no attention to personal hygiene, mortgage their house, and neglect their children the moment they hear that fish are nibbling at Jokkfall.

House builders in Tornedalen are a similarly perverse category. Evasive characters, preoccupied when you talk to them, restless, impatient, and with shifty eyes. Only when they have their hands wrapped around a hammer are they anything like normal folk, only then can they possibly say nice things to their wives through a mouth full of nails. It's amazing what a bloke can manage to build in a lifetime! House and cowshed, signed and sealed. Sauna and shit-house, before your very eyes! Woodshed and barns, no problem! Toolshed and summer house, attaboy! Then garage and dog kennel and cycle shed and playhouse for the kids.

This is about the point at which the local authority decides that the site is fully developed. The husband is devastated, as sour as vinegar, starts shouting at the children, turns to drink, can't get to sleep, loses his hair, kicks the dog, has sight and hearing problems and is prescribed Valium by a doctor in Gällivare—and then his desperate wife inherits an undeveloped holiday home plot.

And so he can start all over again.

Summer cottage, sauna, shit-house, woodshed, dog kennel. A pause for breath, then boathouse, earth cellar, guest cottage, toolshed, deck, and fantasy house for the kids. Then all the extensions. Up with the lark every day of the holiday. Hammering in nails, sawing and chopping, and feeling good.

But years go by, and inevitably every square inch is filled. The housing committee of the local authority pore over aerial photographs. And the husband becomes so obstreperous, it's beyond a joke; and his wife is on the point of leaving him.

But all of a sudden, it's time for renovations. New roof, more modern roof insulation, underfloor heating in the living room, loft conversion, game room in the basement, replace the putty in the windows, strip and repaint, new doors for the kitchen cabinets, fitted carpets, new taps and washbasins, replace rotten timber in the sauna, build a patio and balcony, and glaze in the deck.

But then it's all finished. Then it's irrevocable. Then it's impossible to add anything else, it's all completed, there's nothing else to hammer in, and his wife is forced to accept that there's no alternative. It has to be the psychiatric ward in Gällivare.

But then they change the law and relax the planning restrictions.

It's amazing how many new sheds can fit into a normal-sized garden. Off we go again. And the marriage is once more filled with something warm, something calm, something one might even call love.

* * *

Our rock music was something else. It was certainly not useful in any way. Nobody could see any value in it, not even us. Nobody needed it. We just played, opened our hearts and let the music come out. Old people saw it as a sign that we were spoiled and had too much free time, typical of the extravagance and waste of the modern era. This was the kind of thing that happened when young people were not sent out to work. It resulted in an excess of energy that buzzed around and raised the blood pressure.

In the early days Niila and I often discussed whether our rock music could be regarded as *knapsu*. The word is Tornedalen Finnish and means something like "unmanly," something that only women do. You could say that in Tornedalen the male role boils down to just one thing: not being *knapsu*. That sounds simple and obvious, but it is complicated by various special rules that can often take decades to learn, something that men who move up north from southern Sweden often come up against.

Certain activities are basically *knapsu* and hence should be avoided by men. Changing the curtains, for instance; knitting, weaving carpets, milking by hand, watering the house plants, that kind of thing. Other occupations are definitely manly, such as felling trees, hunting moose, building log cabins, floating logs down-river, and fighting on dance floors. The world has been split in two since time immemorial, and everybody knew the score.

But then came the welfare state. And suddenly there were lots of new activities and occupations that confused the concepts. As the *knapsu* concept had developed over many hundreds of years, as subconscious processes in the minds of generations, the definitions could no longer keep up. Except in certain areas. Engines, for instance, are manly. Gas-burning engines are more manly than electric ones. Cars, snowmobiles, and power saws are therefore not *knapsu*.

But can a man sew with a sewing machine? Whip cream with an electric mixer? Milk cows with a milking machine? Empty a dishwasher? Can a real man vacuum-clean his car and still retain his dignity? Those are some questions for you to think about.

It's even more difficult when it comes to new trends. For instance, is it *knapsu* to eat reduced-fat margarine? To have a heater in your car? To buy hair gel? To meditate? To swim using a snorkel? To use sticking plaster? To put dog poo in a plastic bag?

Besides, the rules change from village to village. Hasse Alatalo from Tärendö told me that where he comes from it's regarded, for some reason, as *knapsu* to turn down the tops of your rubber boots.

On the basis of all this, we men can be divided into three categories. First there's the real macho type. Often from one of the small villages, surly, silent, and dogged, with a knife in his belt and salt in his pocket in case he gets stranded out in the wilds. His opposite is just as easy to recognize, the unmanly man. He is obviously *knapsu*, under the thumb of his big sisters and useless in the forest or when out shooting moose. On the other hand he is often good with animals, and also with women (apart from the sexual side of things), and hence in the old days he often became a healer or a naturopath.

The third group of men are all the many in the middle. That's where both Niila and I belonged. What you do indicates how *knapsu* you are. It could be something as harmless as wearing a red woolen hat. That could drop you in the category for several weeks, during which time you'd be forced to fight and watch your back and submit to death-defying rituals before you slowly managed to climb out of the pit reserved for men who were *knapsu*.

Rock music is usually played by men. It radiates something aggressively manly. It wouldn't take an outsider long to decide that rock music is not *knapsu*. But there again, it has to be said that messing about like that is not exactly real work. Put a rock musician in a forest and give him an axe, and he'd piss blood. And even singing was deemed to be unmanly, in Pajala at least, assuming you were sober. Even worse was doing it in English, a language much too lacking in chewability for hard Finnish jaws, so sloppy that only little girls could get top marks in it—sluggish double dutch, tremulous and damp, invented by mud-sloshing coastal beings who've never needed to struggle, never frozen nor starved. A language for idlers, grass-eaters, couch potatoes, so lacking in resilience that their tongues slop around their mouths like sliced-off foreskins.

So obviously, we were *knapsu*. But whatever, we couldn't possibly stop playing.

CHAPTER 19

About a girl with a black Volvo, about pucks and fucks
and what you can amuse yourself with in Pajala

Our next gig was at the Community Hall in Kaunisvaara, after a meeting of the young Communists, known as the Red Youth. Holgeri had arranged it: he knew a girl on the committee, one of the thirty or so standing around in Palestine shawls, with their bangs and round glasses, beating time with the pointed toes of their Lapp shoes. It would be fair to say that the reception was pretty enthusiastic. It was two months since we'd performed in public for the first time, and we'd got it together much better. We'd written two of the tunes ourselves, and the rest were covers I'd pinched from *Top Twenty*. A few ancient Red Pioneers came to stand in the doorway and listen out of curiosity, but they soon turned their heels and left. Apart from one old boy who'd been deaf ever since a hand grenade went off by mistake when he was doing his national service. He stood and gaped, adjusting his cap now and then, thinking what a damn waste of electricity it was.

After the last number Holgeri's girlfriend started clapping and shouting for an encore, and a few others joined in. We were still on stage, and I glanced nervously at Erkki and Niila. We didn't know any more, we'd exhausted our repertoire.

Then we heard a howl. Holgeri! He was standing next to the loud-speaker with the sound turned right down. An electronic whine filled the hall, the windowpanes rattled. Then he started playing. Solo, maximum distortion. He never so much as glanced at the audience. Went down on his knees and slammed his guitar on the floor, shook it like a newly murdered corpse in front of the funnel-shaped lips of the loud-speaker. Clawed at the screeching strings. The tune seemed familiar. Fragmented, coming and going like a distant radio broadcast, but nevertheless packing a punch. We just stared at Holgeri. He lay down on his back. Thrust his guitar skyward, thrust after thrust. Eyes half closed, sweat pouring off his brow. Then he bent his head back and started playing with his teeth. The same strangely familiar tune.

"Hendrix!" Niila yelled into my ear.

"Better!" I yelled back at him.

Then it dawned on me what he was playing. The Soviet national anthem, echoing around the old wooden walls of the Community Hall.

Afterward several of the audience came up on the stage to ask where we stood politically. Holgeri sat there with a faint smile on his face, as if he'd just woken up out of a dream, while two girls tried to sit on his knee. I found myself face to face with a girl with strange, Indian-inked, Arab eyebrows. Her hair was so shiny black, it seemed she must have just dunked it in an inkwell. But her face was powdery white. There was something doll-like about her, a thin outer layer of cellophane. Her body was hidden behind the regulation voluminous uniform Red Youth fashion dictated, but her supple gestures gave her away. She wiggled her pelvis as she crept toward me, slight, careful movements. But I knew there was a woman in there, a hunger. Without a word she held out her hand to be shaken, like a grown-up, and she smiled, displaying her small, sharp teeth. She shook firmly, like a man. It hurt.

Afterward we packed up our instruments and the amplifiers. The old guy with the cap wandered around, an innocent grin on his face, as he checked on how the girls' titties were coming on. The treasurer presented us with liver-sausage sandwiches and fifty kronor from the club's funds.

"Are you going to Pajala?"

It was the black-haired girl. We were standing at the top of the steps. She pulled her leather jacket more tightly around her.

"Can I offer you a lift?" she asked.

She nodded toward the road. I followed her hesitantly. She stopped beside a black Volvo.

"My dad's car."

"I like it," I said.

We were on our way before I knew where I was. The seat felt chilly under my bottom, and my breath was misting over the windscreen. I switched on the heater and turned up the heat to combat the wintry cold. An approaching car sounded its horn loudly, and flashed its headlights. The girl fumbled around with the controls until she found the right switch, then dimmed the headlights.

"Surely you're not eighteen yet?"

She didn't answer. Leaned back in her seat, her hand on the gear shift. She hugged the middle of the road, the icy surface sped away underneath us, the mountains of snow piled up on each side of the road sparkled in our headlights. The ice on the marshy swamps beyond glowed blue and unyielding.

"Is it cool to be a Communist?" I asked.

She tried to find the knob to turn on the radio. The car edged toward the ditch at the side of the road. I whimpered and she jerked the wheel and straightened us out again.

"You don't need to be scared," she said. "I've been driving for years."

She took the old road from Autio to Pajala. When we got to the long, straight section at the beginning, she plunged the accelerator pedal right down to the floor. The engine raced and whined, and the speedometer registered a fever. The cold air outside licked a layer of ice all over the car and not least the windows, and the inside temperature dropped.

"There are often reindeer on the road here," I said.

She laughed and increased the speed even more. I realized she enjoyed scaring other people. If I were to fasten my safety belt now, she'd have won. Instead I tensed my body and prepared to adopt the crash position while staring hard at the side of the road, and pretended to be relaxed.

After fiddling around for ages she managed to find Finland Radio. Tango in a minor key, a woman singing about love and sorrow. The car bounced its way over hill and dale, around endless curves, leaving behind a melancholy-looking cloud of smoke. A heart emptying itself into the vacant landscape, a trail of blood. I glanced surreptitiously at the girl. Examined her profile in the darkness, her round chin, her fleshy lips, her cheeky upturned nose, so typically Finnish. I felt the urge to explore. Kiss.

"What's there to do in Pajala?" she asked.

"God only knows," I said.

We were already at Manganiemi and were soon swishing over the old bridge. The lights from the village flickered through the trees, and there was a glittering white sheen on the river. She slammed her foot down on the accelerator despite the Scania Vabis truck coming toward us over the narrow bridge. We somehow squeezed past, but you couldn't have slid a single copy of the *Haparanda Daily News* between us. The truck driver played a fanfare on his horn, but the girl's face was expressionless.

"Is there a film on tonight?"

I didn't think so. What else was there to do? I remembered a classmate who kept rabbits in his boiler room. He used to feed them on half-rotten vegetables from the Co-op that they'd only have thrown away otherwise. You could sometimes catch the bunnies going at it, but I supposed that was a bit childish.

"We can take in the Pajala Sporting ice hockey practice. They have a match this weekend against Ötå-Kuiva."

I explained how she should continue straight on then turn right at Arthur's general store, which looked a bit like a shoe box, then keep going toward the center of town past all the shops, including the Harjuhahto shoe shop, the office supplies store and Larsson's gentleman's hairdressers, Wennberg's bakery, Mikaelsson's corner shop and Lindqvist's café. We turned at the school and came to the ice hockey rink. We parked the car, which had warmed up at last, and followed a well-trod snow path down to the rink.

It was all go there. Padded giants in yellow and black shirts were practicing skating backward in a circle around the whole pitch. The coach was called Stenberg, a bearded police constable who'd moved into the area from the south. He blew his whistle and urged them on.

"Any pansy who cuts a corner gets a sack of shit dropped on his little-girl curls from a great height! Get those skates moving, you idle bastards!"

Then they warmed up the goalie with a salvo of cannon balls, whamming and blasting with their fancy Koho sticks while the ghoul behind his death-mask was bruised black and blue through every inch of his padding. Some of the pucks whizzed over the sideboards and disappeared into the fields beyond, where some kid would be ecstatic to find them when the snow melted.

"Thwack that puck into the top corner like you were belting the devil and his grandmother and all the choirboys of hell!" Stenberg yelled. He was brilliant with youngsters and on his own initiative had started training programs for young lads in every village and hamlet for miles around.

Then they had a practice match. A crude, all-farting performance characterized more by good intentions than clever tactics. They crashed into the sideboards, slid over the ice on their bottoms, and pelted the goals with shots until their sticks started smoking. The long-haired forward on one of the teams had a gum shield of the old type that made him look like a German shepherd with a muzzle on. One big mass of muscle, he put his head down and charged forward, scattering the defense like a train barging through a reindeer herd. His puck control was not of the best, but he did manage, with a bit of luck, to deliver a back pass so that his own defense could shoot straight through the clear-felled tunnel he'd created. His opposite pole on the team was a skinny blond guy with incredible reflexes. He'd stand still as a statue when the puck was dropped, then his stick was transformed into a lightning flash and the puck would shoot off like a rubber thunderbolt.

We stood on a pile of snow behind the sideboards and watched for a while. I snuggled a bit closer to her, as if by accident, so that our jackets were touching. She had a mouthful of bubble gum, and there was a smell of liquorice every time a bubble burst. I noticed she was shivering, and pulled her Palestine shawl tighter around her neck.

"Are you cold?"

"A bit."

"We could… I've got a friend who keeps rabbits…"

"How childish," she said, wrapping her bubble gum round her index finger.

I ought to have put my arm around her instead. Too late now. I felt stupid. Had an urge to go home and practice riffs in front of the mirror. She noticed I was backing off. Softened up, watched the match for a while, and pretended to be interested.

"They ought to practice precision passing," I said. "Like the Russians. This is more Canadian. Brute force, you know. Lumberjack ice hockey."

I branched off into an in-depth analysis of the game and elaborated on how the Russians had such brilliant technique because they used to remove the blades of their sticks and practice with the handles alone. Then I noticed she was bored stiff. And I started to feel cold as well.

"Why don't we call in on the ladies' aerobics?"

She nodded, and looked into my eyes for longer than she needed to.

Then averted her gaze as if she'd realized she'd given herself away. I felt my heart starting to thud, and led the way to the gym just a few hundred feet away.

The door to the ladies' changing rooms wasn't locked. We sneaked in. Jazz music blared from the school tape recorder. There was a smell of fish and varnish, as there always is in old PE halls, a sort of fetid smell of torture by ropes and vaulting horses and flying rings. Plus an acid stench of female sweat and sex. The housewives' clothes were hanging from hooks all around the changing room. Wrinkled woolen trousers, tent-like underskirts, flowery dresses, surgical stockings, bra cups bigger than my woolly hat. The floor was covered in shopping bags and PVC handbags and worn-down ladies' boots, Wellingtons, and Lapp shoes, marooned in pools of melted snow.

I tip-toed toward the hall. It was dazzlingly bright in there. A sudden earthquake hit the building, the floor shuddered. The ladies were jumping on the spot. My God, but the flesh quivered! Tits jiggled like flour sacks, spare tires swelled like rising dough. It was lucky they had no sense of rhythm—if they'd all jumped in time with the music, they'd have gone through the floor. Then they started prancing around the room with giant strides. Colossal legs clomping around like elephants. Sweat poured in torrents over the double chins and into the canyons of their cleavage, varicose veins glowed blood-red. "Stretch and streeetch!" yelled the instructor from behind the tape recorder, and forty powerful housewives swayed like birches in a storm. "Now, forward stretch and touch your toes," and twenty gigantic bottoms from which had sprung a hundred children waggled in the air. Bum sweat cascaded over blubbery backs, the air was alive with a whiff of pussy. "Up again, then left and right," sideways thrusts with ample hips. There were collisions of course, producing amazing mass energy. Women fell like two-ton bombs, lay slithering in the pools of sweat on the varnished floorboards before scrambling up on their feet again, indomitable. The room stank of marshy swamps and menopause. Death and birth in an ancient mix, female excitement.

The girl grabbed me by the hair on the back of my neck. Interlaced her frozen female fingers. A shudder ran down my back and into my hips. I went weak at the knees, was forced to sit down. She slid down onto my knee and spat out her bubble gum. Her pupils dilated, became black water holes. I started stroking her chin with my thumb, light as a feather along her jaw-line, up toward her curvy little ear. Snuggled my face up to hers. Closed my eyes and searched for her skin. Her cheeks melted, heated up. She started breathing more eagerly. I could feel her smiling under my lips. We opened our jackets. Body against body. Her breasts were young and pointed. I wrapped my arms around her and squeezed till tears came to my eyes, felt a happy glow flow through me. Get together. Get a girlfriend.

Suddenly her hand was under my sweater. Freezing cold but gentle and loving. She caressed my sensitive back muscles, made them twitch. Moved faster, more impatiently. Pinched a little. Scratched.

"Would you like to… be my girl?" I stammered.

By way of response she slid her hand inside my pants. Turned her hand into a little mouse scuttling over my buttocks, my hip bone, darting into my groin. I flinched.

"It won't hurt," she giggled, showing her white teeth.

I wanted to tell her I'd hardly got any pubic hair, warn her she'd be disappointed, but she was already there. Deftly stroked my scrotum, like a spider trussing up a fly. Fingered my little erection. Now I was caught, impossible to run away. She kissed me, thrusting her long, blood-tasting tongue into my mouth. I felt dizzy, stroked her breasts, but roughly, clumsily. She forced me backward, down onto the wooden bench. Pulled down her jeans. I wanted to feel her but she knocked my hand away.

"You're too slow," she said harshly, holding me down.

My shoulder blades were pressed down against the bench. She sat on me like a bouncer subduing a drunk. I could hear the women stamping away in the background.

"You're so… nice," I mumbled shyly.

Eyes closed, she steered me inside her, greedily. Deep down into the darkest, dampest depths. It felt warm and soft, like a pillow. She started wiggling with snake-like movements, rocking back and forth, a slow and tender dance making something grow, getting bigger all the time. A picture being painted redder and redder until the whole canvas became a damp membrane. I thrust into her again and again, felt my head swimming. She stepped up the pace and started emitting shrill shrieks. Grew more eager, more abandoned, like a dog screwing a sofa. I put my hand over her mouth, but she shrieked right through it. Cat-like screams.

"Hush, they'll hear us!" I gasped and could feel my skin growing tauter. Bulging outward. Pressure, bleeding. I tried to wriggle out but she clung on to me. It grew ever bigger and stronger. Pricking with the point of a knife until it made a hole. Her hair hung down thickly all around me. Dark clouds. Full of flesh.

And now. Now, yes now now now the whole world burst and the rain came cascading down from the black clouds above.

* * *

When I opened my eyes a woman was standing there. One of the flesh-laden matrons from Vittulajänkkä. Eyes staring from under her sweaty permed hair, beads dripping from her nose and chin. I knew she would start shouting. Call in the other harridans, create a lynching atmosphere. They'd squash us against the floor with their hundred-pound bottoms and check to see if we were pickpockets. One of them would say: *Kulli pois! Out with your prick!* and then one of the Lappish women from the Arctic forests would chew my balls to mincemeat like they do when they castrate screaming, white-eyed reindeer stags.

Scared stiff, I withdrew, pulled on my pants while the woman stared critically at my shrinking erection. The stamping from the gym was deafening, horrendous.

"Much ado about nothing," she said with a grin.

Then she took a drink of water straight from the tap, farted loudly, and went back into the hall. A strong smell of stables followed us all the way out.

* * *

The girl got into the Volvo and said: "Ta-ta." I stopped her from closing the door.

"Will I see you tomorrow?" I wondered.

She stared straight ahead, her lips tense but indifferent.

"Can't you tell me your name at least?"

She tinkered with something and started the engine. Engaged first gear and started moving. I ran alongside, clinging on to the door. She looked at me with her big, dark eyes. And suddenly her mask fell. It cracked, collapsed, and underneath was nothing but a big, fleshy wound.

"I'm coming with you!" I yelled in desperation.

She accelerated, the door flew out of my grasp. With tires spinning she skidded away under the streetlights in a cloud of whirling snow. The sound of the engine grew fainter then died away into silence.

I stood motionless for a long time, and then the penny dropped. She hadn't had an ignition key. The engine had been hot-wired. And as the pain grew, sinking its cold roots deep inside me, I realized I would never see her again.

CHAPTER 20

*Regarding a birthday party at which the Tornedalen
national anthem is sung, how the moose hunters turn up,
and how four young men shoot for the stars*

As the years went by, my grandad became more and more of a hermit. He enjoyed being on his own, and when Grandma passed on he got it into his head that other people were a nuisance. He lived on his own, looked after himself, and his final wish was to die in his own home. Whenever we went to visit him, he was friendly but reserved. As far as he was concerned, the bottom line was that he wanted nothing to do with an assisted living facility: just let us get that into our thick skulls. Some people might think his house was a mess, but he liked it that way.

But he couldn't do anything about the passage of time, and eventually his seventieth birthday approached. His family had a guilty conscience, because they hadn't been to see him as often as they might have; they all agreed that they should make up for this by giving him a birthday party nobody would ever forget. It would be an opportunity to add a few celebratory photos to the family album before the old man was too senile.

It took a great deal of persuasion before the object of the celebration agreed to take part, not for his own sake, but for the family's. Looking on the bright side, he watched the preparations being made. The week before, his house was full of relatives scouring the foot sweat off the floorboards, scrubbing the rag carpets with soft soap, polishing the old windows with methylated spirits in the freezing winter cold, airing his black funeral suit to get rid of the smell of mothballs, washing congealed fat off the lamp shades, changing the wax table cloths, dusting every nook and cranny and discovering an incredible number of spiders' webs and dead flies, carrying junk out into the barn, standing shoes in unnatural rows and patterns, and moving things in cupboards and drawers until everything was in the wrong place and impossible to find. Grandad managed to lose his temper several times, moaned and cursed and threatened to throw out all these intruders, but it was like a D-Day operation: impossible to stop once it had started.

* * *

The birthday fell on a Friday. Sis and I had been given the day off school, and we accompanied Mum and Dad to Grandad's house quite early in the morning. It was fine weather and minus four degrees, a dry, windless chill that poured hoarfrost over car windscreens and covered trees with stiff ice needles. The last of the morning stars were fading away in the sky. The light lay blue over the forests. Dad parked the car in the courtyard where the snow plow had already been; we crunched our way over the frozen flakes and stamped our feet on the porch. The old dog began growling behind the door. He was half-blind and had started biting, so I picked up the sweeping brush and was prepared when Grandad opened up.

"*Tekkös sieltä tuletta?* Is it you, then?" he said in Finnish, pretending to be surprised. Mum handed him the flowers she'd had inside her coat to protect them from the cold, Dad shook his hands and wished him many happy returns, and I swept the attacking Finnish spitz down the steps. It fell over and started howling.

We sat down at the kitchen table and listened to the clock ticking. The whole place looked unnaturally tidy. Grandad sat in the rocking chair, his wrinkled neck rubbing against his stiff shirt collar, and he fiddled nervously with his tie. Everything was artificial and stiff, which is how it should be on ceremonial occasions.

At lunchtime my uncles and their wives started turning up, and big cream cakes were produced. Some of the ladies started making coffee and filling the thermos flasks, while Sis and I helped to butter the local rieska bread and make open-face sandwiches with juicy slices of oven-baked moose steak. Others filled trays with newly baked biscuits and buns, and the house was filled with a lovely smell of cinnamon, cocoa, and vanilla.

Outside, a pale February sun had fought its way up out of the snow-drifts and made the wintry day start glistening. A few reindeer were kicking at the crust of snow in the meadow, licking at the faded wisps of grass they uncovered. Some were lying on folded legs in hollows in the snow, preserving body heat, with only their dark antlers visible. The old dog hadn't the strength to bother about them, and instead nosed around by the house, sniffing at the holes made in the snow where Grandad had gone out for a pee, and a bunch of great tits clung onto a piece of bacon rind nailed to the wall. The whole countryside was bathing in the white tundra-light under an ice-cold sun.

As the afternoon wore on, more and more visitors put in an appearance. The parking area in front of the house soon filled up, and cars packed the road outside. The closest neighbors came on kick sleds, and a couple of them made their way on skis. It was now time to start getting serious with regard to the formalities. Guests sat down at the long tables that had been prepared: thin men with runny eyes and frozen eyebrows starting to melt, and portly ladies with arms like loaves from the local baker's, compressed into flowery Sunday-best dresses. Coffee was duly slurped from saucers, and salmon sandwiches and biscuits were passed around. The ancient wood-fired oven was lit for old times' sake, and the old ladies started going on about the old days and how nice it would be to bake some genuine crispbread instead of the rubbish you found in the supermarkets nowadays.

After a second cup it seemed appropriate to bring out the brandy. A bottle bought at the monopoly store was uncorked and carried around by Dad. Schnapps glasses were filled to the accompaniment of silent nods, while those condemned to driving home placed their hands over their glasses. The atmosphere became noticeably livelier. Mum sliced up a couple of cakes and put them on plates. A few toasts were proposed, but Grandad remained anchored in his rocking chair, sweating. Dad filled up his glass with brandy, to make things look better in the photographs. Then followed a rendering of the traditional birthday song in broken Swedish, accompanied by admiring expressions. The old man was embarrassed by all the fuss and tried to hide behind all the bunches of flowers. Then he was instructed to open his presents. He'd left them untouched in case it occured to anybody that they were the only reason he'd agreed to the party in the first place—a sensible move given the usual Tornedalen assumptions. All thumbs, he struggled with the parcels until one of my uncles took pity on him and produced a *puukko*. A few assured slashes and the old boy made short work of the fancy wrapping paper, as easily as slitting open the belly of a pike. He produced a glass relief of a bull moose, a carved kitchen clock driven by batteries, a cake slice made of Tornedalen silver, a fancy pewter tankard, some lace tablecloths, a wall-hanging complete with hanging chain, a fancy pack of shaving luxuries, a guest book with a genuine reindeer-skin cover, a bed-hanging made of shells from somebody who'd been on holiday in Thailand, a poker-work doorplate with the motif "Welcome," and various other useless gifts. Grandad commented in Swedish that this was pure overkill—another way of saying that all this expensive bric-a-brac was quite unnecessary. Nobody had dared to give him really useful things such as a chopper or a new exhaust system for his car, since that could have been interpreted as suggesting that he was incapable of seeing to mundane, everyday things.

Early in the evening the local folklore society turned up to pay their respects, twenty or so mild-mannered ladies and gents who shook hands politely like southern Swedes. Several had brought bunches of flowers with neatly written cards. After a sandwich and a piece of cake, they produced song sheets and sang with tremulous, slightly shrill voices. Swedish folk songs from Grandad's school days, well-known sing-alongs, tributes to the landscapes and climes of their motherland. Dad served brandy, tactfully avoiding the Laestadians. To end, we all joined in the Tornedalen national anthem, slowly and reverently:

> *To Tornedalen's vales and hills*
> *We sing our grateful praise.*
> *Our northern homeland, shorn of frills,*
> *Is where we'll end our days...*

Some of the elderly were deeply moved and started wiping away tears. Grandad was surprisingly touched, his eyes grew red-rimmed and his hand shook so much that Mum had to take away his glass. The whole house was on the point of bursting into tears. Especially when the Finnish verses were sung last of all, everyone's heart fluttered and felt hot and wet.

Everybody sat in melancholy silence for a while. Let themselves fill up with Finnish suffering, and pondered all the catastrophes that had befallen the family: all the merciless blows of destiny that had been suffered, all the backward children born, all the teenagers who'd become deranged, all the starvation, all the poverty, all the horses that had to be put down, all the TB and polio, all the failed harvests, all the failed attempts at smuggling, all the beatings suffered and all the scorn from the authorities, all the suicides, all the traitors and blacklegs, all the occasions they'd been cheated, all the cruel teachers and greedy company directors, all the times they'd been blacklisted, all the laborers who'd gone to Russia to help Stalin but been shot for their pains, all the damn "efficiency consultants" at work, all the sadists at the hostels they'd stayed in as school kids, all those who'd drunk themselves to death, all those who'd drowned while floating timber or been killed down in the mine, all the tears, all the wounds, all the pains and humiliations that had afflicted our long-suffering family on their arduous trek through this vale of tears.

Outside, the long, steel-blue winter dusk had turned into darkness. The pole star hung down like an icicle from the winter ceiling, encircled by thousands of glittering sparks while the temperature fell a few more degrees. The forest was stiff and frozen, not a single twig moved. The whole taiga was draped in grisly silence, the endless forest extending through sparsely populated Finland, on over the vast Russian land mass, through the even more vast Siberia, and on to the shores of the Pacific Ocean, a motionless tree-desert weighed down with snow and sub-zero temperatures. Deep down in the forks of enormous fir boughs crouched tomtits like tiny, fluffy orbs. And there, only there, deep down inside, was there a warm little flutter.

Suddenly a mumbling spread through the kitchen. The moose hunters! The moose hunters were approaching! The chairman of the folklore society rose to his feet and delivered a polite but brief thank-you speech, and Grandad promised to present an old and illegal fish spear to the local folklore museum, as he couldn't see well enough in the dark now to use it himself. They turned their coffee cups upside down on their saucers, flung on their outer clothing and were gone in a blink. The only ones left now were a few neighbors and retirees, plus Dad's brothers, who now dared to start swearing again and ask for more to drink.

Soon there was a stamping on the porch steps, then the front door was kicked open. In boomed about twenty silent men. The spokesman for the moose hunters said:

"Hello."

The others sat down at the long table without a word, and stared straight ahead. The youngest was just over twenty, the eldest was already over eighty. Many of them were related to us.

Rieska bread, cake, and coffee, and then a toast with brandy from the last of the bottles, and everybody wondered why on earth the French insisted on coloring their spirits brown and making them taste like paint.

The spokesman for the sharpshooters got to his feet and started to deliver his ceremonial speech before the old men forgot where they were. He insisted that Grandad had been an effective member of the team; he wasn't quite gaga yet, but as soon as he was he should stay at home and concentrate on the washing up and count on his former colleagues to look after his meat supplies. They couldn't see any signs of senility just yet, repeated the spokesman, and the old boy seemed to be thinking straight, but by God, once he started rambling and talking nonsense, then he had better stay at home! Let's face it, even a doddering old devil needed to be able to distinguish between a moose and a motor car, for instance, before he could be let loose in the woods with a gun in his hand—that was the difference between this particular group of sharpshooters and certain others he could name in this area.

The hunters all nodded grimly, and the spokesman took a swig before continuing. And so, the old boy could still manage to carry a rifle and put up with the rain and the cold and do his duty, but for hell's sake, if he were to become senile! He'd be better occupied wearing out the sofa with the force of his farts. Because even if nobody could see any signs just yet, it was only a matter of time before his brain became addled, and that would be it, the old bastard ought to be quite clear about that!

After this heartfelt ceremonial speech, they handed over a pewter goblet with all the names of the hunters, including the dogs, engraved on it. A few of them had been spelled wrongly, as they'd made the mistake of having the engraving done in Luleå, where they weren't familiar with Finnish names, but for the discount received they'd been able to buy a bottle, complete with contents.

Grandad responded by claiming that the wrong spelling was no doubt due to the awful handwriting of the sharpshooters, that his physique was equal in all respects to that of an eighteen-year-old, that he could see like an eagle and hear a moose cow fart at a distance of several hundred feet, and that if they took into account the number of brain cells destroyed by all the boozing among the hunters, he was highly unlikely to be the first one to go doddery. He then thanked them for the bottle, and more especially for what was in it, as this was the last remaining drop of strong drink left in the house, and once it was finished they'd be offered coffee for the rest of the night.

The moose hunters shuddered in shock. Grandad served them all with a thimbleful, and emptied the bottle. Silently, almost in tears, the men raised their glasses and emptied them. This couldn't be true! The mean old bastard! Not now, when they'd managed to sneak out of the house without their old ladies noticing.

Grandad looked around and gave a signal. Dad quietly opened the hatch into the cellar and clambered down into the darkness. He was back in a shot and slammed the bottles down on the table. Two from each hand. And Grandad roared with laughter.

"Here you are, my boys! Some sweeties for you!" He was laughing so much, his belly was hopping up and down.

The hunters were so relieved, they almost burst into tears. Nobody bothered about the fact that the corks had not been sealed by the state monopoly liquor store. At last Bacchus could come into his own.

This was bliss. The joy of drinking. Getting drunk. Getting legless in the company of good friends without having to put up with whining objections. To pour the stuff down till your prick went stiff and your tongue flapped about your mouth like a flag in the wind. Emptying a bottle and immediately having it replaced, no need to go easy and measure it all out with a ruler, no need to pay, no need to sit half-sober but broke in some fancy pub and wonder where all your pals had got to.

The wonders of excess. None of your smallholder's skimping with bacon rind and moldy seeds, but the ecstatic whoop of the hunter faced with a couple of hundred pounds of steaming meat. To drink till you drop, fill yourself up to the brim, pour it down with gay abandon— and just for once have no thoughts about the morrow.

Mum and the rest of the women still around could see the signs of imminent doomsday, and sullenly withdrew to go home. The men promised with one voice not to drink too much, but their tongues were so far into their cheeks they almost emerged on the other side. My big sister also withdrew, so as not to become a sex object; so I took over her role and started washing the coffee cups. Some of the men wondered archly if I was *knapsu*, and went on about my small titties. I suggested they go away and sniff shit or lick little girls' privates.

Soon we heard the noise of cars outside, and when I investigated I saw it was our band that had turned up. Niila, Erkki, and Holgeri had arrived in an old Volvo Duett, chauffeured by a cousin. I helped them unload the amplifiers, guitars, and the drums, fewer of them than usual for this occasion. We put them next to the wood-burning stove to thaw them out before use. Unfortunately Greger was unable to be present: he had some vital phone calls to make, but might put in an appearance later on.

The moose hunters had reached the cordial stage. They started telling tales and boasting and recounting pornographic experiences in both Finnish and Swedish. One of the men started to sing *Rosvo Roope* with half-closed eyes, and followed that up with *Villiruusu*, even though several of his pals urged him to stop singing Korpela songs, as they only revived memories.

Dad was now getting tipsy as well. He staggered backward with a few empty bottles in his hands, and very nearly fell through the trapdoor into the cellar. The men all roared with laughter, but Dad cursed the idiot who'd left the hatch open, even though it was him. Then he passed the bottles on to me instead. I tottered down the unsteady ladder, feeling the coldness and dampness envelop me. There was a strong smell of sandy soil and potatoes. Wooden shelves with rows of glass jars full of cloudberry and lingon jam, the remains of the gravadlax, a few crates of pilsner, a tin of fermented Baltic herring, and a tub of pickled herring. Some planks had been placed on the earth floor, and on them were all the bottles of moonshine. I discreetly filled a lemonade bottle for the band, and put it to one side for later.

When the first of the sharpshooters went out for a pee, we gathered in front of the stove. I fitted a multi-plug into the mains and prayed the fuse would stand the strain. There was a worrying clicking noise in the cold loudspeakers when the current was switched on. Niila and Holgeri plugged in their guitars, and Erkki sat on a kitchen chair behind his drums and other fancy bits. I plugged the mike into the spare socket on the base amplifier, and coughed to get my vocal cords moving.

The hunters had watched our preparations with considerable misgivings, but when Niila started to strum in three-four time, they relaxed. Everybody recognized the old evergreen we'd taught ourselves in honor of the occasion:

"*Oi muistatkos Emma sen kuutamoillan, kun yhdessä tansseista kuljettin...*"

Everybody put their glasses down and remained seated. The party had already reached the melancholy stage, and the music was right on target. I sang facing Grandad, but he looked away modestly.

"*Oi Emma Emma, oi Emma Emma, kun lupasit olla mun omani...*"

We followed that with *Matalan torpan balladi*. The mood became so sorrowful that the windows steamed up. We finished up with the Erkheikki Love Lilt, a slow waltz in a minor key that could have wrung blood from a stone.

Afterward, all the men wanted to drink a toast to us. As was the norm in Tornedalen, nobody said a word about our performance: after all, unnecessary praise would only encourage us to undertake projects beyond our capabilities, and result in bankruptcy. But you could see from their eyes what they thought of it.

We sat ourselves down in a corner and started swigging from the lemonade bottle. The hunters, on the other hand, had the urge to wander around. They'd gone past the subdued stage, and now wanted to stretch their legs and discuss all sorts of things. One of them stumbled over to us and wondered about our political persuasions. Another wondered whether what he'd read in the *Evening News* was right, that girls were hornier now than they used to be. We gave evasive answers to his first question, but maintained in response to his second that girls were no doubt the same as they'd always been, and that their enthusiasm for sex wasn't obvious on the surface but you caught on when you were halfway inside 'em. He then started asking intimate questions about our girlfriends, how horny they were and how often we did it. And although we told him where to go, he persisted and wanted to know all the details.

I started to feel a bit woozy and staggered outside. A few of the men were standing in front of a snow drift, trying to remember if they'd just had a pee or were just about to. They decided for the latter, and pulled out their guns. They seemed to have made the right decision, as jets eventually appeared. One of them claimed the height record, and another challenged him. My young bladder was as bouncy as a highly pumped-up football, and I had no trouble at all in beating them both. Then I signed off with my initials underneath the record squirt. The old boys got annoyed and threatened to tar my scrotum. I drew a box around my initials then increased my record for good measure before they agreed they would fill my underpants with snow—but I was already on my way back in by then.

The second phase of stupefaction was now approaching. The one that is final, and soft as the white shroud of death. A broad-shouldered, bear-like man grabbed me and started telling me something. He was holding me by the shoulder and droning on solemnly while his eyes circled around like heavy bumblebees. It was impossible to make out what he said. His tongue was as thick as a gym shoe, his voice sounded like squelching in mud. One of the younger hunters was feeling argumentative and started saying something to him, but his comments were just as incomprehensible. Soon they were involved in a heated discussion even though neither could understand what the other was saying.

Those still capable of speech complained about being thirsty. Their mouths felt like sandpaper, their blood had turned to dust in their veins, their lips were sticking together, and their muscles were stiffening like dried meat. I dived down into the cellar, brought up the remaining bottles and placed them before the voices of those crying in the wilderness. There was no stopping now: once you'd started skiing down the slope you had no choice but to keep going. Throw caution to the wind, accelerate till your ears start popping. An *oikea mies*, a real man, feared neither death nor a three-day hangover.

Niila and Holgeri were now starting to get drunk as well. It showed least in Erkki, even though he'd been knocking it back faster than the others. He was discussing salmon flies with one of the younger hunters, who sat there with eyelids drooping and snot dripping down his downy moustache. They agreed to try out a place on the River Tärendo, since life offered few things more perfect than grilling a newly caught greyling over a campfire at night by a rushing Norrland river. They drank a toast to that and their eyes filled with tears. Summer is so beautiful, so perfect, and so endless! The midnight sun over the edge of the forest, glowing red night-clouds. Not a breath of wind. The water mirror-like, not a ripple. A fish snaps at a fly, a ring spreads slowly over the vast stillness. And there, in the middle of the silence, a moth swoops down. Gets stuck on the sticky water through the powder on its wings. Glides along toward the rapids, tosses about amid the rocks and the froth. Midges swarm over the tops of the fir trees in the reflected warmth. You can see it all from where you sit in the narrow crack that is a summer night, floating on the fragile membrane between two worlds.

The oldest of those present, the ones in their seventies and eighties, were leaning at alarming angles in their chairs. Dad noted the potential problem even though he was many sheets to the wind, and addressed me in a language that most resembled Tornedalen German. Nevertheless I got the drift, and between us we managed to get hold of the oldest and thinnest of the old boys under his arms. He was surprisingly light and made little resistance when we lugged him over to the sofa and sat him down in the middle, leaning back gracefully. The other two fossils were somewhat rounder in shape and weighed rather more, but we managed to place them on either side of the first. They woke up briefly and started hooting like owls, but soon fell asleep again, forming an orderly line. Heads leaning back against the sofa, but chins sagging. They sat there with wide-open mouths like fledglings in a nest, with their bald heads and wrinkled necks. I sat opposite them and tried to hit their open traps with sugar lumps, but Dad put a stop to that with an ominous glare.

Grandad came back in after an excursion outside for a pee. The tap had run so gently that his fingers were blue with cold, and he cursed old age and its cruel pranks. During his absence those left inside had made a horrifying discovery: they'd run out of booze. A slurred crisis meeting was called by some of the old dodderers and representatives of the moose hunters. They went through the better-known moonshiners in the area, reckoned up their own stores back home in the liquor cabinet, and wondered how they might be able to remove a few bottles without waking up the old woman. Somebody pointed out that the night was yet young, and the gas station down the road was still open. They could buy some meths, spruce it up a bit with a bit of wheat-flour, then pour it through a coffee filter. That would be not only strong, but also drinkable, and doubtless safe for anybody with a sound heart. One of the moose hunters volunteered to take a taxi to Finland provided they all shared the cost, buy some beer from a shop he knew in Kolari that was open until late, and bring back as much as was possible to cram into the car. He knew the customs officers, so if they stopped him he could invite them to join the party. Everybody thought that was a splendid idea as Finnish beer was the best possible thing you could drink to avoid a hangover, and they asked him to make sure he also bought some Finnish bread and *piimä*, and brought along a few Finnish floozies if he happened to come across any.

Grandad now asserted himself and rose to his feet. He produced a three-liter plastic container and asked solemnly for it to be filled with water. A neighbor filled it up while the rest watched wide-eyed. With due ceremony Grandad placed the container in the broom closet, then asked his audience how well up they were on the Bible. Nobody said a word, realizing that the old man was gaga.

"Are you true believers?" he asked again, determined to get an answer.

"Not really," muttered several of those present.

Grandad opened the cupboard door and took out the container. Then he took a swig and passed it to the man on his right, and so on, and everybody took a swig, one after another. And when they'd all had a taste, everybody agreed that Grandad was Jesus—no, to be honest, greater than Jesus, because Jesus had merely turned water into wine whereas Grandad had waved his wand and produced the hard stuff. Admittedly a bit primitive, with a greasy aftertaste; but there again there were not many substances as healthy as fusel oil, with all its trace elements and chromosomes. I was the only one who noticed that not only had the contents of the container been transformed, but also the color of the stopper; but I made up my mind to say nothing, in order not to spoil the implication that a miracle had been witnessed.

An elderly neighbor somewhat on the portly side started to slide out sideways from his kitchen chair. I just managed to get there and protect his forehead as he collided with the floor. It was not possible to revive him, so I took hold of his ankles and dragged him over to a wall so that the hulk wouldn't be in anybody's way. His limbs were totally relaxed and limp. I placed some newspapers under his head in case he vomited. At that very moment his neighbor passed out, sitting in the rocking chair with his chin on his chest. The snuff trickled down onto his shirt like melted chocolate. The young moose murderer with the downy moustache laughed so much at the sight of the old guy that he couldn't stop shaking. I also started giggling at all the old drunks staggering around from room to room, babbling away, spilling all over themselves when they tried to drink, going outside for a pee in their stockinged feet, singing cross-eyed, falling down on their bottoms and crawling like crocodiles on the rag carpets. I and the downy moustache combined to carry the snuff-stained gent away and place him on the floor next to the first one to succumb. We repeated the procedure for one of the men who'd passed out while apparently on his knees praying on the porch, and he became the third in the cluster. They lay there like slaughtered pigs, and we guffawed so much at the sight that we doubled up. Then we took a swig of the fusel oil and snorted and choked, then burst out laughing again.

Dad was getting worried and pointed at the three blokes on the sofa. They were ashen, motionless. He asked me to check if they were dead. I went over to them, grasped their blue-veined wrists and took their pulse: nothing. Oh, yes, a faint pecking.

Niila and Holgeri came back in smelling of diarrhea, and shivering with cold. They asked for some coffee to clear their throats, and I handed them a thermos flask. At the same time I noticed that the downy moustache had stopped laughing. He was slumped in his chair and snoring, just like the guys he'd been laughing at. He was about to collapse onto the floor, so I dragged him away and deposited him next to the previous three, looking young and red-cheeked alongside the gray old-timers.

Somebody wanted a taxi, staggered over to the telephone, and ordered one. Somebody else marched shakily over to me and started yelping—it sounded like a puppy sucking at a bone. It was an age before I realized he wanted some assistance in phoning his wife and asking for a lift home. I asked him for his telephone number, but couldn't understand what he said. Instead, I looked him up in the phone book then held the receiver to his ear. The old lady answered after the eighth ring—no doubt she'd been asleep in bed. The man tried hard to concentrate: "Issshh... lissshhh... msssorrriter trubbbbell..."

She slammed the phone down although she'd certainly recognized his voice. I myself could feel the floor starting to rotate, and went over to Niila. He was sitting with his eyes half-closed, a blaring transistor radio pressed to one ear. He could hear the voices of the dead on medium wave, and had just heard an announcement in Tornedalen Finnish. It sounded exactly like his uncle who'd died the past autumn, a voice whispering, "*Paska... paska...,*" followed by a mysterious silence. I suggested there might well be a long line for the toilets up there in heaven, but Niila told me to hush. Listened hard, looking somewhat confused.

"Hang on, there's somebody else there!"

"I can't hear a word."

"It's Esperanto! She says that I... wait... that... I'm going to die..."

At that point the taxi turned up. A couple of the men steadiest on their feet tried to wriggle their way into their overcoats and staggered out of the door. A third fellow, very portly, explained to me in sign language that he'd very much like to take part as well. I propped him up and helped him down the steps and into the snow. Halfway to the car he uttered a drawn-out, horse-like whinny. Then his body imploded as if pricked by a pin. He collapsed on the spot, his bones giving way as if his skeleton had shriveled. I tried to hold him up, but didn't have a chance. Three hundred pounds of old man's flesh and blood.

I took his pulse. The man was unconscious, not of this world. His body was steaming like a meat casserole in the arctic cold. The taxi was waiting, its engine ticking. I took hold of the guy's feet and tried to drag the pile of bacon toward the taxi through the uncooperative snow. The old fellow's shirt splayed out and acted as a brake. The snow melted against his back, but not even that could wake him. He was as heavy as a corpse. In the end I gave up and signaled to the taxi, which disappeared in a flash. Moaning and groaning, I started dragging the body back where it had come from, back to the house. I kept slipping, and could feel the sweat breaking out on my spine. Inch by inch. He was still alive, I could see the steam puffing out of his nose and mouth. A thin column of breath spiraled up to the starry sky, outlined against the porch light.

I was forced to pause and draw breath. And at that very moment, when I looked up, the Northern Lights blossomed forth in all their glory. Big green fountains growing and swelling, waves of sea-fire foaming forth. Quick red axe cuts, violet flesh just visible inside. The light grew more intense, more lively. Billows of phosphorous in frothing maelstroms. For minutes on end I simply stood and enjoyed it. Suddenly thought there was some faint singing from up above, as if from a Finnish soldiers' choir. The voice of the Northern Lights. Or maybe it was the engine of the taxi being projected through the severe cold. It was all so beautiful. I had the urge to go down on bended knee. What splendor, what beauty! Too much to bear for a small, shy, and drunk boy from Tornedalen.

Somebody slammed the front door behind him. Erkki stumbled over to me, unzipping his fly. I pointed to the drunk lying at his feet. Erkki registered the fact with a degree of surprise, took a couple of steps back, and fell over. Stretched out comfortably in the snow, he took out his dick and peed as he lay. Duly relieved, he closed his eyes. I suggested he should abandon any thought of slumber, the stupid bastard, and kicked some snow into his face. He started threatening a bloody punch in the kisser, but struggled to his feet even so. Between us we managed to drag the old devil back into the house and place him at the end of the impressive row of bodies on the floor.

Dad and Grandad were sitting at the kitchen table looking pale, and stammered something about the old fellows on the sofa having died. I took the pulse of all three. Their bald heads were leaning in various directions, their skin yellow and wax-like.

"Yup, they're dead," I said.

Grandad cursed at the thought of all the problems there'd be with the authorities then started sobbing as old folk do, snot dripping from his nose and into his glass. Dad launched into a solemn if slurred speech on the glorious death of heroic Finns, listing suicide, war, a heart attack in the sauna, and alcohol poisoning as the most common examples. And tonight this trio of beloved and respected relations had chosen to walk simultaneously, side by side, through the Pearly Gates...

The thin one in the middle opened his eyes at this point and asked for some more schnapps. Dad was stopped in his tracks and could only stare. Grandad handed over his snot-filled glass and watched it being shakily drained. I laughed so much at their faces that I nearly fell off the chair, and said it must be a pretty good party if even the dead join in and drink.

Peace began to settle in all around the house. The old boys lined up on the floor hadn't moved since I laid them there, deep in a dreamless drunken stupor. Others were crawling around like tortoises with slow, stiff movements. Niila was sitting with his back to the wall, his face green all over. He was trying desperately to remain upright, drinking occasionally from a pail of cold water. Holgeri lay beside him in the fetal position, twitching. Most were now silent and introverted as their livers worked overtime to clean up the poisons and their brain cells died like swarms of midges. Erkki had half-fallen off his wooden chair, but his jacket was caught on the back. The only one still going strong was a wiry sixty-year-old moose hunter who had propped himself up on the table and was doing gymnastic exercises with his legs. Stretching them forward, upward, and to the side in complicated oriental patterns. He always did this when he was drunk, and everybody left him to get on with it.

I could feel the intoxication reaching its peak inside me. It was bubbling away in the background as I sat studying the old devil's leg movements. The party was over already, even though it was barely eleven o'clock. In less than four hours the moose hunters had downed more than two pints of moonshine per head, but even so not a single one had thrown up, a sure sign of long and dedicated practice.

A car was heard approaching, and its headlights played on the wall-paper. Before long I heard the stamping of feet on the porch. In stormed Greger, and caught sight of me.

"Jump in, let's go!"

Then he stopped dead. Turned slowly around and stared wide-eyed at the impressive battle field.

I shook some life into the boys; we carted the equipment out into the car, and drove off. Greger was whistling merrily and tapping his fingers on the steering wheel until we asked him to stop.

"Boys," he said with a smile, "I've been on the phone all evening. You'd better starrrt practicing."

"Eh?"

"Learrrn some new songs."

"Songs?" we repeated stupidly.

Greger just laughed.

"I've fixed your first tourrr. A few schools, a youth club, and then a festival in Luleå for amateurrr bands."

* * *

We pulled up outside the school. Greger unlocked the deserted music room and we carried in the amplifiers. We were all still elated and dazed by the news, so when Greger went home we stayed behind and played. It sounded awful, but it came from the heart; it was rough and raw, exactly like we were. Niila did his homemade riffs, and I improvised a few songs and began to feel like a rock star. The cold had put Holgeri's guitar out of tune and his fingers were fumbly, but perhaps that was why he produced fantastic solos, distorted and lopsided bellows, fluttering swaying tones. Finally we played our old favorite, "Rock 'n' Roll Music," at least ten times. We didn't pack it in until Erkki had snapped both his drumsticks.

It was just after three in the morning. Pajala church village was des-
olate in the winter darkness. We crunched home through the powdery
snow under the softly buzzing streetlights. The cold streamed into our
lungs, our ears wrapped themselves around the silence of dawn. Inside
our mittens our fingertips were aching, thanks to the sharp strings.

"We ought to run away," proposed Niila, "Just clear off."

"Stockholm!" said Erkki.

"America!" yelled Holgeri.

"China," I said. "I'd like to see China one of these days."

It was so silent. As if everyone in the village had frozen to death. We
started walking down the middle of the road, four abreast. There was
no traffic. The whole place, the whole world was motionless. We were
the only four people alive, four pounding hearts in the innermost hollow of the winter taiga.

We stopped when we came to Pajala's biggest crossroads, the one
between the hardware store and the newsstand. We were all hesitant, as
if we felt we'd arrived at our goal. That it was here something else was
about to begin. We looked around uncertainly in all directions. The road
to the west led to Kiruna. If you went south you came to Stockholm.
Eastward took you to Övertorneå and then Finland. And the fourth stub
of road led down to the ice on the River Torne.

After a while we went back out to the middle of the road and sat
down. Then, as if by mutual agreement, we lay down in the middle of
the crossroads, right across the carriage way. We stretched out on our
backs and gazed at the starry sky. There was no traffic noise, everything
was still. We lay there side by side and breathed up into space. Felt the
chilly ice under our bottoms and shoulder blades. Then finally, peace-
fully, we closed our eyes.

* * *

And this is where the story ends. Childhood, boyhood, the first life we
led. I'll leave them there. Four boys on their backs at a crossroads with

their faces turned up to the stars. I stand quietly beside them, watching. Their breathing grows deeper, their muscles are relaxing.

They're asleep already.

EPILOGUE

Once or twice every year when I can't control my longing any more, I travel up to Pajala. I get there as evening is drawing in, and wander out onto the new, circus-like pylon bridge that spans the River Torne. I stand in the middle and gaze out over the village and the pointed spire of the wooden church. If I look around I can see the forest on the horizon, and Jupukka Mountain with the blinking sewing needle that is the TV antenna. Way down beneath me the river flows wide and nev-erending toward the sea. The low roaring sound rinses the din of the city out of my ears. My restlessness melts away as dusk gathers.

I let my eyes wander over the village. Memories come flooding back, people who've moved away like me, names that flash past. Paskajänkkä with its Kangas, Karvonen, Zeidlitz, Samuelsson. Texas with all the Wahlbergs, Groths, Moonas, and Lehtos. Strandvägen's Wilhelmsson and Marttikala, Äijä and Tornberg. Vittulajänkkä with its Ydfjärd, Kreku, Palovaara, Muotka, Pekkari, Perttu, and many, many more.

I rest my hands on the cold parapet and wonder what became of you all. People I once knew, people who shared my world. My thoughts pause for a while with my friends in the band. Holgeri, who went to technical college and now works on the mobile phone network in Luleå. Erkki, who became a supervisor at LKAB's pellet factory in Svappavaara. And me, who became a Swedish teacher in Sundbyberg with a sense of loss, a melancholy I have never managed to overcome completely.

On the way home I pass by the cemetery. I have no flowers with me, but I pause for a while by Niila's grave. The only one of us who went in for music. Who really went in for it.

The last time we met was during the Pajala fair, he'd flown in from London and was scratching absent-mindedly at little sores on his wrist.

That night we went fishing at Lappeakoski. His pupils were as small as drawing pins, and he was buzzing away manically:

"The breaking up of the ice, Matti, that time we stood on the bridge and watched the ice breaking up, by God, it was awesome..."

Oh, yes, Niila, I remember the ice breaking up. Two little boys and a homemade guitar.

Rock 'n' roll music.

The taste of a boy's kiss.

MIKAEL NIEMI grew up in Pajala in the northernmost part of Sweden, near the Finnish border. Among his published books are two collections of poetry—*Näsblod under högmässan* ("Nosebleed during Morning Service") (1998) and *Änglar med mausergevär* ("Angels with Mausers") (1989)—and a young adult novel, *Kyrkdjävulen* ("The Church Devil") (1994). His most recent book is *Svålhålet,* a collection of short stories.

LAURIE THOMPSON has translated some fifteen novels from the Swedish, including books by Stig Dagerman, Peter Pohl, Henning Mankell, and Kjell-Olof Bornemark. He was editor of *Swedish Book Review* from its launch in 1983 to 2002. He lives in West Wales.